What Child is This?

A Christmas at Bremmer's Novel

Other Books by John R. Mabry

A Christian Walks in the Footsteps of the Buddha

The Kingdom: A Berkeley Blackfriars Novel

The Power: A Berkeley Blackfriars Novel

Spiritual Guidance Across Religions

Faithful Generations

Growing Into God

Salvation of the True Rock

People of Faith

The Way of Thomas

The Monster God

Noticing the Divine

Faith Styles: Ways People Believe

God Has One Eye: The Mystics of the World's Religions

God is a Great Underground River

I Believe in a God Who is Growing

Crisis and Communion

Heretics, Mystics & Misfits: A Sermon Cycle

God As Nature Sees God

The Tao Te Ching: A New Translation

What Child is This?

A Christmas at Bremmer's Novel

JOHN R. MABRY

the apocryphile press

BERKELEY, CA

www.apocryphile.org

apocryphile press
BERKELEY, CA

Apocryphile Press
1700 Shattuck Ave #81
Berkeley, CA 94709
www.apocryphile.org

Chapter One

First there was the sandwich; then there was the crash.

Jerry Keller had been looking forward to that sandwich. As manager of Bremmer's Christmas Super Shoppe he had seen many busy days—especially as the time before Christmas grew shorter—but he had seen few as busy as this. When he tried to remember back to breakfast, it seemed a dim memory from the remote past, a time punctuated by pre-dawn darkness and the howling of wolves. He seemed to recall that it involved bacon and ice cream, but he could be mistaken. Memory is a tricky thing.

He had stolen a moment of peace when no one seemed to be looking. With relish he unwrapped the ham-and-sweet-potato-on-sourdough monstrosity that Carol had lovingly packed for him in that distant time before dawn. Almost quivering with anticipation, and certainly rumbling with hunger, he brought the sandwich to his lips only to have the moment shattered by the sound of falling boxes and the unmistakably painful din of breaking glass.

"Awww, dad-blast it, what now?" he asked the canary-yellow walls of the break room as he let his sandwich drop to the table unbitten and hustled onto the floor.

Bremmer's was a sight to see anytime of the year, but in the weeks leading up to Christmas it was a wonder. It wasn't the largest Christmas superstore—that distinction belonged to what his employees called "the-store-that-will-not-be-named," about fifty miles away in another little town of German heritage—but Bremmer's was a grand store nevertheless, one that the whole town was proud of.

But in that moment, Jerry did not see the store's glory—he was on the lookout for trouble. As his narrowed brown eyes took in the floor, his panda-shaped body swiveled at the hips like a giant dish antenna turning in search of a signal. It wasn't the sound, but the glances of the patrons that gave him his clue regarding the location of the crash. He told himself not to run, but walked as briskly as he could past the sale tables with their slightly damaged and discontinued items. Turning left at the main aisle, he passed through the Christmas tree display, including the newfangled model that hung from the ceiling, which Jerry referred to as "the stupidest thing I ever saw."

And it was there, at the far end of the tree section, that he saw it: one of the heralds—the angels blowing gold trumpets—which had been hanging from the ceiling had fallen straight onto a display of glass tree ornaments.

A small group of patrons was gathered around the crash sight, gawking and naturally causing a traffic-flow problem by blocking the main aisle. Jerry took in the scene with his hands on his hips, trying to figure out the best way to approach it. As he was thinking, Gibbs ran up to him and gawked at the mess.

"Geez…" the gawky stock boy breathed. "What do you want me to do, Jer?"

Jerry knew that this was the time when he should take charge, start barking orders, and manage the problem. Behind his wire-rimmed glasses his brown eyes shifted back and forth over the scene, and he began to sweat.

"Boss?" Gibbs tapped his shoulder.

"I'm thinking," Jerry snapped. He took out a hand-kerchief and dabbed at his forehead. Just then Myrtle arrived, indicating her distress with tiny, bird-like flutterings of her hands and a mumbled, "Oh, my my my…"

Gibbs looked back and forth from Jerry to the angel; one had crashed and the other was not far behind. Without another word, the stock boy picked the angel up and hurried off with it to the back room.

Not sure what to do, Myrtle put her hands out as if in prayer and cocked her head, listening to the words of the Christmas carol emitting from the tinny ceiling speakers. "*Fall on your knees*," she echoed the Christmas carol, a puzzled look on her face. Suddenly her eyes snapped open, "Fall on your knees *and sweep!*" she exclaimed, scurrying off in search of a whisk broom and a dustpan.

Still surrounded by customers feasting their eyes upon the damage, Jerry sat cross-legged on the floor and picked up what remained of a silver Christmas bulb. Once a globe larger than his fist, it looked to him now like a teacup with a ragged and dangerous lip.

Looking up, he was surprised to see the customers looking at him with more interest than they were showing to the crash. He looked back at the broken bulb, and then, clearing his throat, rose again to his feet. He stumbled a bit as the blood rushed to his head from standing too quickly, but he addressed the shoppers directly for the first time. "Sorry about the mess, folks, we'll get this cleaned up straightaway. Please go back to your shopping." He wanted to say, "Move along, nothing to see here," like the policemen on TV, but he would have felt silly. There was, after all, quite a bit to see here, and he stood frozen to his spot as he took in the glass and tinsel carnage.

In a moment, Myrtle had returned with a broom and had begun sweeping up the shards of colored glass. Moments later, Gibbs returned from the back room, breathing heavily from running. "Jer?" he asked. "What do you want me to do?"

Still, Jerry did not know where to begin. He waved at the mess, and Gibbs' mouth pursed in a sideways motion as he tried to understand what his boss was trying to say. He watched Myrtle sweeping for a moment and gave a decisive nod. "Jerry, I'm going to carry these boxes to the back. If you can carry some, too, we'll get it done quicker." Careful not to cut himself, Gibbs squatted and lifted an armful of the damaged boxes, shuffling carefully toward the stockroom. Then Jerry watched himself do the same, as if from a distance.

After a couple of trips, they had cleared the floor of the damaged boxes, and Myrtle moved three of the flocked trees into the empty space, hastily creating a mini-display that would hide the fact that there had been any upset at all. In the stockroom, Jerry and Gibbs dumped the broken boxes into a 30-gallon trash can until it was nearly full. Jerry felt sick at the sight. He glanced at the break room, remembering the sandwich waiting for him there, but found he wasn't at all hungry.

"Boss, you feeling okay?" Gibbs asked. Jerry looked at the gawky youth with his impossibly long arms, his shocking red hair, his long face pocked by alternating freckles and acne. *That is one ugly kid,* Jerry said to himself, but out loud he said, "I'm fine. Just....I'm fine." Jerry realized he was about to confide in a subordinate his fears regarding his own managerial ability, which seemed a bad idea, even when his judgment was impaired, as it certainly was at the moment.

Just then the intercom blared, "Checker, please. We need a checker." Gibbs' eyebrows lifted. "I could do that," he offered hopefully. Gibbs hadn't yet learned the register, so it was an empty offer. Jerry crossed to the intercom on the wall and punched at the black button. "On my way." He nodded at Gibbs. "Thanks for your help, son."

"Glad to, Boss."

"Well...man your post, please—"

"Jerry, why bother? No one is buying those things."

Jerry grunted. "Walk with me," he said as they turned out onto the floor. They had to go past the station where Gibbs had been assigned anyway, so it was one way to get the boy to his place with a minimum of fuss. "Except for me, you are the only one trained on that machine," Jerry said.

"Yeah, but no one is buyin'," Gibbs complained, a little too much like whining for Jerry's nerves in their current state of jangle.

"It's going to take a while for word to get around," Jerry said, wishing he believed that himself. He had sunk a fortune into the Orna-matic machine—that printed custom photos onto Christmas tree bulbs, along with up to three lines of text of thirty characters each for whatever the customer wanted the ornament to say, written in a variety of possible fonts in glittery, high-contrast script. The machine had knocked Jerry's socks off at the Christmas trade show last July. The fact that it did not seem to have a similar effect on the shoppers of Munich, Michigan left him with a sour feeling in his stomach. "Talk it up, do a few free samples," he told Gibbs as they reached the station where the machine stood in all of its bulky glory. He noted with a sigh that the aisle was as deserted as an arctic plain.

"Whatever you say, Boss," Gibbs said. Jerry could hear the pained resignation in his voice. Jerry started away, and then remembered another matter that was nagging at the back of his mind. "Oh, Gibbs, is everything ready to go for the tree lighting in the town square tonight?"

"I don't know. Donna was on that. She's out sick today."

Jerry nodded. He remembered Velma saying something about that when he had come in. "Well look, why don't you put in fifteen minutes here, then go call Donna and see where things stand. Then come do another fifteen here, and then finish up whatever she hasn't gotten to yet. Fifteen on, fifteen off, like that."

"Sounds good, Boss." His face brightened, saved from certain boredom. Jerry nodded and set off again toward the cashiers' station. Except for the area directly around the Orna-matic machine, the store was so crowded that trying to get from one place to another in a speedy fashion was a bit like running an obstacle course. He felt like a linebacker weaving and dodging to get through the opponents' defensive linemen, with the fifty-yard line forever just out of sight.

Rounding a corner, the checkout lines came into view, and if he were a swearing man, he would have let rip a bright blue streak. The three checkout stands that were open were mobbed, each with a line of twenty or more customers. Feigning professional calm, Jerry swung behind the register of line number four and called out above the din, "I'll take the next customer here!"

No "next customers" responded, but the tail ends of several of the other lines surged toward him, and he felt a tug of satisfaction as he settled into the regularity and tedium of ringing up items and making change, quickly entering into something like a meditative state in which time seemed irrelevant and little else in the universe existed.

A half hour later, however, his bubble of busy bliss was unceremoniously popped as Gibbs ran up to him, once more out of breath. "Gibbs, why are you running? It sets a bad example for the children. We don't let *them* run in here."

Linda from the next counter called over, "It's not professional!"

"You heard the woman," Jerry agreed. "It's not professional."

"Boss, I was getting the manger scene packed up for tonight."

"Is everything ready?" Jerry asked, a vague feeling of dread beginning to climb up his undershirt toward the back of his neck.

"Well, yes, almost everything," the young man agreed. "I got the angel, two shepherds, Mary and Joseph and all three wise men in bubble wrap and in the truck. I also got a donkey and two sheep."

"So what's the problem?" Jerry asked.

"The baby Jesus," he panted. "He's missing."

Chapter Two

Sheriff Howard Saks struck his boot against the cement porch step to dislodge the clumps of snow that had gathered on it, mixed white and brown like rocky road ice cream. Sufficiently de-snowed, he struck the other boot until it, too, was reasonably clean. He straightened up to his full six feet five inches and pushed open the door of his house.

"Lara, I'm home!" he shouted, removing his coat. He didn't used to come home for lunch. Sometimes he missed the lunchtime grease-fests at the Hungry Sow, universally considered the finest diner in Munich. More than the food, he missed the camaraderie—shooting the breeze with the retirees permanently fixed at the counter, and dropping his guard for an hour, spending time with his fellow officers as something other than their superior officer.

That kind of thing was possible in a small town. It was one of the reasons he liked it there. As he picked his way through the obstacle course of the living room, he thought back to when he and Lara were first married. He had been a deputy in Grand Rapids, then. He'd felt like he was part of a machine—a big machine, too big for his taste. He didn't like the impersonality of the large force or the anonymity. So when Lucy was born, he was determined to raise her where everyone would know her.

He sighed. Thinking of Lucy often stopped him in his tracks. In the first couple of months since she went missing, the thought of her resulted in a sob that would erupt from his throat with the involuntary force of a sneeze. It was unmanly and embarrassing. Now, six months since she'd been gone, it only struck at his heart, causing a physical pain that lasted for hours.

But he had that pain a lot, because he thought of her a lot. He rounded the corner and stepped into the kitchen. He expected to see Lara, surrounded by a cloud of steam, putting lunch on the table, reminding him to "wash his filthy hands." Instead, the room was silent and dark. It was also undisturbed by mealtime preparations.

"Lara!" he called again. "Lara, you home? Is everything okay?"

His brows furrowed, folding his face nearly in two at the bridge of his nose. Quickening his pace, he stepped into the hallway, and into the bedroom he shared with his wife. It, too, was still. The curtains had not been drawn back, and the room was cold and dark as midnight. Howard felt a shiver run down his spine. Losing Lucy had broken his heart. It never occurred to him that he might lose Lara, too, and the thought of it, as irrational as he knew it was at this point, made his heart race. A cold sweat began to bead up on his forehead.

He knocked on the door of the bathroom, but when he did, it swung open—empty. "Lara!" he yelled, and he noticed that there was a frantic note to it.

At the end of the hall was Lucy's room. They both

avoided Lucy's room, so he decided to rule out other possible places first. He checked the garage, and the basement, and the spare bedroom that served as a combined office space and craft room. But Lara was not there.

Finally, fighting down his panic, he turned again toward Lucy's room. They hadn't touched it since she...he used to say, "disappeared," but now he had begun to use the word "left." He didn't know why. "Lara?" he called softly as he pushed open the bedroom door.

Lara was there. His breath caught in his throat, which was suddenly thick with relief. She was sitting on the bed, running her hand along the bedspread. He sat next to her and pulled her into him. Her small frame folded around his sizable belly and she clung to him. But she didn't weep, nor did she speak.

She didn't need to. He held her to him and rocked her, looking around at the artifacts of Lucy's childhood in what was now a museum of a bygone time that he knew in his heart of hearts would not come again. He saw the row of collectible dolls—unplayed-with for half a decade, but still cherished and carefully arranged on a shelf.

The wall was adorned by a poster advertising a CD of her favorite band, Grief Patrol. The name of the CD appeared to be "This Effervescent Sadness," and for the first time ever, Howard felt a connection to those words. He hated the music—he found it loud and dreary. He preferred country and western, and he liked pretty much everything about it: the patriotism, the melodrama, and the humor. It was hopeful music, he mused. A Grief Patrol CD sounded to him like sixty straight minutes of depression, and he didn't understand how Lucy could listen to it over and over.

There's no reasoning with kids, he reminded himself, and hugged his wife, rocking, rocking. He tried not to think of what had happened to his daughter, but the possibilities rattled through his brain obsessively. Had she been kidnapped? Had she died in a drug overdose—had her cigarette-smoking high school buddies simply dumped her body in a ditch somewhere? Did she run away to Detroit, and was she turning tricks now to earn her next meal?

His thoughts were interrupted by his wife, who did not move, although she spoke. "I was hard on her," she said into his prominent gut. He didn't answer her, but stroked her back and watched as one little gleam of light escaped the curtains and slid down the far wall like a tear.

Chapter Three

Pastor Katie Jorgenson straightened her Master of Divinity diploma and stood back to admire its placement. Then she set the hammer down on her desk and surveyed the room. *My desk,* she thought. *And this is my office.* Her heart skipped half a beat, and she felt a thrill of excitement and pleasure. No one had been more surprised than she when St. Gabriel's Lutheran Parish in Munich had called her.

She had spent the past five years since her ordination in what felt like a torturous indentured servitude as the youth pastor at a large parish near Flint under the suspicious eye of an ambitious senior pastor, who was all too eager to find fault with every decision she made. *Here,* she thought, *I will be my own boss, and no one will question my motives or whisper behind my back!*

"Pastor," a voice interrupted her reverie. Katie turned to see Evelyn Gammerbrau, the parish secretary, sticking her head through the door of her office, seeming, for some reason, hesitant to step inside.

"Come in, Miss Gammerbrau," Katie said, smiling broadly. Miss Gammerbrau didn't look happy about actually stepping into the office, and Katie wondered momentarily about what kind of relationship she had had with the previous pastor. Hesitantly, the woman stepped inside. She looked to be about fifty-five, slim, with mousy brown hair and half-lens glasses that hung on a cord when not planted on her nose.

Pastor Katie, who was barely past thirty, tall, and blond, was almost her mirror opposite. Katie noticed that she and her secretary did share one trait, however: a prominent nose that forbade both any claim on real beauty. Katie smiled broadly and motioned toward a couple of chairs where they could sit opposite each other without the pastor's desk imposing itself between them. *After all,* Katie said to herself, *I'm the pastor. I don't need to remind anyone of my authority here.*

"What can I do for you, Miss Gammerbrau?" Pastor Katie asked, smoothing her skirt and crossing her legs in a professional and ladylike manner.

"You can call me Gammy, Pastor, everyone does." Miss Gammerbrau sat, her notebook at the ready.

"That's fine, if you're sure it's all right…Gammy."

Gammy shot her a forced smile that lasted only one half second longer than it absolutely had to. "Pastor Knudson always had me report to him on his calendar every morning, so he'd know where he had to be, and when."

"That's fine, Gammy, but wouldn't it be easier to just e-mail that to me? Or better yet, to keep everything on a Google calendar, so that we can both access and make changes to it as necessary?"

Gammy cocked her head slightly. "E-mail, Pastor? That's for children."

Pastor Katie sat up straight in her chair and shook her head. "Are you saying you don't use e-mail?"

"No ma'am."

Katie searched the church offices in her mind. To her horror she realized that she didn't remember seeing a computer anywhere. Perhaps she had assumed everyone used laptops? More likely she just hadn't been paying attention. She felt at her clerical collar—a bad habit she'd picked up that evidenced itself whenever she felt insecure about her calling or her ability to carry it out.

"Gammy…let me get this straight. This church doesn't have wifi?"

"Wifi, Pastor? What is that?"

"DSL?"

"Is that a disease, Pastor? 'Cause I can assure you that I am as healthy as an ox."

Katie couldn't understand it. All of the correspondence and announcements from the bishop's office came by e-mail—how had Pastor Knudson known about the clergy retreats or prepared for the bishop's visits without e-mail? For that matter, if they didn't have e-mail they most certainly didn't have a website—an unthinkable oversight for any congregation wanting to attract new members.

"Well, we'll have to fix this immediately. Can you… never mind, I'll call the phone company and get things started straightaway." She smiled, feeling not quite as confident as she had just minutes before. "Now, you were about to report to me my schedule for the day." She saluted Gammy, "Aye-aye, let's have it, then."

Gammy narrowed her eyes at this occasion of silliness, but dutifully opened her notepad anyway, setting her half-glasses on the peak of her formidable nose. "You have a seven-o'clock Christmas tree lighting in the town square. Every year the pastor says a prayer and plugs it in. You're the pastor, now. You should get there a little early, 6:45 at the latest. I'll get the prayer out of the files for you."

"There's a set prayer for lighting the Christmas tree?"

"Pastor Knudson has used it every year since 1971. Composed it himself. People expect it."

"Well, I'll definitely take a look at it."

"I'll have it on your desk by four p.m."

"I've got several hours until then. What else is on the schedule?"

Gammy looked again at her notebook. "Not a thing."

"No visits?"

"There were three lined up, but they canceled."

Katie's eyes widened. "Why did they do that?"

Gammy removed the glasses from her nose and let them drop to hang by the cord, even with her bosoms. "Pastor, the people of this church come from good German stock. They don't just let strangers into their homes, even if they have hi-falutin' degrees and clerical collars." She leaned in, as if concerned that she might be overheard. "Especially not *Swedes*," she whispered.

"Is this a joke?" Katie asked, wondering suddenly where the reality-TV crew was hidden.

"Is what a joke?" Gammy's face was pursed up like a persimmon.

Katie sighed and sat back in her chair, not sure how to process all of this. She sighed, a little too loudly. "Thank you, Gammy. Listen, I wonder if you can tell me where the nearest parishioner lives?"

"The Fischers live across the street—that'd be the chef at the diner, he's widowed, got four kids. Three houses down would be the Saks' place. He's the county sheriff, lives there with his wife, Lara. Their daughter disappeared a few months ago. They haven't been to church in a while."

"Their daughter…disappeared? What happened to her?" Katie's face softened.

"No one knows. One day she was there, next day she wasn't. Sheriff has pulled out all the stops looking for her, but it hasn't done any good."

"They must be heartbroken."

"They haven't been to church in a while," Gammy repeated.

Katie nodded, standing up. "Then that's where I'll start!"

Gammy cocked an eyebrow at the Pastor. "Just what do you mean, 'That's where I'll start?'"

"I'll just go knock on their door, and introduce myself, and tell them I hope I'll see them at church." She grinned broadly, relieved to have a plan.

"Pastor," Gammy said, still seated and her face pinched, "has it occurred to you that your visit might not…be that welcome?"

"Why wouldn't it be? I won't be going in, I'll just be saying hello."

"Pastor, let me tell you something. We here in Munich have never had a female pastor. Lots of folks left the church when they heard you were coming. I swear I don't know how you squeaked by with a majority at the parish meeting. Oh, wait, I do, there was a flu going around. The liberals in the parish seemed strangely immune. I thought it was *very* suspicious." She looked at Katie as if she were accusing her of conspiracy. "Anyway, I can't say for certain that's why the Saks haven't been to church lately, but I can't say it isn't, either."

"I can't believe that, Gammy," Katie said, shocked.

"Believe it, Pastor," Gammy said, rising and making for the door. "But don't you worry, I've got your back." And she slammed the door that separated their offices with a loud bang.

"In that case, I'm going to keep my back to the wall," Katie said to herself, fumbling at her clerical collar.

Chapter Four

Jerry stumbled into the break room, slightly off balance from crab-walking through the stockroom attic. He wove over to a seat at the break table next to Gibbs and collapsed into it with all the grace of a falling sack of root vegetables. Myrtle, at the other end of the table, pointed to her head and moved her finger in a circular motion. Jerry scowled. Deep in his heart, he knew the woman was crazy, but it was rare for her to say so right out in public, especially in sign language.

She repeated the motion again, with intensified finger-circling. Jerry looked at Gibbs for a translation.

"Oh. Okay. So Jerry, you've got cobwebs in your hair," the teenager informed him.

"Gibbs! It's rude to *say* so!" Myrtle objected.

Jerry sighed, correcting her. "It's *helpful* to say so. Thank you, son—the game of charades was *not* so helpful." Jerry ran his fingers through what remained of his short brown hair, teasing out the cobwebs and wiping them on his khakis.

"Did you find it, Mr. Keller? Did you find the baby Jesus?" Myrtle asked, sipping at her Coca-Cola through a soda straw.

Jerry sighed. "No, I'm sorry to say. I searched everywhere. It's a Kendall Nativity Set, Model E, which is the largest they make, just a little more than life-sized— it's not easy to misplace one of those."

"Jerry, did you ever notice how the baby Jesus in the Kendall sets are not size-proportionate to the other figures in the set?" Gibbs asked.

"What an odd thing to say," Myrtle snapped. "I swear, Gibbs, you are an odd child." Myrtle opened a pack of Cheez-Its and, using tweezers, held one cracker to her lips at a time and nibbled at it in strange, bird-like attacks.

"I *have* noticed that, Gibbs." Nick had just come into the break room and opened his Santa suit jacket to reveal a tie-dyed T-shirt underneath. This he untucked and then loosened his belt. "It's a madhouse out there—thank goodness for State-mandated break periods."

Jerry grinned at Nick, who was hands-down the best store Santa he had ever hired—and a hard worker on the loading dock and in the stockroom during the off-season, too.

Nick mussed up Gibbs' carrot-top and continued. "The Jesus in all the Kindall sets is about half again the size he should be. If Mary had given birth to a child that large, she'd have been walking bowlegged 'til Easter."

Myrtle gasped, "Nick, you are the last person I would expect to hear *blaspheming.* You should be ashamed of yourself."

Jerry chuckled, "Well, it *was* a miraculous birth. Maybe the holy mother got a little help."

"What are we gonna do, Boss?" Gibbs asked, glancing at the clock and buckling on a wide leather lifting belt. "We gotta go set up the crèche pretty quick."

Jerry tugged at his tie, starting to sweat. *People I can handle,* he thought. *Decisions make my brain freeze.* "Anyone have any idea where it could be?"

"Maybe it got broken after last year, and someone

just tossed it," Nick offered, settling in across from Jerry and opening a can of Cactus Cooler.

"No, someone would have told me…at least I hope they would." Jerry pursed his lips. "More likely it was just misplaced in transit."

"So what are we gonna *do*?" Gibbs repeated.

Jerry shook his head and drummed the break table with his fingers.

"Wait," Myrtle exclaimed, and leaped up, running to the break room door. She stuck her head out into the store and listened for a minute.

Jerry rolled his eyes and sighed. "Here we go…"

"*A child, a child….*" She mimicked the line of the carol playing just then, singing in a warbling soprano voice, and then explained, "It's from 'Do You Hear What I Hear?' A child, a child, as if it were…*two children*." She paused, thinking. Then, excitedly, she asked, "Mr. Keller, why don't we simply use a baby Jesus from another one of those sets, just for the day?"

"I'd hate to mar it, that's an expensive set." Jerry frowned for a moment, but then turned to Gibbs. "Do we even *have* another Kendall E-series in stock?"

"I'll go look, Boss." The teenager's red hair flashed out of the room looking for all the world like the tail of a rocket.

"That's a good kid," Nick said. "I don't care what anyone says."

Myrtle lowered her head and whispered, "What are they saying—*who's* saying?"

Nick grinned and winked at Jerry. Then he got up and ambled over to the snack machine. He pulled on his very real white beard as he surveyed his options. "I certainly was worried about him for a while, I have to say."

"You mean Lucy Saks disappearing?"

Nick nodded. "What happened to the Starbursts? They used to stock this thing with Starbursts."

"I wonder about that myself," Jerry said. "I know they were close."

"They were an *item*," Myrtle corrected him.

"Good on you, Jerry, cutting the kid some slack. Meant to say that to you before. He's just a kid, but a kid can have a broken heart same as the rest of us." Nick punched in a code, and had no sooner collected a bag of Twizzlers from the machine's delivery chute than Gibbs tore into the break room again.

"Bad news, Boss," he panted. "No E's. A D-Series would work—would actually be closer to the proper-sized Jesus—a preemie instead of giganto-baby. But there's no D's, either—the Methodist church over in Silas bought the last one last week. The C's are just too much smaller to work. Jesus would look like a leprechaun baby."

Myrtle fixed him with a menacing eye, but Jerry held up a finger in her direction and she held her tongue. "What about other sets, from a different brand?" Jerry asked.

"I thought of that. Nothing big enough, except…"

"Except what?"

"Well, it'll raise some eyebrows, Boss, and that's for sure."

Nick chuckled, "I like it already." He fed a Twizzler into his soda can to use it as a straw.

"I'm listening," said Jerry.

Chapter Five

Pastor Katie picked her way down the sidewalk toward the Saks house, taking care to avoid putting her foot in either snowbanks or slushy puddles, but since the sidewalk was in poor repair, she was not entirely successful, and she felt a slow, spreading, cold sensation in her left boot. "Drat," she mumbled to herself, making a mental note to keep some spare socks in her office.

The snow was lovely, she noticed, as was the town. For a moment her frustration at Gammy faded and was replaced by awe and beauty. Munich was a small, sleepy village. The word cozy came to her mind and she smiled.

At the third house, she paused and tried to assess what kind of people lived there. It was a small, cracker box affair, in good repair, painted a tasteful lemon with a smart dark teal accent around the windows. It was the house of hard-working middle-class folk who cared about their home and their town, she decided. She started up the path to the front door.

Once there, she pressed the doorbell, but heard nothing. *It could be broken,* she thought, but avoided the temptation to try it again. *It could just be a quiet doorbell, or maybe it rings far back in the house. I don't want to annoy people right out of the gate.*

After a few minutes, not detecting any sound or movement from within, she knocked on the screen door. The cold metal stung at her knuckles, and she hugged her arms to her chest and lowered her face into her coat collar against the cold. Steam billowed from her mouth with each breath she exhaled, and she wondered at the beauty of it as it drifted away from her.

The door yanked open with a loud "snack" and Katie jumped. "Sorry," she said to the man's eye in the slit of the door. "You scared me."

The man opened the door the rest of the way. He was tall—very tall, she realized. His hair looked like the kind of buzz cut you saw on Marines in the 1960s, and his eyes were pained. "I'm your new neighbor," she said. "I'm Katie Jorgenson, I'm the pas—"

"Now's not a good time," the man said sharply and closed the door with a bang that made her jump again.

She stood alone and blinked. "Katie, my dear," she said out loud to herself in a faux-British accent as she descended the steps to the street, "You are off to a *smashing* start."

Chapter Six

There was nothing left to burn. The books were gone by then, and all of the furniture that she could move. She was just about to start dismantling the handrail on the staircase when she felt a tension in her belly release and moisture began seeping down her legs. *This must be my water breaking,* she thought. *It's coming. It's finally real.* She had been in active denial for months, she knew, but always in the back of her mind she knew this moment would arrive. She was not ready.

She'd been having little spasms the past few days, but

she had ignored them. Her face twisted into a mask of helplessness and grief and she started sobbing. When the first wave of cramps hit, her sobs alternated with screams of pain.

She gasped for air until she was dizzy, so she forced herself to stop crying and breathe normally, or she knew she would pass out. Snow danced in front of her eyes, looking exactly like the screen of the tiny black and white TV her parents had given her for her room when she was very young—a TV with no signal. A roaring had begun in her ears.

She breathed deeply and exhaled slowly and gradually the snow and the roaring subsided, leaving her aware that she was squatting on the wooden floor of the big, cold, empty house. She noticed the pale light that barely illuminated the room. Afternoon light, she had come to understand, was the loneliest.

With a start she realized that she had no idea how long she would have before the next round of cramps began. *I'm not ready for this!* her brain screamed silently, but she forced herself to think logically. What did she *need?*

A soft place to lie—she had that. A month ago when she had first broken into this house she had dragged all the bedding downstairs into the kitchen, and there she had created a nest that was small and relatively easy to keep warm. A half-bath was there, and the owners of the house had blessedly kept the water on, even if the gas and electricity were not.

Food—she had three cans of beans left that she had stolen from another empty house down the street, and a couple of potatoes from a neighbor's root cellar that were only slightly moldy. It was not enough, but it would suffice for three days. She placed the cans and a can opener within reach of the pile of blankets that served her for a bed. To boil the potatoes she would need a fire, which brought her to....

Warmth—that seemed to be the eternal problem, at least since autumn had begun in earnest. She wondered if she had the strength to really attack the white balusters of the staircase in her current state. She had straw for kindling, stuffed into a paper bag near the stove. And she had a lighter, used far less these days since her cigarettes had run out.

As she was thinking the cramps hit again and she slid down the wall and wailed until they stopped. The moment they did, she grabbed the hatchet from the nail by the door and headed for the staircase. Her back erupted into spasms of fire as she raised the hatchet but she screamed as she hacked, and the noise emitting from her throat served somehow to cancel out the pain. Two chops, three, four, five, and she had knocked loose the bottom of the first baluster. Two more chops loosed the top and she was able to wring it free of its place.

She learned how to be more efficient as she worked and she had a small pile of seven balusters before the pain overtook her again. Without shame she rolled on the floor and howled until it passed, after which she picked up the hatchet again without a sound and knocked out another eleven balusters, working her way up the staircase.

Three attacks later, she had them all. It took four trips to get them all back to the kitchen, and the uncooperative things kept slipping free of their fellows and dropping behind her as she worked. She didn't curse; she didn't have the energy. She just picked up the fallen balusters on her return trips until she had them all.

The next round of cramps was the worst yet, and she realized her time was running out. She fought to keep her panic under control, and as soon as the contractions subsided, she scrambled to get a fire lit.

Placing one of the balusters on the first step leading up to the pantry, she brought her foot down hard as close to the middle of it as she could. It cracked. Another kick snapped it in two. She snapped several others until she had a pile of wood small enough to fit into the antique wood-burning stove that adorned the corner of the kitchen.

Several of the old houses around Munich had these, although most of them were merely decorative, now. The manufacturer's German name was proudly stamped across the top of it: König. The fact that this house had such a stove had been one of the reasons she had chosen *this* house to squat in. The stove no doubt had rarely been used, but it *did* work, and she was grateful for her good fortune at finding it.

She had just got the fire lit when the next contractions hit. But this round was not like those that had come before. This was deep, and she had the sense that she was poised over an endless abyss from which she could never return. The pain didn't stop this time, but settled into her bones like a monster setting up house within her. Another squatter, just like her—and apparently here to stay.

She screamed and clutched at the blankets in her two balled fists.

Chapter Seven

The sun was completely down, and Pastor Katie's spirit was as black as the sky was dark. At about five o'clock she had given up for the day, every avenue of connection with her new parishioners thwarted. After her ill-fated visit to the Saks she had returned to the office, grabbed a copy of the parish roster, and begun to systematically knock on doors.

It was fruitless effort. Either no one was home, or children were home who would not admit a stranger— she had to admit the wisdom of this and did not begrudge it—or people were simply busy and sent her on her way, usually politely, but others less so. But with every unanswered knock, with every "no thank you," with every "another time, Pastor," she felt personally slighted.

She knew she was acting out of a sense of panic, that her feelings were irrational, that she should just go home and go to bed. But she couldn't do that—she had to light a stupid Christmas tree in front of an entire town that, if Miss Gammerbrau was right, didn't want her. Why had the church called her, if that was the case? Her head spun and her heart ached. Finally, she had simply sunk into her office chair, some part of herself savoring the depression that coursed through her in waves and rendered her immobile, almost insensate.

For she didn't notice that the sun had set, and was surprised when she realized that she had been sitting in the dark for some time. She sprang for a light switch and looked at her watch: 6:45. "Oh no! Oh, God help me!" she exclaimed out loud, and, all self-pity forgotten for the moment, she snatched up her coat and ran for the door.

Fortunately, St. Gabriel's sat on the town square, and she didn't have far to run. Rushing toward the massive Christmas tree, she wasn't sure if her racing pulse was the result of running or panic—probably both. She felt to make sure her clerical collar was in place. It was. She sniffed and cleared her throat, running her fingers over her hair in a pointless attempt to unmuss the unmanageable.

A crowd had gathered around the tree and the crèche. There seemed to be a high degree of excitement in the crowd, and despite her hurry and concern, her interest was piqued. She began to wind her way through the crowd, hearing laughs, catcalls, and plenty of "tsk-ing."

She finally got close enough to see. Standing on tiptoe to look over the shoulder of a tallish woman in front of her, she saw what everyone was buzzing about: an enormous crèche scene had been erected on the north side of the Christmas tree, its figures nearly half again life-sized. It was impressive and ornate. She looked at each of the figures in turn.

There were the wise men, ahead of schedule, apparently. She remembered that, as a child, she had always kept the wise men across the room, and that starting on Christmas Day, she had moved them a little bit closer to the crèche, until they finally joined the other figures on January 6th, the Feast of the Epiphany. These punctual wise men were turbaned and tanned, one bearing a box, another a cruet, another a satchel with a bow.

For a moment, she forgot her panic, and felt a trickle

of wonder and joy ripple through her. Her eyes moved to her right, taking in the poor shepherds, clad in what looked like sackcloth, bearing crooks, their brows adorned with leather headbands. Above them an angel hung, with bright wings and beatific countenance, her hand extended in benediction, her mouth open with praise.

And there was Joseph, looking down in reverence at…. Pastor Katie gasped. Joseph was gazing in reverence at what was clearly an African baby Jesus, his skin as dark as mahogany—and perhaps even *was* mahogany, she realized. Yet Joseph seemed oblivious to anything being amiss. Nor did the surprising skin color of her offspring seem to upset the holy Mother. Her devotion was total, painted tears welling in her plaster eyes.

Suddenly the titters and catcalls around her came rushing back to Katie's consciousness. She heard the woman in front of her whisper to her neighbor, "That's what comes of getting a female pastor. You watch, everything will be all 'political correctness' and that 'social justice' nonsense from here on out. You wait and see. Now even the crèche is political. It's a shame."

"At least she's Lutheran and not UCC," her friend responded. "I hear that Congo female pastors are all communists or man-haters—or both."

"Yah, I wouldn't be a bit surprised. You know, come to think of it, this new pastor doesn't have a man…." Katie watched her eyes widen as she looked at her friend.

"Do you think?"

"She'll keep it secret, I'm sure, but I will lay you odds," the second woman said, nodding.

Katie felt like she had been punched in the gut. "I am *not* a man-hater!" she shouted at the women in front of her. The women looked at her, looked at her collar, looked at each other, and turned three shades of ash.

"P-p-pastor," the first woman stammered, "So nice to…. I mean, we were just…best to you." She grabbed her friend and pulled her away.

"Yes, I'll just *bet* you wish me *the best*," she said with scorn, trying to master her feelings. *I will not cry. I will not cry. I will not cry.*

"Pastor, there you are!" A voice emerged above the din, and a thin, tall man in a bulky coat and earmuffs pushed his way through the crowd to her. "Easy to spot you with the collar and all," he said, holding out his hand. "I'm Tom Drescher, interim mayor. Our mayor died two years ago…it's a long story, another time." He grinned at her as she shook his hand. "Welcome to Munich. I meant to stop by before, rude of me. Settling in nicely? Ah, there's Jerry."

A plump man with thinning brownish hair and spectacles squeezed in beside the mayor. He had on a striped scarf, and his face grimaced against the cold, drawing his lips back from his teeth in what looked like a fearsome and unnatural smile—not unlike Teddy Roosevelt, she realized. "Pastor." The plump man reached to shake her hand. By reflex, she took it.

"Jerry here is the general manager of Bremmer's, the Christmas Superstore—you know about that, yes? We're pretty proud of that store, you betcha," the mayor said by way of introduction. "He and his team put together this whole affair—the tree, the lights, the crèche, the…weird baby Jesus," he shot Jerry an uncertain look, but quickly turned his attention back to the Pastor. "The town owes Bremmer's a lot, always has. They're a great employer, and a tourist attraction besides—because of them Munich hasn't seen the hardship that some other towns around have…but that's another story for another time."

The interim mayor glanced at his watch. "I've got seven sharp, so we'll give it five minutes and begin. Here's what we'll do. I'll welcome everyone, plug Bremmer's—" he punched Jerry playfully in the arm.

"Ow," said Jerry, rubbing at his arm and scowling at Drescher.

"Then I'll introduce you. You'll say a prayer, then I'll say a few more words, then I'll give you the signal, and you plug the tree in—there's an oversized plug Jerry dummied up just for these occasions right in front of the tree. Looks more impressive than it is. You'll put the giant plug in the giant extension cord, but you'll actually need to flip the switch just behind it to make it go on." He winked at her, "A little bit of stage magic. Sound okay?"

But she hadn't heard a single word after he said, "You'll say a prayer." A prayer! Her mind raced. Gammy had placed the old Pastor's prayer on her desk this morning. It was still there. In her distress over the day's events, she hadn't even glanced at it. She looked over the crowd and gauged that it was three or even four hundred strong. All of them would be watching to see her succeed or fail. Panic once again gripped her, followed by a double helping of performance anxiety.

Her heart pounded. Her feet were frozen. Tears welled up in her eyes. *I will not cry. I will not cry. I will not cry.*

"Pastor, are you all right?" Tom looked at her with concern. So did Jerry. "I was asking if all of that sounded okay to you."

She nodded, brushing the back of her mitten across her eyes and across her nose, which was running from both cold and emotion. "Fine, that's all fine." She fought to call back anything the man had said after mention of the prayer. "You'll walk me through it, though, right?"

Tom grinned. "I will. You don't actually have to remember a thing. Just stand up there and look pretty." And with that, he and Jerry moved through the crowd toward the tree.

At any other time, she would have been offended by a remark like that, but she was oddly comforted by the tall, friendly man, and she wondered if she had stayed in Munich if they would have been friends. Then she realized what she had just thought. When had she decided she was leaving? When did she know that it would never, never work in a little town like this? A town that abhorred the very *idea* of female clergy. A town so backward and conservative and mean....

She caught herself, remembering that she had mere moments to compose a grand, public prayer. Again, she fought down panic, and as she picked her way to the tree, she thought furiously. As soon as she was standing next to Jerry, Mayor Tom raised a wireless microphone to his lips and exclaimed, "Merry Christmas, everybody!"

The crowd responded gleefully, with catcalls and boisterous cheer out of proportion to the event. "You all know me, Tom Drescher, your interim mayor. I'd like to be a real mayor some day, but I hear that involves blue fairies, and that's another story."

"Tell us another story, Tom!" someone called, to great peals of laughter.

"I want to welcome all of you to the official kick-off of the Christmas season here in Munich, with the lighting of the town tree. We all know who to thank for this marvelous tree and this…curious…display!" He grinned uncertainly.

"Why is Jesus black?" another man called.

Tom ignored him. "Let's open our festivities with a word of prayer—"

"Are we praying to the black Jesus, Tom, or the white one?" someone yelled.

"Don't you have a Chinaman Jesus?" someone else parried, and an enormous roar of laughter followed. Even the town's few African American residents seemed bemused.

"As you know, our town has a strong Lutheran heritage, and St. Gabriel's has a new pastor, Pastor Katie… Katie…"

Katie leaned over and whispered, "Jorgenson."

"Pastor Katie Jorgenson, won't you please bless these proceedings?" He handed the microphone to her.

The heft of it surprised her, and she wasn't able to grip it properly with her mittens. The microphone fell into the snow and a loud "pock" sound blasted the crowd. Frantically she fished around in the snow for the mic, found it, and held it between her two mittens as if she were praying. The propriety of this posture did not occur to her in the moment, however, and instinct took over. "Let us pray," she said.

She bowed her head, and spoke to the clump of snow by her left boot. "Heavenly Father…" she paused. For all of her furious thought during Tom's introduction, she had drawn a complete blank. She lashed herself internally for not at least reading the old pastor's prayer. She wouldn't have used those words, but it would have given her some clue as to what these people were expecting. And now she was painfully aware that the seconds were ticking by and she wasn't saying anything.

Her next prayer was silent. *Okay, God, you said that you would give me the words when I needed them. I need them now. Right now. A little help, please. Pretty please.*

"Heavenly Father," she repeated, hearing her words echo unsettlingly over the PA system. "It's a cold night. And it's dark. This must have been what it was like when Mary and Joseph made their way to Jerusalem."

"Bethlehem?" someone called out.

"Yes, t-to Bethlehem." Panic rushed through her. She forced it down as the crowd tittered. "They must have been scared and uncertain, their future was so… unknown. It must have been hard for them to trust you. It-It's hard for a lot of us. As we wait for the coming of the Christ child in this season…grow us in love and trust. Grow us in warmth and hospitality. Grow us in the tender care for those we love…and those we're not too sure about. Bless this season, bless these people, bless this town as we celebrate your nativity. Come among us again, make your home with us again, inspire our hearts again as we open to you and to one another in hopeful Advent expectation. For we ask this in the name of the baby Jesus…no matter what color he happens to be. Amen."

There. She had done it. It had started badly, but she had prayed her heart, and the words had come. She had done her part, and God had done his. She breathed a deep sigh of relief, then realized that Tom had taken the microphone from her and was talking again.

"—ask Pastor Katie to plug in the tree!" He nodded at her, and motioned toward the giant, oversized plug and extension cord on the ground. She picked them up and without any ceremony, plugged the one into the other. But nothing happened.

"The switch," Jerry whispered loudly. "Flip the switch."

She fumbled with the plug, running her mittens over it, looking for a switch. To her great horror, she dropped it, but apparently she dropped it on the switch because no sooner had the prop plug hit the ground than the Christmas tree blazed to life.

The crowd cheered, hooted, and whistled. Pastor Katie wished fervently for a snowbank she could slink away and bury herself under. Everyone but her seemed to understand that the proceedings were over, because the crowd noise did not abate, but grew as the revels began in earnest.

Jerry turned to her and offered his hand. "Thank you, Pastor. It was very nice meeting you." She looked at him, then at Tom, then back at Jerry. Without a word, she nodded, turned her back to the crowd, and set off for the parsonage.

Chapter Eight

Jerry leaned against the car, feeling the weight of every weary bone in his body. Most of the crowd had dispersed, but he still heard the sound of revelry now and then. Mostly, though, he heard the distant roar of the freeway, the whine of the wind, and his own heavy breathing.

He didn't even notice Carol until she touched his face with the back of her glove. "You look beat, honeypot," she said. He looked up into her face, glowing in the light of the streetlamp. Here she was, the love of his life, the mother of his children, the guardian of his sanity, always supportive, always understanding, always full of grace. His heart melted at the sight of her, just as it had done for the past twenty-five years. He could not imagine his life without her.

"I am," he said. "I'm whupped. This has been one stressful day."

She nuzzled him. "I'll drive home. You relax."

He couldn't argue with that, and didn't want to, so he made his way to the other side of the car and sank into the passenger seat with a loud and grateful sigh. Carol slid in beside him and started the car, turned on the headlights, and made a technically illegal U turn on Main Street.

"One day Howard is gonna get you for that," Jerry said, without much conviction.

"He does and the cookies stop."

"The extent of civic corruption in this little town staggers me."

Carol smiled. "And marriage is just prostitution, don't forget."

"I love the way you put a good spin on things," Jerry chuckled. "Other people have boring marriages—you know how to keep the thrill of fornication alive, despite the marriage certificate."

"That's why you stay married to me, dear."

"That and the cookies. Just make sure Howard only gets the cookies, though. I'm not enlightened enough not to be jealous."

"Good thing," she patted his leg.

They rode in silence for a while. Jerry watched her face as the lights passed over it, noticing how the chubbiness of middle age had only made her more beautiful. Then he noticed that her brow was tight, as if she were worried about something. "How was your day?" he asked.

"What? Oh, busy. Jack Turner from Silas, you know him?"

"Yeah, I know Jack," he said, picturing the stocky farm equipment salesman, a regular at Bremmer's, sometimes even volunteering at their charitable events.

"He was trying to carve a toy for his grandkid and nearly sliced through a finger."

"Ouch! Is he going to lose it?"

"Gary doesn't think so, but we're going to have to watch it pretty closely. Also had a burn—get this, from Mrs. Ohlstead, setting fire to her figgy pudding."

"You're kidding me."

"I am not."

"I've never even had a figgy pudding."

"Neither had she. Her granddaughter got a recipe off the Internet. The store was out of brandy, so she used Everclear instead, because it was cheaper than whiskey."

Jerry laughed out loud and pounded the seat beside him.

"She's a Seventh-Day Adventist," Carol explained. "What does she know about alcohol?"

"Please tell me she's going to pull through."

"She'll hurt for a couple of days, but she'll be fine. Sent her home with a salve and a change of bandages."

Jerry grinned and stared out the window, watching his store as they passed it on the road.

"What are you thinking, Jerry?"

"I'm thinking I'd give my big toe for a slice of that figgy pudding."

Carol laughed and reached for his hand. "How was *your* day, honey-pot?" she asked.

"Oh, dear, where do I begin?"

"I thought the baby Jesus was a nice touch."

"Couldn't for the life of me find the Christ child for that set. I even crawled through the attic looking for it. Do you think the Johnsons were offended?" he asked, referring to an African American family they knew well.

"Maggie looked like she was having the time of her life. And George was smiling, too. Yeah, I wondered about that, and they could very easily have taken offense, given some of the catcalls flying around tonight, but they didn't."

"They're sensible folks. I've always said so."

"I have never once heard you say so."

"I never said they weren't."

"You never said they weren't circus clowns or tadpoles, either."

"What?" Jerry shook his head. "You just lost me, sweetie."

"Not hard to do, honey." She smacked his leg playfully. "How did you like the new pastor?"

Jerry considered. "I'm not sure what I think about her. She seemed awfully nervous tonight. Not very…I don't know, professional, I suppose."

"Can you blame her? This is a brand new town to her. Plus, she's got to prove herself to these folks, some of whom are openly hostile to the very idea of a woman pastor. I'd be shaking in my boots."

"That she was," Jerry agreed. "Her prayer started out rough, but it ended up okay. I'd sure hate to have to pull one of those out of my hat in front of a crowd of people."

"A crowd of *strangers*," Carol corrected him.

"Right," Jerry said.

"Many of them hostile."

"I'm agreeing with you, honey-pants," he pleaded.

"Did you notice she was crying?"

Jerry turned in his seat. "What? How do you know?"

"I saw her as she was walking away. She wasn't sobbing. She kept her head up. That woman has her pride, and she's strong, I can see that. But I also saw the tears streaming over her cheeks."

"Could've been a trick of the light."

"Fiddlesticks. They were tears."

Jerry watched the road as they approached their street. He saw the Crenshaw's Christmas lights, giving their corner house a magical glow that thrilled the child within him. "What do you think that was about?" he asked.

"Well, if I were to guess, I'd say it's a combination of loneliness, homesickness, insecurity in a new position, ambivalent parishioners—"

"Not to mention hostile."

"—and an insular community that, filled as it is with wonderful people, isn't, frankly, that chummy with outsiders."

"True."

"We need to make her feel like an insider, Jer."

"That would be…very charitable."

"Oh, pooh on charitable. Don't be so clinical. It's the Christian thing to do."

"Are we Christian?" he asked. "We haven't been to church in years. And the last time we did go, it was to the Unitarian Fellowship. They're not Christian—heck, they're not anything."

"That's not fair. That was a lovely little church, and there were both Christians and Jewish folks there."

"Don't forget the witches and the atheists."

She sighed as she pulled into their driveway. "My point is that we should be supportive of Pastor…Katie, was it?"

"I think so."

"Sunday morning, we will be Lutherans." She switched the car off and set the brake.

"I don't think just going to the Lutheran church one time makes you a Lutheran."

"It will make us Lutheran for the day. You have to give yourself over to experiences, sweetie."

"I will not program our doorbell to play 'A Mighty Fortress is Our God.'"

"I didn't ask you to."

"You just want me to go to church."

"You will if you're smart."

He narrowed his eyes at her. "You're a tyrant, you know that, right?"

She leaned over and kissed him—a kiss that was long, wet, and deep. When their lips parted, he felt like he was coming up for air. "And you have no mercy," he added. She kissed him again.

Chapter Nine

Jerry set the last box down at the end of the "workplace" ornaments aisle. "Thanks for restocking these, Myrtle."

She flashed him a smile. "These are going like hotcakes." She pulled a box cutter out of her apron and, with a deft flick of her wrist, slit the packing tape and opened the box. "One week left until Christmas," she said, with a mocking tone of danger. "Do you think you can survive it?"

He didn't answer but stretched his back. He had lifted too much again, and it hurt. From the box Myrtle pulled a plastic bag filled with small, cute stethoscopes, each with a hook for hanging on a tree, and began arranging them on the display shelves.

Just then two boys ran past them, one of them accidentally kicking the box, sending the little stethoscopes flying. "Hey!" Jerry called, and forgetting his back, ran after them. He ran past the barnyard animals ornament kiosk, past the display of Christmas bulbs bearing the logos of various Protestant denominations, past the Fairy ornament kiosk, the stand sporting prosthetic limb ornaments, and through an entire room devoted to bulbs of every size and color sporting baby names, both boys and girls.

Jerry was quickly falling behind, but, determined and dogged, he continued his pursuit. Up ahead he saw them approach the narrow aisle where Gibbs manned the Orno-matic machine—the one employee with apparently nothing to do.

"Gibbs!" he shouted. Gibbs was staring off into space, apparently lost in a daydream. "Gibbs!!" he shouted again, his voice hoarse and labored from his effort.

Gibbs looked up and squinted, taking in the situation immediately. Calmly, he stepped out from behind the Orno-matic counter, and stuck out his leg as the boys rumbled past. One of them went flying, landing on his face with the sound of a loud *slap*, and the other, realizing he was running alone, stopped in his tracks and looked back at where his friend lay face down on the linoleum.

Jerry stopped short, wheezing, and clutched at his hair. "Gibbs, what did you do?"

Gibbs didn't answer, but knelt immediately by the boy on the floor, who was balled up, wailing, and clutching at his mouth. Jerry cringed to see a tooth on the floor near the boy's head. Then he noticed the blood oozing over the boy's chin.

"You okay?" Gibbs asked the boy. The boy's eyes grew round, a mixture of outrage and disbelief.

A woman called from a distant aisle, "Tyler!" The other boy, still frozen in place, looked toward the woman. "Tyler, there you are! Have you seen Jeremy, the little devil?" A stout woman wearing a Tigers ball cap cleared the last of the kiosks separating her from the scene—and dropped her bags. Jerry heard the sound of breaking glass, and lowered his head into his hands.

"Jeremy, what happened to you?"

A split second after setting eyes on the woman, the injured boy let loose with a caterwauling wail. "My baby!" the woman said and dropped to her knees next to the boy.

"It's just a split lip," Gibbs said with unnatural calm. "And the tooth. He'll be fine."

"What happened here?" Rage flashed in the woman's eyes, as she looked from Gibbs to Jerry and back again.

A small crowd had begun to form. Jerry noticed that he was sweating. A lot. The woman looked at the standing boy. "Tyler, what happened here?" Tyler, slightly older and taller than the injured boy, shrugged. "We were playing."

"I tripped him," Gibbs confessed, without a hint of remorse.

"You did *what?*"

"He and the other kid were running down the aisles like it was a track meet, like they were racing or something. They were going to hurt someone, or break something, so I stopped them."

"You hurt *him*! You broke *him*!"

Gibbs blinked. "He was running."

"I don't care! I'm calling the police! This is assault!"

Jerry stepped forward, not sure what to say. "I-I saw it," he told the woman. "Gibbs didn't mean to hurt him. He didn't even think. He just *reacted*."

"No kidding, he didn't think!" The woman fished in her purse for a cell phone. Jerry watched helplessly as she dialed three numbers, which he assumed must have been 911.

"Ma'am, why don't you all come to my office, where you can have some privacy for your call, and the boy can lay down?"

The woman nodded, put away her cell phone, and, with Gibb's help, raised the boy to his feet. The boy was still crying and sniffling, and Jerry noted a great smear of blood on the floor. "Clean this up, Gibbs," he ordered, and, lifting the injured child into his arms, led the woman toward the back rooms.

"I'm still calling the police," the woman glared at him.

"Of course," Jerry agreed. "You can use my office phone, if you like."

After depositing the angry mother and two boys in his office, he closed the door and then leaned against it to catch his breath. Lillian, a tall, wispy woman who worked seasonally as a cashier, hurried past. "Becky called in sick," she threw over her shoulder.

"Of course she did," Jerry replied to no one, since Lillian had already entered the floor.

Jerry knew he should call in someone from his seasonal list, but it was behind this door, in the same room as the Very Angry Woman. He sighed and decided they could survive being short staffed another fifteen minutes. At least, he hoped to have his office back by then.

He took a deep breath and stepped back out onto the floor, narrowly missing bumping into a couple walking arm-in-arm past the door. "Watch where you're going, jerk!" the man snapped.

"Sorry," Jerry said reflexively. For a moment, he stood motionless and imagined a deserted beach. Seagull cries punctuated the air and waves rolled in with power and grace. He sighed and felt himself relax.

His reverie, however, was broken suddenly by the sound of shouting and a crash, just audible above the din of Christmas music and hundreds of shoppers. "God help me," he thought. "What now?" Summoning his internal reserves, he took off running toward the sounds.

They were coming from the checkout lines—specifically the one nearest to the entrance. A tall man dressed in a blue down jacket over a grey hoodie appeared for all the world to be threatening people with a brick. The other patrons cowered before the man's rage, and Kathie, the cashier, stood ramrod straight against the partition separating the registers, as far away from the man as she could get without turning her back and climbing.

The man was shouting at her. "I want my money *back*!"

Jerry slid to a stop on the linoleum within feet of the wild man, narrowly avoiding crashing into a display.

Finally, he was close enough to see that the man wasn't holding a brick at all, but a bright red, foil-wrapped fruitcake, their best-selling brand.

"What's going on?" he asked no one in particular.

Kathie's face registered relief when she saw him. "Jerry, thank goodness you're here. This guy is out of control!"

It was only then that Jerry noticed that the glass on the UPC code reader set into the counter was smashed. "Did he do that?" he asked Kathie.

She nodded. "He smashed it with the cake!"

The man's eyes were wild and he held the fruitcake aloft, threatening anyone who dared step toward him. Jerry felt paralyzed. It was a familiar feeling. There were always so many options. There was never any time to think. He sank to the floor and sat cross-legged, watching the man and pursing his lips.

The man looked at him strangely, not expecting this action. He looked around uncertainly. But seeing the fear in Kathie's eyes, he resumed his threatening posture.

Just then Jerry heard Nick's voice booming out behind him. "Young man!" Jerry turned to see Nick, in full Santa drag, walking briskly toward them. "Young man, drop that fruitcake and back away. Do it now!" The man wavered, lowering the fruitcake slightly.

Nick stopped about two yards short of the young man, assumed a rock-steady position and placed his hands firmly on his wide, white-fur-ornamented hips. "Neal Traugott, don't think I don't know you." Nick's voice thundered with confidence and command. "You're being very, very naughty! If you don't do what

I say right this instant, you'll be very sorry! Put it down, and put it down now!"

The young man dropped the fruitcake, which fell to the floor with a loud thump, sounding every bit like a brick. "Back away! Back to the door!" Nick was advancing, now, his face beet red, his eyes afire.

The young man backed away until he bumped into the plate glass window. He looked down at his empty hands. "I just wanted to return a fruitcake."

"I told him!" Kathie moved to the middle of her cashier's pen and began yelling at the young man, although her words didn't address him. "I told him it is against our *policy* to return food items! It's *not* personal!"—her bottom lip started to waver, and her voice pitched higher, cracking as she lost her emotional control—"It's store policy!" She covered her face and sobbed.

"Oh my," Jerry said out loud from his position on the floor. Nick was hugging the young man now, speaking softly to him, but Jerry couldn't hear what he was saying. Not that he cared that much. He noticed that the fruitcake had fallen within easy reach. He liked fruitcake. He knew a lot of people didn't, but he loved it.

With slow, deliberate movements, Jerry picked up the fruitcake, and with deft, practiced motions, stripped off the foil and the plastic underneath. With his fingers, he tore off about two inches' worth and took a bite.

His mouth filled with pleasure. He could taste the pleasing bitterness of the brandy, and reveled in the gooey goodness of the candied fruit. He savored every bite until he had finished the slice, then quietly wrapped the rest of it back in the foil, and set it aside.

He wasn't thinking about it. He was just acting. Thought didn't seem necessary. The fruitcake was good. "Tasty," he said out loud, and he smacked his lips. Then he pushed himself to his feet, and walked toward the young man. "How much is that fruitcake selling for now, Kathie?" he asked.

"Fourteen ninety-five," she replied. She stood wide-eyed and unmoving, watching his every motion.

Jerry took his wallet out of his pocket and took out three five-dollar bills. The wild look was gone from the young man's face, and now he simply looked scared of Jerry. Jerry handed him the bills, smiled, and said, "The store can't take it back, but I'll take it off your hands, if you'll sell it to me. I love fruitcake."

The young man nodded and took the money. As soon as Jerry turned away, he scrambled past Nick and ran for the door.

Nick placed a hand on Jerry's shoulder. "You okay?" Jerry was looking at a spot on a far distant horizon that existed only in his mind, but he nodded. "I know that fella," Nick told him. "Do you want to press charges?"

Jerry shook his head from side to side slowly, still staring at that imaginary spot. "You thinking about a beach there, Jerry?" Nick asked.

Jerry nodded.

Just then a loud crackle interrupted Amy Grant's "It's the Most Wonderful Time of the Year," and Gibbs' voice sounded over the store-wide intercom. "Jerry Keller to the back. Jerry Keller to the back. Stat." There was a loud *pop!* and the music resumed.

"Stat?" Nick asked. "What does he think this is, *General Hospital?*"

Jerry shook his head, surveyed the scene before him briefly, and began moving uncertainly toward the back rooms.

By the time he reached the door to the break room, his temporary fugue state had mostly passed. He walked in to see Gibbs holding something up to his chest, and it appeared to be wrapped in a blanket. "What's that you've got there, Gibbs?"

"Boss, I…it's…he's…it's a baby."

Jerry had to laugh then. It was a full belly laugh, filled with all the stress of the day. He laughed long and hard and as he did so he felt the tension drain out of him. "Well, a day late and a dollar short—isn't it just my luck!" He laughed some more and sat down at the large, oaken break table. "Is it damaged?" he asked.

"I don't think so. Seems fine."

"Where was it hiding?"

"It wasn't hiding anywhere. I found it lying in the open on the loading dock."

Jerry scowled. "Dagnabbit, I looked everywhere for that thing yesterday. So did you! Heck, I crawled through cobwebs looking for that thing. It couldn't have been just lying out in the open. We would have seen it! Unless…" He looked away. "Unless someone's playing tricks on us.…"

"Boss, it's not the baby Jesus."

"It's not?"

Just then a wail erupted from the bundle in the blanket.

"No Boss, this is a baby. A real baby."

Chapter Ten

Pastor Katie inhaled deeply, the steam rising from her coffee filling her nose with pleasure. She salivated in anticipation of that first lovely sip of the morning. Raising the cup to her lips, she tasted the burnt chocolate of the coffee, the sour spice of clove, the pepper of cinnamon. She allowed herself a moment of ecstasy. Lowering her cup, she thought, *That is a Christmas blend worthy of Solomon the King.*

Stöllen Goods was an upscale bakery and coffee shop, long on cuteness but short on variety. Katie didn't mind, since it was largely just the coffee and the atmosphere she was after, and those were the things the little shop had in spades.

Ever since her "difficult" discussion with Gammy, she felt her office tainted by a hard-to-define negativity. She knew it was just her imagination, and if she stayed it would probably pass. Her shoulders drooped. The thought of leaving undid the momentary lift provided by the excellent coffee. In her heart, she knew she was leaving. The only question was, how soon?

In the meantime, she had a sermon to write, and she simply couldn't face that office. Or Gammy. She opened her laptop—did Stöllen Goods have Wi-Fi? She looked expectantly at the signal monitor and watched it jump to a full five bars. *Yes!* she exclaimed inwardly. She decided that this was her new favorite place.

She quickly navigated to a lectionary site and perused the readings assigned for Sunday—the 4th Sunday of Advent. She loved this part of the sermon-writing process. The lectionary editors, in their often baffling wisdom, selected scripture texts for the three-year cycle that sometimes complemented one another, and sometimes seemed totally random. The fun was in figuring out the common theme running through all of them.

It was like a puzzle, and she loved puzzles. But it was better than a puzzle. It was like doing a crossword where all of the clues were drawn from an area of your life that you loved—like football, or the Victorian novel. The lectionary readings were a puzzle where all of the solutions somehow involved God, and when you figured it out, it told you something about yourself that you either didn't know before or needed to be reminded of. It was a most magical game.

She read prayerfully and carefully through the Old Testament reading from Isaiah. "Look, the young woman is with child and shall bear a son, and shall name him Immanuel." A promise of Good News. She nodded. She could use some Good News right about now. *What is this passage saying to me, to my own life?* She asked herself. She didn't have an answer, but let the question hang as she read on.

Her eyes flitted to the Psalm appointed for the day. The passage struck her like a slap. "Give ear, O Shepherd of Israel, you who lead Joseph like a flock!" She was a shepherd; was the passage talking to her, to pastors? No. She relaxed. It was a call to God—God was the shepherd. The psalmist is calling upon God to hear their cry, to come and save them. That was a prayer she could pray. *Come and save me, God,* she prayed silently. *I feel lost here and I don't know how to make things better.*

The reading from the Epistle was a single run-on sentence from the apostle Paul, the opening of a letter. She read it three times and it said nothing to her. But she was praying the readings here, so she said, *Among your many revelations to this man, God, couldn't you have included a lesson on how to use a period?* She sighed and moved on.

The Gospel reading washed over her like warm, rose-scented water, delicious and poignant. The angel comes to Joseph in a dream, saying, "Do not be afraid to take Mary as your wife, for the child conceived in her is from the Holy Spirit. She will bear a son, and you are to name him Jesus, for he will save his people from their sins." God's care for Joseph's fears, his sense of betrayal and hurt, touched her deeply. *Thank you for caring for Joseph,* she prayed. *Thank you for caring for me, too.*

What was the common theme? Except for the Psalm, all three readings were a promise that salvation is coming, and coming through a child. The Psalm calls on God to bring salvation—not unrelated, she noted. She desperately wanted that promise to be true. Suddenly the Psalm took on new significance—if she wanted it to be true, she should ask for it, just as the Psalm did. She read the Psalm again carefully, only this time she read it before God as a prayer. As she did so, she felt stronger, more hopeful.

Just then a snatch of conversation from the next table intruded upon her attention. "—that new pastor. What were they thinking?" A woman's voice sounded haughty and offended.

"Did you hear that awful prayer?" Another woman said, chuckling.

"I think she was making it up on the spot!"

"So undignified. Prayer should be dignified."

Not again, Katie thought, cringing. *Don't the people in this town have anything better to do than to gossip about* me*?*

"We're thinking of going to the Presbyterian church this Sunday."

"All the way to Silas?"

"It's only ten miles. Besides, it's either that or the Methodists, and Rev. Niles is so old no one can understand a word he's saying. They're calling him Rev. Spotty behind his back."

The second woman cackled. "I hadn't heard that!"

"Well, keep a lid on it. No need to hurt the old man's feelings."

"How long before that woman Pastor moves on, do you think?"

"Gammy gives her three weeks, tops. I hear she even has a bet running with the organist! He thinks she'll hold out six."

"Gammy knows that church inside and out. My money's with her."

"That's smart," the first woman said. "My guess is that she's mustering the faithful. She'll force that she-cow out in no time."

"It will serve her right. People should know their place."

"It's not natural. And did you hear she's a *man-hater*?"

Katie lowered her forehead to the table and banged it quietly but repeatedly. Her heart sank into a black pool of despair. The hope the scriptures had instilled in her fled like cats from a broom. Gammy had won already, she realized. She felt hurt. More than that, she felt *betrayed.*

For a few minutes she just checked out. The words from the other table no longer reached her. She felt numb and disordered. Then, slowly, she began to think logically again. She was grateful she hadn't put on her clergy shirt this morning. Without it, she was invisible. Just another young professional woman. With slow, deliberate movements, she packed up her laptop, slid it into her satchel, and with all the poise and dignity she could muster, walked out the door.

Chapter Eleven

When Howard pushed open the door to the Sheriff's office, it was like stepping into a tomb. Not a creature seemed to be stirring, and the air felt cold and brittle. Then he heard the rustling of papers and saw Diane's dusty blond head bob into view just above the counter that separated her desk from the small lobby. "Diane," Howard said. It was a greeting. He hung his Stetson by the door, but kept his coat on. "Heater broke?"

"Just sluggish, I think, Chief." She was wearing her morning smile. It would wear off by noon. "Sooner or later we're going to have to replace that thing. It's a dinosaur."

"You're right. But not today." He headed straight for the fax machine and began to sort through the in-box to its right. It was his morning ritual. He'd given up praying for some word of Lucy, but he couldn't stop hoping. He couldn't stop looking. He read every bulletin, every wanted poster, every memo for clues. His imagination made crazy leaps. It was like starting his day with a steaming cup of grief.

"I didn't see anything there, Chief," Diane said, a note of uncharacteristic tenderness creeping into her voice. "I look too, you know. We all do."

"All" was not a large category—besides himself there was just Diane and two deputies in the office. But he was grateful for her concern, and he half grimaced, half smiled at her. "Where are Czarnecki and Mueller?"

"Dick's down with the bug. Maggie's on a call—a fence-and-calf matter."

"Hmm. Dick going to be okay?"

"Well, he's not coughing up blood or anything, but his voice certainly sounded like sandpaper. I don't think this is really a mental health day. I think he's sick, but he'll probably live."

Howard nodded. "Okay. Well, I'm going to be...." But he didn't need to finish the sentence. He closed the door to his office and switched on the tiny space heater on the floor. He blew air through his cheeks and took in his office—the cinderblock walls, the unused philosophy degree diploma on the wall, hanging slightly askew, the trash can overflowing with crumpled paper, the yellowed slats of the venetian blinds.

But there was color here, too. On his desk was a bright red poinsettia, so glaringly out of place that it took a while to register. In that moment, it seemed like almost the perfect plant, as if the archetypal poinsettia had forsaken Plato's world of forms and condescended to dwell in the world of men, bringing light and cheer to all who beheld it. He felt his heart melt a bit, and his mustache twitched with unwelcome emotions. A note was attached to this red agent of transcendent cheer, and with unhurried motions he opened it.

The note was simple. "Don't give up on me. Lara."

His lip quivered, and he wiped his eyes with his sleeve. Then he put the note in his pants pocket and sat at his desk. But he couldn't take his eyes off the poinsettia. He thought his wife had been completely lost in her own little world of recrimination and guilt and blame. But here she had reached out to him. Not directly, but truly.

He had had enough of blame. Certainly there was enough of it to go around, but blame, he thought, was like caffeine or sugar. It grants fierce energy but fades quickly, leaving you feeling nauseated and depleted.

No, he was done with it. If he could ever find Lucy, if she were alive, if she would just come home, he wouldn't ask her a single question. He wouldn't yell at her, he wouldn't punish her, he wouldn't ever treat her…*like a child again*, he thought. *But she is a child. Not for much longer. But she is for now.*

He couldn't sort it out and so he dropped it. For months he had blamed Lara—for her perfectionism, for riding the poor girl so harshly, for demanding more of her than anyone could be expected to deliver. *For not knowing how to be tender, or warm, or forgiving,* he thought. Anger at his wife swelled in him. He wanted to hold her responsible, to blame her for Lucy's running away, and for months he had. But he was tired. The blame had simply run out of steam, and the knot in his stomach turned queasily.

He reached out and touched one of the poinsettia's deep green leaves. It was soft, like velvet, like the fabric of a couch he used to have, like a dog's ear. His heart ached for soft things, and until this very moment, he hadn't known it. The ringing of the phone broke his reverie. Distantly he heard Diane's voice answer it.

He turned to the short stack of memos Diane had placed on his desk. One was from Sheriff Michaelson from the next county over, with no message. Howard guessed he just wanted to grouse about the budget cuts the state legislature was imposing on them, or perhaps Bill just wanted to schedule lunch, where he would doubtlessly do the same.

He set that memo aside and looked at the next. A reminder of his upcoming dentist's appointment. *Yup,* he thought. *Looking forward to that one.*

The next memo was a call from Karl Wysocki, who owned several properties just outside of town. Most he rented to poorer farming families, but since the last economic downturn, he hadn't been able to rent all of them. Underneath his phone number there was only one word: squatters.

Howard exhaled noisily—halfway between a moan and a sigh. Of course, he'd have to deal with this, but turning some poor family out into the cold the week before Christmas? That was definitely not his favorite part of the job.

The phone rang again, and a few moments later, Diane's voice buzzed through the intercom. "Rouse your creaky bones, Chief. Maggie's still out, so you're up. They need you down at Bremmer's. And Chief… I'm not sure what this means, but they want you to bring some diapers."

Chapter Twelve

Howard was expecting Bremmer's to be a madhouse. The parking lot was the fullest he'd ever seen it—hundreds of cars stretched out in front of him for what must have been a half a mile. He parked his Range Rover by the loading dock and, package of disposable diapers under one arm, went in through the back—mostly to avoid the crowded shopping floor.

He strode quickly through the dock, through the cavernous stockroom, piled floor to ceiling with boxes and crates on pallets. Passing the offices, he caught a glimpse of a mother and two boys on Jerry's couch, but he didn't stop. He continued into the break room.

"Howard!" Jerry called when he saw him. The portly, bespectacled manager offered him a firm shake and motioned him to the break table. Agnes, one of the cashiers, was there too, apparently on break, flossing her teeth and reading a magazine. Tip, a floor person, came out of the bathroom and saluted Howard, making for the vending machines.

Also by the machines was Gibbs, and Howard had to quell a gut reaction within himself at the sight of him. This was the boy, after all, who caused the conflict with Lucy. If it hadn't been for him, she wouldn't have run away. Howard's teeth gritted as he took in the measure of the boy again. He seemed taller than the last time he'd seen him. Less ugly, somehow. And was he holding a baby? What was that about?

"Are those the diapers?" Jerry asked. Howard nodded and handed them to Jerry, who put them on the table. Howard sat down near Jerry on the break table bench, facing outwards. "What's going on, Jer?" He asked.

"Two things," Jerry answered. "One small—I think. One big. Which one do you feel like tackling first?"

"Let's get the small thing out of the way."

Jerry nodded. "Come with me, then."

Just then Myrtle stuck her head through the door. "Jerry, we've got a little girl out here who's got her finger stuck in a Russian stacking doll."

"Deal with it please, Myrtle," Jerry said to her pleadingly.

"Ooo-kay…." Myrtle slunk away.

"Gibbs, you'd better come, too," Jerry said. "But listen, son, unless we ask you a question, it's probably best if you keep quiet, got it?"

Gibbs, strangely, seemed the very picture of equanimity. "I've got to get a diaper on her, then I'll be in."

Howard's eyes narrowed. "Who's baby is that?" he asked Jerry.

"That's the big thing."

"Oh."

Together they walked to Jerry's office and went inside. "Howard, this is Mrs. Kroll, her boy Eric, and his friend Michael."

"Sherriff, I'm so glad you're here," Mrs. Kroll shook his hand. "My son was attacked—by one of *his* employees." She pointed at Jerry. "I want to press charges."

Howard was skeptical. He didn't like the red-headed wonder his daughter had chosen over her own family, but it didn't sound like anything he'd ever heard about the kid, either. Impulsive, yes. Gangly, yes. Ugly, yes.

More hormones than he knew what to do with, sure. But violent, no. "Did you see this…attack, Mrs. Kroll?"

"Of course I did, I…." She looked at Jerry then, and stopped herself. "Actually, no. I got there just after."

Howard turned to Jerry. "Did *you* see the…attack?"

"I saw it happen, but it wasn't an attack." Jerry described what he'd seen, and Howard nodded. He leaned over to where Eric was lying on the couch. He pulled his flashlight from his belt and examined the boy's lip. It was cut, all right, but it didn't look like it needed stitches. It had already stopped bleeding. "This looks worse than it is," Howard said. He looked back up at the woman. "Is this the extent of the damage?"

"He knocked out a tooth when he hit the floor!"

Howard turned back to the boy. "How are you feeling, Eric?"

"My lip hurtsh."

"You're pretty brave." The boy nodded.

"Does your tooth hurt?" Howard asked. The boy shook his head. "Was that tooth there loose this morning?"

The boy nodded.

"Make sure you put it under your pillow tonight. I hear front teeth are going for twice what other teeth get." The boy's eyes grew wide. So did his smile.

Just then, the door opened, and Gibbs walked in quietly, sleeping baby still in his arms. He sat down in Jerry's chair without a word.

Mrs. Kroll was nearly shaking with rage. "I want that boy arrested!" she said, pointing at Gibbs.

"Well, ma'am, he's not my favorite person in the world, so that's in your favor."

"He's a monster!"

Howard and Jerry both looked at Gibbs then, who was rocking back and forth slightly, seemingly oblivious to what was being said about him.

"Yeah, he's a real menace to society," Howard said drolly. "You can tell just by looking at him."

Gibbs cooed slightly at the baby and rubbed her cheek with his own as he held her.

Howard turned to Michael. "Jerry here just told us what happened. You want to add anything?"

Michael's eyes were huge. "No, sir."

"Did he tell it right?"

The boy nodded.

"You think you should have been running through the store like that?"

The boy looked down. "No, sir."

"Leonard," the Sheriff said. Gibbs looked up. "Do you think you might have found a less dramatic way to stop these boys from running?"

"I guess so. I couldn't think of it in the moment, though."

"Can you think of one, now?"

The boy kept rocking, but looked up at the ceiling, thinking. Then he looked back at the Sheriff. "Not really, no, sir. Let them keep running, I guess."

Howard pushed out his lower lip. He hated the King Solomon role. It required good and creative ideas, and he knew his strengths. Creativity was not among them. "Leonard, you can go. I'll speak to you in the break room in a minute."

Gibbs, dismissed, rose in a dignified manner Howard had never before seen in the lad and left the office.

"Okay, Mrs. Kroll, you've got a couple of options. You can press charges, and Mr. Gibbs there will probably be convicted of a misdemeanor. It'll go on his permanent record and could prevent him from getting into a good school or getting a good job down the line. So, you *could* do that."

The woman looked pleased. Satisfied.

"Or.... You all are in that Victorian out on Lake Circle, right?"

"Yes, that's us." The woman looked suddenly suspicious.

"That fence of yours is about to fall down. It's an eyesore, and three of your neighbors have filed complaints about it. Now, I've put it off as long as I can, but sometime before the next city council meeting, I'm going to have to issue a fine."

The woman's eyes widened. "But that fence is huge! We haven't got the money—"

Howard held up his hand. "Hear me out. Let's just say that fence was repaired before the next Council meeting. I wouldn't have to issue you a fine. That's a good outcome, wouldn't you say?" She nodded, but looked uncertain. "And let's just say that Bremmer's would pay for the materials for that fence. And let's say that a certain Mr. Gibbs donated his time and labor. As punishment. And let's say that were to come with a formal, written apology."

Mrs. Kroll scowled. Howard went on before she could say anything, "No paperwork, no charges, no ruining a youngster's life. Just a brand new fence and a heartfelt 'I'm sorry.' What would you say to that?"

The woman's lips pressed so tight that the color had left them. "How much is the fine?"

"Five hundred dollars."

Mrs. Kroll's mouth dropped open. Howard could see Jerry struggling not to smile.

"That fence does need repairing," she conceded.

"Fine, then. Jerry, can you get the materials delivered the week after Christmas?"

"No problem, Howard."

"Can you give that young man with the baby a little time off?"

"He's got some vacation time coming."

Howard put his hat back on his head, not because he was leaving, but to signal that she was. "Then I think we're done here. Thank you for being a concerned citizen, Mrs. Kroll." He offered a hand to young Eric and helped him to his feet.

Still obviously angry, but cowed and a little shamed, Mrs. Kroll shooed both boys out of the office in front of her. Howard called after them, "Last I heard, front teeth were going for five dollars from the Tooth Fairy."

Mrs. Kroll turned on a dime and shot Howard a nasty look. He smiled at her and tipped his hat. She spun again and exited in a huff.

Howard turned to Jerry. "One down, one to go."

Jerry slapped him on the back and together they walked back to the break room. All the other employees seemed to be on the floor, and from the sound of the din coming from the store, Howard wasn't surprised.

Myrtle stuck her head in through the door again. "Jerry—"

"Deal with it, Myrtle."

She looked uncertain. "You've been deputized," Howard told her. "Go get 'em!"

Her eyes darted back and forth uncertainly, but she ducked out again just the same.

Gibbs was making faces at the baby. She gurgled and giggled and waved her hands at him.

"That was a near miss, young man," Howard said.

"Yes, sir. I'm sorry, sir."

Howard felt a dark cloud descend on his heart. Was he sorry about Lucy, too? He wanted that boy to be sorry. He wanted him to be very sorry. He wanted him to hurt as much as he did.

Howard breathed deep, in an attempt to clear his emotions and his head. "All right, now, Jerry, what's up with this baby? It's the busiest week of your year, why is Mr. Gibbs back here playing nursemaid instead of out there on the floor tripping more young miscreants?"

"Tell 'im, Gibbs," Jerry ordered.

"I was carrying some boxes out to the recycling, and I saw this pile of blankets on the loading dock." The kid was guileless, Howard noted. He'd never noticed that about him before. Of course, he'd never really talked to the kid before. He felt a twinge of guilt. He ignored it. "So I went over to see what it was. The baby was in the blankets."

"Whose baby is it?"

"I don't know, sir."

"Did you see anyone back there?"

"Nope. I looked, too."

Howard pursed his lips and sank down onto one of the benches a couple of feet from the baby. He removed his hat and held it between his knees. The baby looked so much like Lucy when she was that age. Emotion tugged a thread loose from his heart, threatening to unravel it.

Jerry leaned against the vending machine. "What do we do, Howard?"

Howard sighed. "Well, legally, we need to call child protective services."

"*Legally* sounded like a bad word in that sentence."

"It is." Howard chewed on his lip and thought. "Once a child gets into the system…well, let's just say the future isn't bright. It would be better for everyone if we could handle this locally. Find out who the parents are, get this child back to where she belongs." His fingers tapped the brim of his Stetson nervously. "First, though, we should make sure the baby's healthy. The problem is that if we take her to the hospital—boom, she's in the system." He looked up at Jerry. "Do you think Carol could come by and check her out?"

"Shouldn't be a problem. Could probably even get her to bring Gary, the doctor from Silas she works with, just to be on the safe side."

Howard nodded. "Sounds good. You okay having this young man play nursemaid a while longer?"

Jerry nodded. "He's shocking me with a previously undiscovered aptitude for parenting."

The end of Howard's mouth turned up in a smile. "He does have that."

"Young man, you okay doing what you're doing, maybe for a day or so?"

"I'm fine. We need to send someone for milk, I think."

Jerry nodded. "We'll do that. What about tonight?"

Gibbs looked up, his face suddenly fierce and protective. "We're good. She can go home with me. My mom can help."

Jerry looked at Howard uncertainly. Howard waved his hat and shrugged. "Well, call your mother, just to be sure."

The fierceness left Gibbs' eyes and he smiled, relieved. He returned his attention to the baby.

Howard stood and put on his hat again. "Walk me out, will you, Jer?"

The two men retraced their steps through the bowels of the store. "I'm going to go see if there are any missing persons reports matching the baby's description," Howard said. "And I'll make some discreet inquiries at the hospital. I'll let you know if I turn anything up."

Instinctively, both men paused when they reached the loading dock, and looked at the empty space where, they assumed, Gibbs had found the baby.

"You sure you're okay watching the kid?"

"Do you mean Gibbs or the baby?"

Howard chuckled. "Both, I guess."

"I think we'll be fine." Jerry sighed. "It couldn't have come at a worse time, though."

"There're no *good* times for things like this."

"You know what I mean."

"I do. Which is why I'm asking."

"Don't worry about us," Jerry said with certainty. "Just let us know what you find, okay?"

Chapter Thirteen

Sunday morning dawned cold and bright. The intensity of the sunlight seemed in direct contrast to the shadowy dimness by which Pastor Katie's soul was navigating. It was a forced march to get out of bed. Bringing her toothbrush to her lips, she felt like there were lead weights strapped to her wrists. Every few seconds she sighed deeply, as if trying to pull up from her lungs some reserve of vitality or hope or even nerve.

But it was no good. She felt like a fake slipping the plastic tab collar into her clergy shirt. She looked at herself in the parsonage's full-length mirror and, except for the black bags under her eyes and the tightness of her jaw, saw a professional clergyperson. Yes, she could fool just about anyone looking like that.

Except herself. A wave of despair rolled through her, and she did not resist it, because she knew if she did it would stay and not pass through. In a moment the feeling had subsided. The heaviness in her chest remained, though. Donning her coat, she locked the door and crossed the garden courtyard to the church office.

In less than a minute she unlocked her office door and stepped inside. All seemed normal except—she stopped and stared. By the fireplace was a large gift, wrapped in bright Christmas paper. For a moment she forgot her anxiety and touched her hand to her heart. *How thoughtful,* she said to herself. *Should I wait for Christmas, or should I open it now?* She wondered. She looked for a card, but there was none. She decided it was best to open it now, as it was no doubt from parishioners, and she would have opportunity this morning to thank them.

Feeling for a moment like a little girl again, she ripped the paper off the large box, and discovered that beneath it was not a box at all, but…a suitcase. A brand new, rather expensive American Tourister model, with an extending handle and wheels. There, tied to one of the zippers, was a small card on a string. It said, simply, "Bon Voyage." There was no signature.

Katie stood quickly upright, and fought a series of emotions pulsing through her like fire. In a fit of frustration and rage she gathered up the paper and, opening the door into the courtyard, threw it on the ground. She then picked up the suitcase in both hands and sent it flying after the paper. She slammed the office door and stood panting in the silence of her office for an unknowable amount of time.

When her consciousness surfaced from its plunge into her darker emotions, she glanced at the clock and saw that her time was short. She could already hear the musicians rehearsing in the sanctuary. She also heard rustling in Gammy's office through the wall. Mechanically, she prepared for worship.

She went to the bathroom a final time, just in case, and then slipped into the vestry to robe. She nodded at, but did not speak to, the ladies of the altar guild. They didn't seem to notice, or mind. In fact, they exhibited a distinct air of snooty detachment as they flittered about on their business that suited her just fine. She removed her coat and donned a white alb, securing it around her waist with a ropelike cincture.

The organ began pealing in earnest as she fixed her stole. She lowered the dark blue chasuble over her head, and looked at herself in the mirror—straightening, primping, but decidedly not looking at her baggy eyes or the grim set of her mouth.

She made her way to the back of the church, nodding the occasional greeting. She noticed the tubby man who reminded her of Teddy Roosevelt, sitting with what she supposed must have been his wife. He waved at her, and she gave another nod in his direction. When the procession began, she marched as if in a dream. She did not notice that the church was more packed than usual—her brain was busy rehearsing the words of her welcoming comments.

She took her place in the presider's chair, and once the organ wheezed to a full stop, she rose and greeted the assembly. "The grace of our Lord Jesus Christ, the love of God, and the communion of the Holy Spirit be with you all." The Congregation intoned in response, "And also with you."

"Brothers and sisters," she began, "we started this Advent season in anxiety, but we end it in hope." In truth, she had begun this season in hope, and it was crashing around her feet in a steaming mass of anxiety. "The promise is almost here—it is so close we can almost taste it. Our salvation is close, but we do not yet know what form it will take. God, it seems, takes great delight in surprising us." *That's the understatement of the year*, she thought.

"Today we will hear about a teenage girl and the scandalous birth that threatened to undo her. Today we will hear about how God fashions salvation out of tragedy. Let us open our hearts to receive the Word, just as Mary did. Let us pray...."

She read the opening prayer appointed for the day, and took her seat as a succession of laypeople—most of whom she had not yet met—proclaimed the scripture readings. First the Old Testament reading from Isaiah, then the Epistle. Then the Psalm, sung to an old German tune that she loved. Her heart began to warm, and the rhythm of the service ministered to her. She no longer needed to struggle to pray—the service was praying *for* her. She relaxed into it, just a bit.

She stood to read the Gospel, and she finished with a regal "The Gospel of the Lord!" As the people responded, "Praise to you, O Christ," she made her way to the pulpit. She reached up through her alb and took the folded sermon from her breast pocket. She took her time, unfolding it and smoothing it on the rich oak lectern.

Finally, she raised her face and looked into the eyes of several members of the congregation, one after another. They seemed on the edge of their seats. Suddenly, it occurred to her that they had come hoping to see her fall on her face. She set her mouth in a grim smile and began: "In the name of the Holy One— Creator, Liberator, and Comforter. Amen."

"Amen," the congregation intoned, with some light tittering at what must have been for them a very novel formula.

"Before I moved here," she said, "I had a lovely little apartment in Flint. And I do mean, *little*. I loved it; it was homey. But roomy? No. Fortunately, when I moved in I had very little furniture. I am, however, a sucker for antique shops. One day I was browsing and came across a gorgeous old writing desk, and I simply had to have it. In fact, I think it really wanted to come home with me. It was impulsive, but I paid for it on the spot and arranged for its delivery.

"When the delivery truck arrived, and the men carried it upstairs, I was horrified to discover that it was too large for the space I had imagined it would go. The men left it sitting in the middle of the room, looking like an eyesore, and I felt embarrassed, to say the least. I have never had a case of buyer's remorse as bad as this one!" *Until now*, she thought.

She paused before making her transition. "I thought of this story when pondering our Gospel reading for today. There was no way that having a baby fit into Mary's life at that time. There was simply no room for a baby in the life of a single middle-eastern teenager. Saying 'yes' to the angel, to God, would have meant scandal, it would have meant rejection. It could, in fact, have meant death."

She paused a moment to let that sink in. "Jesus is often inconvenient. In fact, he is *usually* inconvenient. He doesn't fit into any of our plans. He only gets in the way, with his troublesome moral admonitions. He's like a piece of furniture that just doesn't fit into our nice and tidy house. I heard someone say once, 'Christianity is bad for business,' and I think, except for the Christmas season, he's probably right.

"Jesus kept being inconvenient for Mary, too. He almost derailed her marriage to Joseph. And when they journeyed to Bethlehem, there was no room for him in the Inn. There was no room for a pregnant teenager.

There was no room for a poor family. There was no room for any of them...." Her eyes glazed over and her shoulders slumped as the full truth of it hit her. Her mouth worked at something that would not come out, and her eyes brimmed over with tears. "There's no room for *me*...." she said. And without another word, she descended unsteadily from the pulpit, and walked into the sacristy, shutting the door behind her.

She pulled off her vestments and left them in a pile. Then she picked up her coat and walked into the cold clear morning with absolutely no idea where she was going.

Chapter Fourteen

When she got back to the cold and empty house, she felt bereft. Bloody sheets covered the floor of the kitchen. The bulge in her belly was gone—and it seemed to her that the best part of her was now missing. It occurred to her that her purpose had been served, and she was nothing but a husk, a shell ready to be discarded, but too stubborn or too stupid to simply lie down and die.

Her body hurt. Her heart hurt. Her soul was screaming. Her throat swelled up and she fought down the emotion, not that there was anyone to see. Not that she should care. Who cared what happened to refuse, after all?

Acting on an impulse that was neither conscious nor

rational, she started cleaning. She wadded up the soiled sheets and threw them in the empty pantry. She went to the linen closet and got a fresh set, clean but faded, with a brownish stain here and there that looked like coffee spilled in some ancient time.

She still had some of the balusters from the staircase left, so she put those in the stove, along with some straw. But before she could light it, her stomach rumbled. She had been so wrapped up in the baby, she hadn't noticed how hungry she was.

Her breasts hurt. They were also scarily huge. But they wouldn't do *her* any good. That was food for the baby, and the baby wouldn't get any of it. She craved red meat. And pudding. And, strangely, brussels sprouts. But she had none of those things. In fact, she didn't have any food at all, except for one lone potato, half-black with mold.

She felt sorry for herself. She felt desperate. Mostly, though, she felt *hungry*. She grabbed the hatchet from its place on the wall and put on the coat she had found. It was three sizes too big for her, but it was warm enough. She didn't lock the door behind her. She didn't have a key, for one thing. The irony of the very idea amused her.

She set out walking toward the other abandoned houses. Over the past several months, she had broken into all of them, one by one, raiding their stores. She gave those houses that had people in them a wide berth, but recently, she realized, something would have to change. The three cans of beans she had left had come from the last empty house.

The way she saw it, she had two options. She could go further afield, maybe walking toward Silas, or in the other direction towards Kent, looking for more empty houses. Or, she could break into a house where people actually lived—when no one was home, of course.

The thought of it scared her. She was scared of getting caught, certainly. She was even more scared of being shot by someone, who naturally would be within his or her rights to shoot an intruder. But what scared her the most was what such an act would make her. She'd be a criminal.

She had been reasoning it out. She knew that squatting was against the law, but it didn't seem like a crime to her. Not really. The house wasn't being used. No one was eating that food. Her being there didn't take anything from anyone. But breaking into a house and stealing a family's food? That was something altogether different.

Right now she was a squatter. Early on, she had, on her better days, enjoyed the romance of that notion. She was like a hobo—free, answerable to no one, taking what she could find. Not a threat, but a fanciful and loveable stereotype. She didn't feel exactly good about herself when she considered herself that way, but she didn't feel bad, either.

But breaking into a house that was being lived in? That would make her a burglar. She hated herself for even thinking it. "I can't do it," she said out loud to herself, turning back to the house she called home. But her tummy rumbled its disagreement. She changed direction then, yielding to its call. Then she thought better of it and turned back. Then she realized that she was only going to get hungrier and hungrier, and she turned around again.

All of the sudden she was glad no one was watching her. They would either think she was dancing or crazy. She felt crazy. Crazy with indecision and with sadness. She sat down in the street and breathed a huge sigh.

She could double-check the other houses. Maybe I missed something? She said to herself. It was worth a look. She got up, dusted off her skirt—baggy now and needing a belt—and set off toward the nearest of the empty houses. Her mind began spinning, trying to think of all the weird places that people might hide food.

Chapter Fifteen

The Sheriff's office was still freezing when Howard arrived. He closed the door behind him and Diane waved a greeting, not bothering to turn from her computer screen. "I shouldn't need to bundle up to come *into* the building," he complained.

"Say the word and I order that heater," Diane said, still not looking at him.

"Ho, Chief." Maggie Czarnecki, his junior deputy, called from her desk near the far window of the little office. Her dark brown hair, he noted, was freshly cut in a fetching pageboy. If he were twenty years younger, he would have found the petite deputy impossible to resist.

As it was, he struggled to be professional rather than paternal toward her.

"Ho, yourself, Czarnecki. Nice haircut."

"Women don't get haircuts, Chief. Our hair is 'styled.' I thought you were married."

"What happened with the calf? Please don't tell me you had to put it down."

"Not as bad as that. Salvaged both the fence and the livestock," she answered, and then added, with mock gravity. "It's days like this that make you glad to be in law enforcement."

He tried not to smile, but was unsuccessful. Mechanically, he went to the fax machine to check for signs of Lucy. As usual, there were none. "Got another call from Karl Wysocki about squatters," Diane informed him. "Memo's on your desk." She finally looked away from the screen. "What was the ruckus at Bremmer's?"

Before answering, Howard walked into his office to retrieve his mug. Returning to the coffee pot, he poured himself a full cup of the strong brew. "Minor incident with a minor. We took care of it. A bigger problem presented itself, though." Briefly, he told them about the baby. Both women listened with rapt attention, and Maggie came closer as he was talking and leaned on Diane's desk. The two women looked at each other.

"Is the baby healthy?" Diane asked.

"She appears to be. Jerry's wife Carol is going to bring the doctor round later today to check her out. Not sure we want her in the system just yet."

"Not if we can help it," Maggie agreed, looking down. Howard saw a lifetime of struggle on her face as she said it. She had been a foster child herself and knew well the hardships of the social service system. He remembered when she had been a troubled teen. She was destined to be involved with criminals one way or the other. Howard had been relieved when she had chosen *this* side of the law, and he had done everything he could to help her.

"Any clue where she came from?" Diane asked.

"None that I could see," Howard shrugged. "That kid Gibbs found her on the loading dock."

"Gibbs?" Diane and Maggie looked at each other, tensing.

"At ease," Howard said, noticing. "I don't hate the boy. Much."

"What about clothes?" Maggie asked, cautiously.

"What *about* clothes?" Howard responded.

"Anything distinctive? Or the blanket? If we have some idea where they came from, we might be able to trace them back to the parents."

Howard nodded and contemplated his coffee as he spoke. "That's good. I'll check that out when I stop by later. In the meantime, Maggie, I'd like you to run down every lead you can find on this kid. Check out missing persons, hospitals, social services, you name it. I want no stone unturned here."

Maggie nodded, turned briskly on her heel and strode back to her desk, all business. "Diane, give her whatever support she needs and keep this place from falling around our ears, as usual. I'll…well, I guess I'll call that old snake Wysocki and let him yell at me for the next fifteen minutes."

Diane's lip turned up in a slight smile and she faced back to her computer screen. Howard entered his office, closed the door, picked up the phone, and dialed. As it was ringing, he sat in his chair and sighed. Several of the poinsettia's petals had fallen on his desk and a couple of the leaves had begun to curl—casualties from its descent into the world of shadow objects. He stuck a finger into the soil. It was dry as dust—a barometer for his soul.

The phone had rung six times, and Howard was just about to hang up when the line clicked, and an impatient voice on the other end said, "What?"

"Karl, this is Howard. I hear you've got squatters."

"More than squatters, we've got burglars. Every house I've got out there on Grizzly Flat has been broken into."

"All six?" Howard slurped at his coffee.

"Five. Sold one last year to the Whitfields."

"Didn't hear about that. But okay, five houses. How do you know they've all been broken into?"

"Because unlike you, you lazy mule, I been there! What do I gotta do to get some law enforcement in this town?"

"No need to get personal, Karl. So far, the only complaint I've heard is squatting, and that's a misdemeanor. And given the cold…."

"Charity is cheap when it's someone else's dime, Sheriff. So save it for a heart-bleeding liberal, will ya?"

At least he's not swearing, Howard thought to himself. *He's just unpleasant now, but this could turn ugly.* "Listen, Karl, I'm on your side. I've got some sympathy for squatters, but not for burglars. I'll head right out and snoop around. Do I have your permission to enter the buildings?"

"Of course. Why don't you swing by the realty and pick up the keys? Don't need you breakin' in, too. S'nuff damage done."

"I'll do that. I'll call you later this afternoon."

Howard hung up and felt the familiar midafternoon lethargy pull at his limbs. *Should I slam back the rest of the coffee?* He wondered. *Nah, work through it. I'm jittery enough.* He threw open his door and, without looking at Diane or Maggie, grabbed his hat.

"Going up to Grizzly Flat to check out Karl's complaint. Hold down the fort."

Diane didn't answer and didn't need to. He paused at the door. "Diane?"

She looked up; a look of mild annoyance creased her brow. "Uh—never mind." When she looked away, he turned and looked back at his office. The plant was a gift from his wife. The soil was dry. The plant was dying. His heart ached. He leaned over, his butt against the wall and his hands on his knees.

"Chief," Czarnecki called from across the room. "You okay?"

He nodded, but didn't answer. Slowly he stepped over to the break table and took a paper cup from the dispenser at the water cooler. He filled it and took it to his office. He sat at his desk and poured the water into the pot that held the plant. "That's for us, honey," he said out loud.

Ten minutes later the keys were in his pocket, and he saw the first of Wysocki's properties clearing the hill in front of him. It was a modest ranch home—nothing fancy. *Bigger than our place,* he thought, as he swung into the drive. *But it's seen some better days.* The fence was missing boards off to his right, and the whole place was badly in need of paint. One shutter hung askew.

Howard stepped up onto the porch, grey from years of hard weather and little care. Several of the boards were warped or chipped. He tried the door. It was locked. None of the windows in front were broken. He set off to his right to circle the house.

He tried the garage door, its ornamental piping faded and shabby, but it too held fast. The side of the house revealed nothing, and the side door into the garage was secure, its windows dusty and spotted with old rain.

The backyard was a tangle of weeds and rusted, discarded car parts. Blocks that once held a car were set up just behind the garage, but they seemed as lonely as the house itself—waiting to succumb to weather and entropy.

Howard began surveillance of the rear of the house. The wooden steps leading up to the back door looked suspiciously unreliable. And near the ground, the basement windows were mud-splashed and…. Howard inhaled sharply, a feeling of triumph coursing through him. One of the windows was broken. He stepped over and examined it. No glass on the outside—it was definitely broken to gain entry, the glass had fallen *into* the house.

It was too small for him to fit through—much too small. *But a boy could fit through,* he thought. *Or a petite woman. Lara could fit through there.* He paused, enjoying for a moment the thought of society-conscious, ultra-hygienic, prim and proper Lara wriggling through that window. He smiled. He enjoyed the fantasy immensely.

He rose and surveyed those steps. Dare he try them? He cautiously tried his weight on the first. It held solid. The second one creaked a bit, but it didn't budge. With increasing confidence he continued to climb until he had cleared the five steps leading to the small, railed porch. He didn't lean on the handrail—no need to try his luck.

He tried an assortment of keys in the lock, but none of them worked. He scrunched up his face and pushed out his lips. "Huh," he grunted. Descending the steps quickly, he made his way around to the front of the house. He tried the keys in the front door.

One of them turned the lock. He felt a surge of satisfaction as he stepped into the four-foot-by-four-foot tiled foyer. Before him, a stretch of dingy shag carpet led to a doorway, the kitchen beyond grimy and dilapidated. There was a closet to his right, and to his left, the living room stretched twenty feet, ending at a painted-over, 1970s-style fireplace.

He walked into the kitchen, and opened some of the cupboards. They were not completely empty. A can of condensed milk was above the stove. And there were three cans of green beans. Howard smiled. He hated canned green beans. Fresh green beans were delicious, but he never understood why anyone would ruin them by putting them in a can.

He remembered back to a tense evening when Lara had served canned green beans and both he and Lucy had refused to eat them. "Mad as a hornet," he said out loud, remembering his wife's face, tight and angular.

Opening the pantry, Howard froze. It was empty, but clearly the dust had been disturbed recently where *someone* had removed *something*. Howard reached for his walkie-talkie. "Diane?"

His handset hissed and spat. "Go, Chief," Diane's voice came, sounding tinny and distorted. "Tell Czarnecky to get her boots off her desk and get out here with the kit. We need to dust for prints, God knows what else. I'm ready to eat my hat for saying this, but Wysocki wasn't just spinning nonsense, the old geezer. We got ourselves a burglar."

Chapter Sixteen

Lara Saks watched the play of light on the living room wall as the late afternoon sun crawled across the sky. For the third time in a minute, she sighed, trying unconsciously and unsuccessfully to clear the heaviness from her soul.

Without knowing why, she rose and went to the window, drawing back the curtain. She saw the wreath on the door of the house across the street and the lights strung around the roof that would soon blaze cheerily into the snowy night.

The distance between the mood of the season and her own state created a jarring dissonance within her. She loved Christmas. There was, after all, a way it should be. She turned and looked at her house—a tree should be trimmed in the corner. The air should be ripe with ginger and spice. Carols should be issuing softly from the entertainment center.

But instead it was a mausoleum. *It's her fault,* she thought. *She's an ungrateful child, and always was. She did this just to hurt you, and she succeeded. She won.* Bitterness swept through her, and although she pushed it away, it came back. It was like trying to push all the water in a bathtub to one side using only your hands—pointless.

I can't let Lucy win, she said to herself. But what could she do? Her limbs felt as heavy as lead. Just yesterday she had called the flower shop to order a poinsettia for Howard. It had taken all of a minute and a half to do, and she had needed to curl up for the rest of the afternoon afterward—she had felt so… "sapped," she said aloud. "I feel sapped." Sapped of life, of purpose, of hope.

Rage rose within her again, bringing welcome energy. She indulged in a fantasy about how she would thrash that girl within an inch of her life for what she had done to her and her father. Then the thought that she might already be dead hit her, and she grew still again. Her mind drifted to when Lucy was a baby, gurgling with promise and joy. They had been so happy then. Things were as they should be.

Not like now. She knew she was rigid. She knew that she had an idea of *how things should be*—that she liked things just so, and if they *weren't….* *I don't mean to be unpleasant,* she thought. A few months ago, when Howard had lost his temper, he blamed her for Lucy running away. She had lashed out with every foul thing she could think of. His words had stung her, she knew, because she suspected he was right. But she could not afford to admit that to him. She could barely afford to admit it to herself.

Her scalp itched, and she scratched it. Her fingers found a scab on the top of her head. As she felt around, she discovered more of them. How long had it been since she'd washed her hair? She was mildly horrified. *I have to take care of myself,* she thought.

But how could she? She felt paralyzed by Lucy's absence, by Howard's unspoken blame, by her own shame that compelled her to isolate herself and to push away anyone who threatened to come near. *It's all the reminders,* she thought. *If I didn't have to look at her pictures and her things all day every day, I wouldn't feel nearly so bad.*

"That's an idea," she said out loud, rolling the thought around in her head like coffee on her tongue in better days. "She left this house…. I should finish the job."

A burst of adrenaline coursed through her. She went to the garage and, pulling out the smaller ladder, got some cardboard boxes from their resting place atop the four-by-four crossbeams. She carried them inside and taped the bottoms. Satisfied that they were sturdy, she carried them into the living room and looked around her.

There was a watercolor Lucy had done when she was in third grade. Lara lifted its frame from the wall and placed it in the box. As she did so, she felt a thrill of satisfaction, of accomplishment, of…what? *Revenge,* she thought. But she pushed the idea away. It didn't leave, however. It fell into her heart and began to fester as she turned to the next wall.

There on the fireplace mantel were photos of the

family laughing. Another photo showed Lucy graduating from sixth grade, holding her diploma, her cheeks still chubby. She gathered them all up and put them in the box. On the mantel she only left one picture—of her and Howard, taken before Lucy was conceived.

In a few minutes, she had succeeded in packing up all traces of her daughter from the living room. She breathed deep, and this time, she felt the air actually fill her lungs. She went to the curtains and opened them. The pink and orange glow of the late afternoon sun flooded the room with warmth and color.

She sealed up one box, and, lifting another with surging vigor, she headed for Lucy's room.

Chapter Seventeen

Jerry heard a child screaming from halfway across the store. He sighed, grateful he didn't have Nick's job. The role of store Santa was thankless indeed. The lighting aisle had been decimated by this morning's shoppers and he and Vern were racing to replace the stock before moving on to tinsel, which had also taken quite a blow. Vern, a stocky teenager from Kent helping out during the seasonal rush, looked dreamily up at the display lights floating above their heads. "Pretty," he said.

"Vern, focus, please," Jerry said, with a bit more edge in his voice than he'd intended. He reminded himself that Vern was a bit slow, and he couldn't expect to work him as hard as…*well, as hard as I* need *him to right now*, he thought.

The intercom popped, interrupting Nat King Cole's "The Christmas Song." "Jerry Keller to the back, Jerry Keller to the back," and another pop before the crooning resumed, and chestnuts roasting on an open fire were once again being lauded.

"Vern, finish these up, and then come to the back for the tinsel, okay?"

Vern smiled. "Tinsel is pretty."

Jerry paused, and suddenly saw in the young man the child that he really was, the innocence on his face, the wonder welling up within him, as yet unquenched by the *sturm und drang* of adult responsibility and toil. He felt a strange, irreconcilable mixture of pity and envy. *What I wouldn't give to feel that wonder again,* Jerry thought to himself. "You bet it is, Vern. That's why we sell so much of it. That's why we need to restock those shelves."

"We *provide*," he said matter-of-factly.

"We do what we can." Jerry clapped the teenager on the shoulder. "The season does the rest."

"I love Christmas," Vern said, not slowing down for an instant.

"So do I, son," Jerry said, and turned to head back to the break room. As he picked his way through the crowded store, unconsciously greeting people and smiling, he wondered at the fact that he worked at this store two hundred and forty days a year, and he somehow, inexplicably, was not sick to tears of Christmas. Yet he wasn't. It was, he realized, his purpose in life. How could one possibly tire of that?

A woman stopped him and asked directions to the kiosk featuring Christmas tree ornaments for public works employees, and he briskly led her to it. Fortunately it was along his way, and in no time he was turning into the break room with a sigh of relief.

There, seated at the break table in her crisp, powder blue scrubs was the love of his life, smiling up at him, holding the mysterious infant in her arms. He remembered back to when she had looked just like that, holding their own children. Well, maybe she had not looked exactly like she did now. She was heavier, and lines creased her face in patterns that had become dear to him.

"She's *adorable*," Carol cooed.

"She is that," Jerry agreed, and he extended his hand to meet Gary Johnson's. He gave it a good shake, and the doctor smiled at him. "You look run ragged, mister."

"Just about," Jerry agreed. "Tax people got April 15th. We've got Christmas. How does she look?"

"We just got here"—Doctor Johnson patted his medical kit—"but we got everything we need. I understand the cord's still attached?"

"Yeah. Will that be a problem?"

"No. Just need a place to work where we won't be disturbed."

"Take my office," Jerry offered.

Carol nodded and rose, baby in her arms. Doctor Johnson flashed Jerry a smile. "Give us about twenty minutes," he said.

"Take your time," Jerry said. "Oh, and Gary—"

The doctor paused and looked back at Jerry.

"Thanks so much for coming. I know you're busy—"

"Don't say another word, Jerry. It's a good thing you're doing here."

Jerry nodded, and the doctor turned again to follow Carol into the office.

Alone for the first time in hours, Jerry felt a mixture of relief and fatigue. He sat at the break table and ran his fingers through his hair, savoring the relative quiet. The intercom popped.

"Well, there you go…" Jerry said out loud to the intercom.

"Jerry Keller to checkout. Jerry Keller to checkout."

"On my way," he said, and he heard his bones creak audibly as he rose. He breathed deeply a couple of times to fortify himself, and with new resolve burst onto the floor in the direction of the exit and the cashiers.

He passed through the nativity scene department, noting a couple of sets that needed to be restocked pronto. He was proud of their selection—he was quite sure it rivaled even the-store-that-would-not-be-named.

Just past the nativity sets were the Santa figurines, featuring Santas from all corners of the globe—the Sinterklaases from Holland with tall bishops' mitres; the Father Christmases from the UK, their heads adorned with holly; and the Yule Goats from Scandinavia in all their goaty glory, straining under the weight of bags of toys three times their size.

Jerry rounded the corner, being careful not to jostle anyone near the Precious Moments winter fairyland scenes. Catching sight of the checkout stand, he saw Margaret Dunny waving at him. She was a commuter from someplace East of Silas, he couldn't remember the name of the place off the top of his head.

Businesslike and levelheaded, Margaret was scowling as she efficiently worked through her line.

As Jerry drew near, she placed her "checkout stand closed" sign on her conveyor belt, to the loud moans and complaints of several of the shoppers in her line. "Don't be such babies!" she scolded, and one by one the customers slunk off in search of other, presumably more hospitable checkout stands.

Jerry didn't really approve of Margaret's attitude, but he so admired her chutzpah that he let it go without comment. "What's the emergency, Margaret?"

"This!" she said, holding up an ornament. "Them!" she pointed to a small gaggle of teenagers standing in a circle near the plate glass window. Some of them looked sheepish, some defiant.

Jerry lifted one eyebrow as Margaret handed him the ornament. One of the boys made for the door. Quick as a flash, Margaret blocked his way, and corralled him back to his fellows.

Jerry turned the ornament, recognizing it as one made by the Orna-matic machine. He smiled, relieved that at least these enterprising children had shared his appreciation of what the machine could do. The text read, "The Moon at Christmas," followed by the year. He continued to turn the ornament, almost dropping it when he saw the photo glazed onto the bulb: bared buttocks shone like a sideways smile above a bunched tangle of lowered trousers.

Jerry felt heat rise in his face and knew that he was blushing. He looked up and heard the titters and snickers of several of the teenagers—the girls burying their faces in their hands, the boys boldly presenting mischievous grins.

Jerry looked back at the ornament, then at the children. Then back at the ornament. He knew that his job required quick decisions, but he didn't really seem capable of them. He began to sweat. He needed some guidance here. He desperately wanted to talk to Carol. He *needed* to talk to Carol. "Jerry?" Margaret called, as if from a distance.

But he knew Carol would not tell him what to do. She would ask questions and probe, and ultimately he would have to decide for himself. No, Carol was no help. She would not tell him what to do. But it made him feel better just to talk to her. He wished he could talk to her now.

"Jerry?" Margaret's voice sliced through his thoughts, straight into his indecision-generated paralysis.

Jerry looked up. "Yes…Margaret?"

"What do you want me to do with these hooligans?"

He looked at the children again. "I don't know," he said, and balling the ornament up in one hand where no one could see it as he walked, he turned on his heels and picked his way through the crowd toward the Orna-matic machine.

"Jerry!" Margaret called after him, but he just kept walking.

The store was laid out in an enormous circle, and there was no direct route from the checkout stands to the counter where Gibbs held forth on that miraculous ornament-making machine, so he chose what looked like the path of least resistance—the right fork—and almost instantly regretted it as he ran into a traffic jam of frenzied shoppers. Again, he passed by the Santas and the Nativity sets, past the break room door, and through the section reserved for goods derived from other holidays—pilgrims jockeyed with bunnies for shelf space, and giant black cats posed with crazily elongated fur on their backs sticking straight up.

Rounding the corner into ethnic ornaments—past Turkey, past Croatia, past the Ukraine (grouped together with Crimea), past Armenia, past Greece—he finally reached the open stretch where he expected to find Gibbs dozing over the Orna-matic's control board.

But that was not what he saw. Instead, he saw a great mass of teenagers mobbing the machine, and Gibbs, lathered in sweat, working furiously to fill their orders. The Orna-matic machine itself was a blur as it whirled and spit—firing, laminating, shellacking and drying each bulb in mere minutes. Gibbs was taking a thumb drive from one young lady dressed in funereal black incongruously accented with a green garland of tinsel looped around her neck like a Hawaiian lei.

"Boss, I am so glad to see you!" Gibbs said, not bothering to look up.

How had he seen me? Jerry wondered.

"Looks like you've got your hands full, son," Jerry said, squeezing behind the counter with him. "I thought the Orna-matic was tanking. What turned us around?"

Gibbs stopped for a moment and wiped his forehead on his shirtsleeve. He grinned with triumph. "Moon ornaments!" he said, nodding his head as if he couldn't believe the miracle.

"Moon ornaments," Jerry repeated.

"Yeah, Boss, once the kids clued in, there was no stopping them."

Jerry closed his eyes and grimaced inwardly. "How many…moon ornaments…have you done, Gibbs?"

"One hundred and thirty-seven, give or take, in the past three hours," he said, with the tone of a soldier reporting victory in battle. "We ran out of gift boxes about ten minutes ago."

Which explains why Margaret and the other checkers didn't catch this until now, Jerry thought. Jerry's eyebrows bunched as he did a quick calculation. *Ten dollars times one hundred and forty ornaments equals…* his eyebrows shot up. *The machine was one quarter of the way to being paid off in only three hours?* He whistled. He knew he had been on to something, buying that machine. A wave of euphoric vindication rolled through him.

He made a decision.

"Gibbs, I am hereby declaring that, until further notice, 'moon ornaments' are not obscene—subject to further consideration, of course. But, you've gotta find other boxes for them, so as not to…offend the delicate sensibilities of the cashiers. I mean it—not another one goes out that isn't packaged up tight and discreet. Got that?"

Gibbs nodded vigorously.

"Also, if you see anything—and I mean anything— more revealing than the…*the moon* in these photos, you reject them outright. Am I clear?"

"Nothing but moons," Gibbs agreed.

"No, lots of other things besides moons—babies and puppies and snowmobiles are fine. Just no…delicate bits."

"Delicate bits?" Gibbs looked confused.

Jerry rolled his eyes. "Nothing *naughtier* than moons."

"Oh, sure, you got it, Boss." Gibbs looked suddenly horrified. "Oh, Boss, there was…."

Jerry held up his hand. "I don't want to know. Just… no more."

"Yes, sir."

Jerry slid the original moon ornament into the pocket of his red blazer and headed for the break room again. He would need to show it to Carol. She wouldn't tell him what to do, but she'd know what questions to ask.

When he entered the back room, Carol was bouncing the baby on her knee and the doctor was washing his hands. "Well," Jerry asked, "how's our girl?"

"Our girl?" Carol smiled at him. "You're not getting attached, are you, grandpa?"

Jerry blushed. The baby was smiling. And drooling. Jerry felt his heart warm at the sight of her. "Maybe," he said. "Just a bit."

"She's top-notch," Gary announced, drying his hands on a paper towel. "She needs some fat on those bones. I brought some Enfamil, and I've ordered a shipment from the mother's milk bank in Flint. Should be here day after tomorrow. I'll drop it off, or Carol will."

"That sounds terrific, thank you," Jerry said. For a moment he forgot all about the store. For a moment he felt free and happy, just looking into the face of innocence.

Myrtle burst into the break room with a flurry of words and hands. "Madhouse! It's a madhouse out there!" Her palms waggled in the air on either side of her ears. "Oh! Hi, Doc. Am I interrupting?"

"Not at all." Doctor Johnson poured himself some coffee and took a seat at the break table.

"Tell me about the latest crisis," Carol said, looking at her husband sympathetically.

"You don't really want to know," he said, although he was dying to tell her.

"You're right. I was just being polite. But now that I see there's *something*, I really, really do," she laughed.

Jerry fished the moon ornament out of his blazer pocket and handed it to the Doctor. Johnson turned it around, saw the picture, and chortled with delight. He buried his face in his arm as his great shoulders shook with laughter. He held the bulb by one finger and passed it to Carol. "You…got…to see this!" he said to her between fits.

Carol didn't take it, her arms filled as they were with baby, but she leaned in to get a good look, and burst out laughing herself. Myrtle grabbed the ornament off its precarious perch on the doctor's finger and studied it— her face clouded by a grim look of horror.

"This is obscene!" she announced.

"It's *funny*," the doctor said, wiping his eyes.

"Thank goodness you found out about it, Jerry!" Myrtle said, indignantly. "Gibbs should be punished!"

"I didn't punish him, and I'm not going to," Jerry said. A look of uncertainty crossed his face. "I didn't even tell him to stop it."

Carol's eyebrows shot up. "Really, Jer? I'm proud of you."

Myrtle looked from one spouse to the other, not sure what to say. She said nothing.

"Well, I didn't really know *what* to do."

Carol leveled a judgmental eye at him. "Did you sit down on the floor again, in front of God and everyone?"

Jerry shifted nervously. "No." He didn't say more.

"Well, at least there's that," Carol said, not able to help cracking a smile.

"*Should* I have stopped Gibbs?" he asked.

Carol raised an eyebrow. Myrtle swiveled her head in jerky bird-like motions looking incredulously at each of them in turn.

"I think we're too uptight about our bodies," Doc Johnson said. "I don't see anything wrong with it. It's harmless kid stuff."

Carol leaned in and touched the baby's nose with her own. The baby girl's eyes grew wide.

"Well, Jerry, it sounds to me like you need a *moral* expert," Carol said.

"Do we have one of those in this town?" Jerry asked.

"We do," Carol said, wiping away a bit of drool. "And she's fresh off the boat."

Chapter Eighteen

The screen door banged behind him as Gibbs crossed the threshold of the double-wide trailer. Holding the baby close to him with one hand, he opened it again and shook the snow from his shoes just outside, first one and then the other. Satisfied that he'd dislodged what he could, he shut both doors and took his shoes off before moving into the living room. It had been dark for a couple of hours, and the house was quiet, but Gibbs saw light in the kitchen.

"Mom?" Gibbs called.

As he waltzed with the baby through the living room, his mother's lithe form filled the doorway to the kitchen. She took a long drag on her cigarette and smiled at him as she blew it out.

"Never," she said, pointing at him with its cherry-red point of flame, "never in all my days did I think I would see that."

"See what?" Gibbs asked, pushing past her into the kitchen. The baby was starting to fuss. He opened cupboards, pulled out a cooking pot, and slammed the cupboard door.

"Gently, baby," his mother said, sitting at the kitchen table, flicking ash into a teacup.

"Sorry," Gibbs moped. It only lasted a second, though, and he was back on task. He filled the pot half way and put it on the stove.

He handed the baby to his mother and unslung his backpack.

"Geez, Leonard, you can't fling her at me like that, give me some warning."

"Sorry," he repeated, but this time he didn't bother to mope, even briefly.

"I was sayin'," his mother resumed, bouncing the child, "I never thought I'd see you, ya' know, as a dad."

"I'm not a dad, I'm just…helping."

"Ya' look pretty dad-like to me." She shot him a wry pout.

"Stop teasing me."

"I don't think I was," she said. "But I can."

"Mom," he complained, dropping a plastic formula pack into the water to warm.

"You hungry?" she asked.

He stopped what he was doing and looked up. Was he hungry? He hadn't given his own meal a moment's thought. There had been too much to do at the store, and there was the baby to think about. He checked in with his stomach. It roared back at him.

"I didn't notice it, but yeah, I could eat a house."

"Fresh out of house, darlin', but how do you feel about kielbasa and kraut?"

"And ice cream?"

"Uh…not at the same time, but yes." The baby was beginning to mewl, so she started bouncing her, making soft "shushing" sounds.

Gibbs put the formula pack into the bottle, and tested it on his wrist.

"Who taught you to do that?" his mother asked.

"TV," Gibbs answered.

"And they say it ain't educational."

Gibbs picked the baby up and sat down at the table across from his mother, placing the nipple in the infant's mouth. She sucked at it greedily.

"Just in time," his mother said. Unburdened, now, she got up and began to rummage in the fridge, pulling out leftovers and placing two fat sausages on a plate. Opening some Tupperware, she filled the rest of the plate with sauerkraut.

"Mustard, baby?" she asked, putting the plate in the microwave.

"Yeah, but the hot stuff, not the yellow stuff."

"That will put hair on your chest if you're not careful." She pointed a warning finger at him. "Says so right on the package. Very small print." She squeezed two fingers together. "Teeny."

Gibbs rolled his eyes and shifted the baby to rest in his other arm. She protested the move, but not for long, finding the nipple again quickly. "How was work?" he asked her.

"Did anyone tell you that you was the perfect man?"

"*Mom*," Gibbs moaned.

"I never had a single man ever asked me that."

"That's cuz you just date losers."

"I 'spect you're right about that." The microwave dinged and she removed the plate, which was steaming. The sausages spit as she placed it on the table. "Don't mean you should say it."

"You taught me to be upright and truthful."

"I don't know about that, but someone did something right." She smiled at him again, and Gibbs could see the pride in her eyes. He looked away, feeling heat rise in his face.

"Baby, let me hold her so you can eat."

Gibbs nodded and handed the child back to his mother. It was a smooth transition and before long both baby and youth were tucking in eagerly.

There was a long silence. "Any word?" his mother asked. She caught his eye and held it.

He looked back down at his food. Then he shook his head.

"I'm sorry, baby. I pray for her every night. You know I do."

He nodded, chewing.

After he finished eating, Gibbs laid the baby down on his bed and put a fresh diaper on her. Lifting her gingerly, he placed her in a cardboard box filled with blankets—a makeshift baby bed right next to his own.

Then he sank into the chair at the small desk that took up most of his room not already claimed by the bed. The computer screen leaped to colorful life, and he opened a web browser. He exhaled deeply and sniffed. He wasn't hopeful. But a sense of duty drove him. He knew it wasn't rational. He also knew that he couldn't stop it.

He navigated to Facebook and pulled up her page. Lucy's face appeared in a small square to the left of his screen, and he felt an ache in his heart. He had told her he loved her only once. The night they had…gone too far. He felt a mixture of excitement and shame at the memory.

She had not posted anything. She hadn't posted anything for months. He checked his e-mail. Nothing. He sent her an instant message: "Lucy, are you there?"

No one responded.

"Are you anywhere?" he typed.

But there was nothing.

He sat staring at the screen for what seemed like a very long time.

"I miss you," he typed. He pushed send. His cursor blinked. So did he.

Chapter Nineteen

Pastor Katie looked at her cell phone—twelve messages. Dread washed over her. She had spoken to no one since she had walked out of the service yesterday. Today she had gotten in her car and driven to Silas for some "retail therapy" at the mall.

She put the cell phone back in her shoulder bag and opened one of her shopping bags lying on the kitchen table. She pulled forth some baking pans, and a chichi brownie mix from the high-end kitchen supply place at the mall. She looked at the price tag and experienced a mild panic attack. It was three times the price of a Betty Crocker mix. What had she been thinking?

Shame washed over her. The shame from the expensive purchases blended into the shame she felt for her behavior at yesterday's service, which blended with the deeper, more primal shame of a child who has been told she has crossed a line, has given herself airs, has overstepped her place.

As she became aware of this shame, she told herself it was irrational. But the others weren't. And now they were all mixed up. She teetered in the kitchen, feeling the water of her emotions circling a sucking drain in her chest.

Fighting for a moment of clarity, she realized she had a choice at this point. She could descend into a steaming mass of self-recrimination from which she might not emerge for days, or…she could bake—and eat—a plate of brownies.

The brownies won.

It's good to have something to do, she said to herself as she threw her coat on a chair and rinsed her new baking pans. She read over the recipe on the chichi mix, and suffered a moment of panic as she wondered whether she had everything she needed. She willed herself to be calm as she pulled the ingredients from the fridge. She sighed with relief—she had more than enough butter, and just exactly the right number of eggs: one.

Fortunately, the brownie mix was otherwise pretty complete. *It better be,* she thought, *at that price.* She emptied the mix into a bowl, folded in the one egg, added butter, and stirred vigorously.

She realized she had not pre-heated the oven and cursed herself. Then she caught herself. *Katheryn Anne*— the voice in her head was, she realized, her mother's, years gone from this earth, but never far from her thoughts or her heart. And not, apparently, willing to be silenced by something as tenuous as mere death.

Katheryn Anne, listen to me.

Katie stopped and breathed. "Listening," she said aloud.

I want you to stop being so hard on yourself. If one of your parishioners came to you, would you ever in a million years say the things to them that you are saying to yourself?

"No ma'am," Katie said out loud.

I should say not, said her mother's voice in her head. *Now confess it to God and to me.*

Unlike most Lutherans, her mother had been a big advocate of private confession, just as Luther himself was. But not to a priest or a minister—just to any other Christian who happened to be near. Many church members had found her mother's "private chats" to be most uncomfortable and unsettling over the years. She smiled at the memory of it.

"I confess to you, Momma, and to our brother Jesus, that I am being too hard on myself."

That's fine, dear. Make your brownies.

She realized the oven didn't really need to be pre-heated. She'd just tack five minutes heating up time onto the total baking time. She poured the mix into a baking pan, set the timer, and slid it into the oven.

She allowed herself a moment of satisfaction, and put on the teakettle. As it was heating, she sat at the kitchen table and looked around the room. It was a beautiful parsonage. She felt lucky—and a little out of place—in it. *It's a little too….* she searched for the right word. The word "grown-up" flashed through her mind, but she rejected it. "Fancy," she said out loud.

The kettle sang, and she poured herself a cup, adding a packet of instant hot cocoa. After all, what was it that Martin Luther had said? "If you're going to sin, sin boldly." She boldly sipped at her chocolate, feeling deliciously sinful.

As she sat, though, the spirit of heaviness returned to her. Suddenly, the "fanciness" of the house seemed oppressive. It seemed to loom. The shadows threatened to suck her into them. It seemed…*it's huge,* she thought. *It's huge and it's empty and I feel out of place, unwelcome, and alone. I'm living here under false pretenses.*

She felt an urge to run upstairs, throw all of her clothes into a suitcase, and hit the road. For good. She could always waitress. *Or tend bar,* she said to herself.

There's a fine line between bartending and pastoral counseling, after all.

She felt small. Suddenly the sucking hole in her chest grew larger, and she could not resist its pull. Self-pity snagged her by the scruff of the neck and pulled her down, down, down, into a well of misery.

She had no idea how long she stayed there. But in the midst of her despair a voice emerged. Not her mother, but another. Not unknown, but unknowable. *I did not say you would not be tempted,* the voice said calmly, lovingly. *I promised that you would not be overcome.*

Was this what this was? she wondered. *Temptation?* She realized with a start that it was. She was being tempted to the most devilish of places—to despair. Of all the Enemy's strategies, this was the most devious and alluring. Martin Luther had thrown an inkwell at the devil when he had been tempted. She threw her mug.

It smashed against the far wall, and shards of pottery chinked to the floor. The sound of it startled her back to consciousness of the kitchen around her, where the alarm was ringing and a thin wisp of smoke was beginning to waft from the oven.

"Oh, poop!" she cursed aloud, jumping up and flinging open the oven's door. "Poop poop poop poop!!!" A noxious cloud surrounded her, bearing a rich, not unpleasant odor of charcoal and chocolate.

Fumbling for a dishrag, she quickly pulled the too-hot confection from the oven, and burned her thumb. "Aaargh!" she yelled, popping her thumb into her mouth. She sat once again in her chair at the table and watched the smoke rising from the baking pan with quickly tearing eyes.

Without thinking, she reached for another of the shopping bags on the table. Picking it up by its handle, she walked into the living room and curled up on the couch in the fetal position. She pulled a large teddy bear from the bag and held it close to her bosom as she stared at the shadows of the Too Big House.

Chapter Twenty

Howard switched off the Range Rover's ignition and put the key in his pocket. He reached over, above the passenger-seat visor, and pushed the button on the garage door opener. As the garage door rolled upwards along its track, he climbed out, and opening the back door, lifted out some packages.

He held them precariously in one arm as he shut the door of the SUV and pushed the button on the car alarm. He waited to move until he had two hands on the packages, but then walked around the side of the vehicle and into the harsh light of the garage.

He was surprised by what he saw there. Instead of the large empty space in the middle, it was filled with boxes. He set the packages down on the workbench that ran along the length of the right side of the garage. They were presents for Lara, and he was hoping to put them in a place she didn't normally go. Since the garage was the closest thing to a "man-cave" he had in their little house, it seemed like a good plan.

Howard reached to open one of the boxes, but then stopped himself. What if Lara had the same idea? What if they contained presents for him? He scowled at the boxes. They weren't new boxes, he noted. He looked up at the crossbeams. The stack of broken-down boxes was visibly diminished.

So, he thought to himself, *these are old boxes.*

He walked around them again, looking for clues. *Just because they're old boxes doesn't mean that there aren't presents in them*, he reasoned. *But there are too many of them. Lara wouldn't get that many presents for me.*

Were some of the presents for Lucy? It wasn't impossible. After all, one of the gifts he bought was. He had seen a sweater that just…looked like her. *Or my idea of her*, he supposed. He wondered how far off his ideal was from reality. If she were dead, that would be very far off indeed.

Still, he had bought it, and had had it wrapped at the department store. They didn't know him there, since he had gone all the way to Trent. The young woman at the checkout stand didn't know that she was wrapping a present for a ghost.

Howard shook off the memory. It depressed him, and he needed to be strong for Lara. *Someone has to be the strong one*, he told himself.

He continued to circle the boxes. But if they weren't for him—or for Lara—what was in them? He looked up at the door leading into the house. Lara might step out of it at any time. If he looked, he might get caught looking.

He shook his head to clear it. *What am I, five years old?* He thought. *Lara isn't my mother and I'm not going to get into trouble for looking at boxes in my own garage. It's not as if Lara went to any trouble to hide them or even to seal them up.*

The boxes had been shut only loosely, by cross-hatching the four leaves sticking up from the boxes. He pulled on one of them, and all four sprang up, revealing the contents of the box. He pulled out the article of clothing on top—one of Lucy's blouses. Beneath that was a pair of her blue jeans. Wedged underneath that was a framed photo of the three of them at the beach, taken during a weekend outing to Lake Superior when Lucy was about ten.

He wondered at the photo. They all looked so happy. What had happened to them? Where had that little girl gone? What had happened to his wife's smile? The carefree look on his own face seemed impossible to fathom.

He tugged open another of the boxes. This, too, was filled with Lucy's things. On top was a Grief Patrol CD. He turned over the plastic case in his hand, looking at the sepia toned artwork—a stone angel wept, with tombstones blurry but visible in the background. For the first time he felt a connection with the band. That angel looked like he felt inside. Not sure why, he put the CD in his coat pocket. Perhaps he'd give it another try as he drove around tomorrow. He was desperate to connect with her—and if he couldn't, perhaps he could connect to something she cared about.

It was desperate, and he felt embarrassed. But he didn't remove the CD. Instead, he poked around in the box. Everything there was Lucy's. He didn't need to look at the other boxes. He could guess what was in them.

He felt anger rising in his neck, its energy pulsing out into his fists. He longed to hit something. He clenched his fists and unclenched them again. He looked at the floor, at his shoes, and breathed deeply. Content that he had calmed himself, he stepped up the short stairs to the door and turned the knob.

He expected to walk into the same dim, funereal atmosphere that had greeted him every night for the past five months. Instead, he opened the door into a world of sound, of color, of delicious odors.

Christmas music blared cheerily from the entertainment center, lights circled the large windows in the living room. There was no tree, but a large wreath hung above the fireplace. A bright fire spit and danced behind the screen.

Lights were on in the kitchen, and stepping cautiously into the doorway, he saw Lara, in her best apron, pulling apple dumplings out of the oven. "Chicken dumplings for dinner, apple dumplings for dessert," she said, flashing him a welcoming smile. Putting down the hot pan, she stepped over to him, rose up on her toes, and planted a kiss on his mustache. "I was in a dumpling kind of mood. I hope you don't mind."

He had been expecting to heat up a Hungry Man TV dinner, so dumplings—savory or sweet—were welcome. But he wasn't thinking about food. He stared at his wife, a feeling of dread washing over him, negating the warmth of the kitchen.

"Lara, are you feeling all right?" he asked.

"Officer, I have not felt this good in—" A flash of sadness pierced the cheer on her face, but in a moment it was gone. "—in months." She slapped him on his rear. "How was your day?"

He ignored the question and sank into a kitchen chair, watching her. Without asking, she went to the fridge, pulled out a bottle of Canadian beer, twisted off the cap and placed it in front of him. He felt like he had fallen into a hole in time to a year ago, and suddenly they were acting out their normal roles. Any minute now, he expected to see Lucy come into the kitchen, sullen and prickly, to pick at her food and moan about her lot in life.

Lucy did not walk in. Yet strangely, Lara's cheeriness didn't seem forced. *She seems…fine,* he said to himself. *Eerily fine.* Panic welled up in him, and he willed it down. *I'm way out of my league here,* he thought. *I need to talk to someone.* But who? A doctor? A psychologist? A pastor? He didn't know. And that he didn't know made him feel even more out of control.

Chapter Twenty-One

Gammy glanced out the window of her office. The morning's new snow gleamed as it caught the sun. A grocery truck passed by, rumbling its way down Main Street. She smiled. The world outside was as it should be. Gammy felt her muscles relax as she basked in the "rightness" of it all.

Then she heard the outside door to the pastor's office bang shut, and her left eyelid began to twitch. A sour feeling in her stomach testified to the "un-rightness" of things in the church. *Her* church. Gammy felt the weight of Divine responsibility. Somehow she had let things get out of control. She had failed in her diligence, and Satan's foxes had set up shop in *her* henhouse. Her mind replayed the events from last Sunday, how Pastor Katie had simply up and walked out of the worship service, leaving an overflow congregation in the lurch. It was shocking, unprofessional, *unforgivable*.

"I will fix this," she said out loud. Her words, although they rang out with conviction, did not soothe the trouble in her breast. She looked at her desk. Everything was arranged just so. The stapler was at right angles to the desk blotter. The tape dispenser lined up beside it in parallel, a perfect inch's distance between them at every point. A coffee cup from the 1975 pan-Lutheran Conference—at which she was the parish delegate, and in the glow of which she was still basking—held an assortment of pencils and pens, each of them in perfect working order. All was in its proper place. She sighed with satisfaction. *If the Lord walked in right now,* she thought, *he would be pleased.*

Except that he wouldn't be. She heard the new pastor rattling around in the office—that office that should *not* be hers. Jesus hated interlopers, she was sure of it. And Jesus would not be pleased at Gammy for not guarding his church against them. Against *her.*

Gammy's lips pressed together tightly, making her mouth go white. A pottery vase sat on one corner of the desk, holding a bloom of plastic flowers—blue flowers, of course, for Advent. Plastic flowers always inspired joy in her, and she gazed upon them now for comfort.

Slowly, she felt the tension in her shoulders ease up a bit.

Noticing a smudge on one of the blue petals, she snatched a tissue from the box on the bookshelf. The shelf contained all 57 volumes of Martin Luther's complete works, which she dusted monthly but had never once cracked. They were a shrine of sorts, after all, to right teaching and good church order—order that had been upset. *On my watch,* she thought. She spat on the tissue and rubbed at the offending petal vigorously, shredding the tissue and littering her desk with fairy-sized spitballs.

"Oh, *sugar,*" she swore, quietly, so the Lord wouldn't hear.

She had just swept the last of the miniature spitballs into her hand when the phone rang. The sudden ringing startled her, and she jumped, clutching at her heart, and accidentally tossing the tissue's detritus all over her blouse. "*Brown* sugar!" she swore, louder now, less concerned about the Lord's tender sensibilities.

She picked up the black telephone receiver—the same one in place when she had begun the job twenty years ago. "St. Gabriel's Evangelical Lutheran Parish," she said, all business, "where angels still bring messages of comfort and joy," she added, her voice oozing like a television car salesman. "Who is this and what do you want?"

"Is…this the church office?" Asked a man's voice, uncertainly.

Gammy frowned. He sounded like a weak man. She despised weak men. *All men should be strong and manly, like the Lord Jesus,* she thought. *This fellow sounds like a wimp.*

"Yes, sir. I'm the church secretary, Miss Gammerbrau. How can I help you?"

"Is the pastor there?"

"Our pastor retired," Gammy stated flatly.

"Yes…yes, I know," said the man, almost stammering. "I mean the *new* pastor."

Gammy frowned. *Who would want to talk to her?* She thought. She should warn this man before he got himself into a situation he would be sorry for. She straightened her back, filled with righteous conviction. *I'll simply lie*, she thought. *The Lord would approve in this case, surely, since I'll be averting certain trouble for this weak creature. The Lord loves the merciful. And the strong.*

"I'm sorry…." She paused as a brilliant thought occurred to her—she could save this sorry sap without actually lying. Her broad smile was audible when she spoke. "…but I haven't seen the pastor yet this morning."

Just then the door separating her office from the pastor's flew open. "Oh, Gammy, Gammy, I'm here!" Pastor Katie seemed out of breath. "Didn't you hear me? Who is it?"

The scowl returned to Gammy's face. *It is not always easy to do the Lord's work*, she thought. The *Devil is like a prowling lion, seeking someone to devour.* "She just walked in," Gammy said, lips tight again. She pretended to put the phone on hold. "There's a man to speak to you, Pastor." She leaned over her desk and whispered. "He's kind of *girly*."

"Uh…thanks, Gammy." Pastor Katie's eyes darted back and forth uncertainly. "I'll just…take that in my office." And she closed the door again. Gammy's nostril's flared. The woman reeked of something that she couldn't quite place. Cinnamon? No. Chocolate? Maybe that was it. Charcoal? Gammy's nose was confused.

She willed herself to focus, and covering the handset's mouthpiece with her hand, she raised the earpiece to listen.

"Pastor Jorgenson, here. How can I help?" The pastor sounded professional and compassionate at the same time. *That's how the Enemy works,* Gammy thought, *masquerading as an angel of light.*

"Pastor, hi. I'm Jerry Keller, we met at the tree-lighting."

"Oh…of course. Hello," the pastor said, but the confidence was gone from her voice now.

The man laughed. "Don't worry—I'm sure you've heard so many new names you can't keep them all straight. I'm the manager of Bremmer's, the Christmas store over on Schillerstrasse Street."

"Aren't 'Strasse' and 'Street' redundant?" the pastor asked. Gammy wanted to bean her. Education made women uppity. The Lord was surely not pleased.

The weak man laughed and seemed more relaxed when he said, "I suppose they are! There was a time in this town when being German and American was oxymoronic. Not to mention dangerous."

"I'll bet," Katie said. "Let me guess—during World War II the town was suddenly filled to bursting with Dutch people, with nary a person of German descent in sight."

"Sounds like you know little German towns pretty well."

"I'm Lutheran, Mr. Keller, and stories of what happened to little German towns at that time are legion. I may be Swedish-American, but I do have my wits about me."

"I'm sure you do." The man laughed again.

Gammy was flummoxed. They sounded like they knew each other, but they just said they didn't. They'd been talking for minutes and she still had no idea why the man was calling. Her eyes shifted back and forth and her lips pursed in aggravation.

"Do you hear breathing?" the man asked.

Gammy felt a stab of panic and quickly moved the receiver away from her mouth.

"No," the pastor replied.

"Must be line noise," the man said. "It's gone now."

"What can I help you with, Mr. Keller?"

Finally! Gammy thought.

"Well, Pastor, I'm sure you're busy, and I'm sorry to bother you with something so insignificant—"

"Mr. Keller, I've been here over a week, and my secretary hasn't lined up a single pastoral visit for me—"

Gammy's eyes stabbed at the Pastor's door like daggers. *Of course I haven't lined up any visits, you demonic cow,* she thought. *I want to protect our parishioners, not serve them up to the devil on a platter!*

"—so I have plenty of time. I'd be glad to help you any way I can."

"Have you been to our store, yet?"

"No, but I've heard about it."

"Why don't you come on by, then, if you're free, and I'll give you the grand tour—depending on how crazy it is, that is."

"Oh, yes, I imagine this is a busy time for you."

"The worst. Can you come?"

"I'd love to. What's this about, if you don't mind my asking?"

Gammy held her breath.

"Well, it's kind of…delicate."

I'll bet it is, Gammy thought. *Girly man like him.* Her mind reeled at the salacious possibilities.

"I'd rather tell you when you get here."

"Of course. Is it far?"

"About three minutes. Just head down Main, past the library, make a left at Schillerstrasse, we'll be on the left. Can't miss us."

"See you in five, then?"

"Wonderful. Thank you, Pastor."

The line went dead and Gammy hung it up quickly. A moment later Pastor Katie's head appeared through the door. "Gammy, I'm heading out." Her smile was fake, Gammy could see that. "I'm guessing I don't have any visits set up for today?"

"No, Pastor." Gammy pretended to shuffle through a stack of papers.

"Didn't think so. I expect to be back by lunchtime."

"I'll be here." *Long after you're gone,* Gammy added silently.

Pastor Katie nodded and her head disappeared again back into her own office. Gammy held her breath, listening for the outside door to bang. It seemed like ages, but eventually she heard it, sending tremors through the frame of the old clapboard house attached to the sanctuary.

Gammy ran to the front door and waited until she

saw the Pastor's car turn out onto the main street. Gammy breathed a sigh of relief. "Just me and you now, Lord Jesus," she said out loud. "Just the way we like it."

She sat at her desk and checked again to make sure everything was square. Somehow a post-it note had moved slightly and was no longer at right angles to the blotter. She felt her breath quicken and a surge of anger wash through her. In a moment, however, she had righted it. She sighed, content.

That woman pastor is a piece of work, she thought, twirling a pencil in her fingers. *It's only a matter of time before she's gone, but it would be better if I could find a way to... hurry her along.*

Her eyes flicked to the door separating her office from the Pastor's. Was it locked? She looked around, even though she knew no one else was there. She got up and almost ran to the door. She tried the knob. It was locked. Her eyes narrowed. "That sow," she said out loud. She ran back to her desk, yanked open the drawer, and fumbled around, looking for a ring of keys. She found it and raced back to the door. She found the proper one on the first try, and the door opened smoothly and quietly.

Gammy wasn't sure what she was looking for. Her first thought was to look at the yellow legal pad she had—very thoughtfully, she thought—placed at right angles to the Pastor's desk blotter. But it hadn't been touched. She inspected the binding—no sheets had even been used. Gammy's eyebrows knit together in concerned confusion. On what had she written that miserable excuse for a sermon?

Maybe she has her own paper, she thought. Inspiration struck, and she bent to inspect the trash cans. Chewing gum wrappers. A Twizzler wrapper. A Slim Jim wrapper. But no paper. A rush of anger punched at Gammy's gut. *That woman is rail thin,* she thought. *It's not fair that she should be able to eat like that.* Momentarily, her faith in God's justice wavered.

Determined not to be distracted by pointless theological questions, however, she returned her focus to the room. And that's when she saw it—the silver notebook-looking-thingy on the desk. Without touching it, she looked it over. A cord ran from one of its corners, off the side of the desk, and to a white box stuck in the wall socket. On its lid there was a white plastic logo of an apple with a bite taken out of it.

That must be a computer, she thought, vaguely remembering having seen such a thing on television. She poked at it, wondering how to make it work. She saw a flat bar facing her along its impossibly thin rim. She pressed it and jumped back with a start as the lid popped open. She lifted it, opening it like the lid of a clam, as the screen leaped to brilliant-colored life.

It was strangely beautiful. *Be ye not swayed by the glamour of evil,* she thought to herself, her lips pressed into a tight little line. She put on her reading glasses and squinted until the text on the screen was in focus.

With a thrill, she read the words out loud:

Dear parish family,
I am very sad that things have not worked out here in Munich as I had hoped. No doubt you are disappointed as well. As much as it grieves me, I must resign and seek employment in some place where my gifts can do the most good. The Feast of the Epiphany

will be my last day with you. I thank you for the kindness many of you have shown, and I wish you the best in your search for the right pastor.

Your sister in Christ,
The Rev. Katheryn A. Jorgenson

The smile had spread across Gammy's whole face. *It seems,* she noted with satisfaction, *that I don't need to hurry this sea-cow-in-a-collar along after all.* She was going willingly, quickly, and with a minimum of fuss. Gammy sighed, feeling the pleasure run all the way down to her toes. The Lord Jesus, she was sure, was very, very pleased.

Chapter Twenty-Two

Pastor Katie saw the store long before she saw a driveway to turn into. She marveled at the sight of it. She was expecting a mom-and-pop-style Christmas store. This, however, was at least twice the size of a Wal-Mart. "Holy cow," she said out loud, finally seeing a drive and turning into it.

The parking lot was crammed, and she had to park several hundred yards from the entrance. Not that she minded. She turned her face to the cold breeze, enjoying its freshness. She was beginning to let go of this place, and in her mind she was already moving on. It felt good. Right. It was, she realized, a relief.

When she saw Jerry by the entrance, she recognized him immediately. She held out her hand and smiled.

"Of course, Mr. Keller. You were so kind to me. And I was such a…a bumbler last time we met."

Jerry smiled. "Don't give it another thought. I thought you handled yourself very well. You certainly won my wife over."

Katie laughed. "You don't say!"

"I do. I'm not sure you noticed, but we were in church the next Sunday. And that hasn't happened in twenty years."

Katie went white. "Oh, dear. Well, that's embarrassing. Your first time back and the pastor bails on the service? I'm afraid to show my face, and that's the truth."

"People are calling it 'performance art,' I hear. Very effective." Jerry winked.

Katie shook her head, trying to juggle shame and charm.

"I'm sorry, where are my manners?" Jerry said quickly. "Please come in out of the cold. Let me show you around the store."

Immediately inside, Katie was met by a gigantic Santa Claus statue, reclining in an almost lascivious manner. *That's provocative*, she said to herself. Walking past the checkout counters, they hit the main floor of the store, and Katie caught her breath.

It was beautiful. To her right, Nativity sets, some larger than life, stretched out into the distance, with display racks of figurines lining the walls from floor to twelve feet up in the air. Ahead of her were a greater variety of Christmas ornaments than she had ever seen in one place in her life. *In fact*, she breathed silently, *there may be more Christmas ornaments here than I have ever seen in all my life combined!*

The diversity of ornaments was staggering. At the edge of her sight off to the right, on the inside of the donut curve, she could just make out kiosks of various countries. Kiosks devoted to various vocations, hobbies, and enthusiasms stretched out around the donut hole to the left. Further to the left were a vast assortment of trees, packages of lights, tinsel, and garlands.

And peppering every aisle, every kiosk, every square foot of the store were strung lights, creating a fairyland atmosphere wherever she looked. "Oh, my...." She said out loud, unable to move, yet unable to take it all in. "It's *beautiful*...."

Jerry beamed with pride. "It is. I'm glad you like it."

"I'm not sure 'like it' describes what I'm feeling right now."

He waved her to follow him, and as they set off down the right side curve, she took in as much of the nativity sets as she could without actually stopping. "A kid in a candy store," she said out loud.

"What's that?" Jerry turned.

"Oh, nothing. I'm just...overwhelmed."

It took a full half hour to give her the most cursory tour. She realized she could easily spend hours and hours in the store before she'd feel like she'd actually *seen* it. She hoped she would have time to really explore it before she left town. A moment of sadness passed through her as she thought that. She liked Jerry. She wanted to meet his wife. It occurred to her that, even if the church didn't want her, there would be people here she could come to love. The thought buoyed her.

Finally, they circled back around to the hub in the middle of the building, and Jerry led her into the back rooms. A clerk sat reading the newspaper at an enormous break table with a cup of cocoa in front of him. A woman with her hair in a beehive style Katie hadn't seen since she was a teenager was eating instant pudding from a disposable plastic bowl. And a tall, lanky teenager with a shock of red hair sticking straight up was burping what appeared to be an infant.

She smiled at them as they passed through. Jerry waved her into his office, where she took a seat in a worn but serviceable office chair opposite his desk. Instead of sitting behind the desk, Jerry planted himself on the couch. "I'm very grateful you came out to…offer your advice, Pastor."

"I'm glad to help, Mr. Keller. What can I do?"

Jerry handed her an assortment of ornaments. She lifted one of them to get a better look, and her eyebrows shot up. A photo of someone's bare buttock stared back at her. She burst out laughing. "What are these?"

"The kids are calling them 'moon ornaments,'" Jerry said, a pained note entering his voice.

"Do you…have a section for ornaments of poor taste?" she asked, looking at him a little uncertainly. "Or…well, you know, naughty ornaments—adult-themed ornaments?"

"Heavens, no. The owner is—she's, well…this is a Christian establishment, Pastor. We keep the Christ in Christmas around here. We don't stock these ornaments. We have a machine that takes photographs and puts them on bulbs. Local teenagers have been bringing in their own…well, moon-shots, I suppose you could say—"

Pastor Katie burst out laughing, picking up another of the ornaments. "Oh, dear," she said. "Okay, so tell me about your dilemma?"

"Well, it's not like we've had many complaints over these—or *any* complaints, really, but I'm waiting for the shoe to drop. Thing is, that darn machine was a bust, a money-loser until the kids started making these silly things. Now…well, it's paid for itself three times over in the last 24 hours."

"That's amazing!" Katie said, grinning broadly.

"Yes, but is it *right?*" Jerry was suddenly serious. "Look, Pastor, I'll be honest with you. I respect the Lord and the Church—churches, I suppose—but I'm not really terribly religious. But that doesn't mean I'm not a person who wants to…well, to do the right thing." He ran his hand through his thinning hair. "The thing is, I don't know what the *right thing* is in this situation."

"Ah. So you called me…." she began.

"My wife suggested you might be able to help, and decide…well…."

She smiled. "The theological term for what you're asking for is *discernment.*"

Jerry brightened up. "That sounds exactly right. I need some discernment, Pastor."

She leaned over and placed a hand on his elbow. "Mr. Keller, I just happen to be in the discernment business. I think I *can* help."

"So is it wrong?"

Katie sat back again. "How should I know?"

Jerry looked confused. "You're the…'discernment'…expert. Aren't you?"

Katie laughed, and then began in a patient tone. "Sure. But what I think about this situation isn't really important. It's what *you* think about it that matters."

Just then the intercom spat and buzzed.

"Jerry Keller to white-flocked trees. Jerry Keller to white-flocked trees. Bring the first-aid kit, and quick!"

Jerry sat up like a bolt. "I—oh, good Lord—I'm sorry, Pastor."

Katie laughed. "Go, go…I hope it's nothing serious."

"Please feel free—"

"I'm going to get myself a soda in the break room. Go!"

Jerry ran behind his desk, yanked open the bottom drawer, and, first-aid kit in hand, rushed out of his office. Pastor Katie looked at another of the moon ornaments, chuckled, and rolled her eyes. Then she stood up and wandered into the break room.

The red-haired young man was still there with the baby. A tall, thin, angular woman sat near them, eating tiny slices of Melba toast with quick, meticulous movements. Just then a stout woman in a checkout stand apron breezed in. "Fifteen minutes for a break is criminal!" she announced to no one in particular. "It's hardly enough time for a cigare—" Her word clipped off as she noticed Katie's clerical collar.

"—a Twinkie," she corrected herself, shooting a "now I've done it" look at the bird-like woman and letting her momentum carry her through the back door toward the loading dock, and, Katie presumed, a much-needed smoke.

"That's Emily," the bird-like woman announced. She leaned over and added, in a whisper, "She *smokes.*"

Katie nodded, conspiratorially. She held her hand out to the bird-woman. "I'm Pastor Katie Jorgenson."

"Yes! I saw you at the tree-lighting. I'm Myrtle. I work here." She pointed to the red-haired young man, who seemed pre-occupied with the baby he held, even though—he? she?—seemed to be sleeping. "This is Gibbs. His real name is Leonard, but he hates it." The red-haired teenager seemed to emerge from his attentions long enough to shoot Myrtle a glare.

"How do you do?" Katie held her hand out to him. Instead of taking it, since both his hands were full of baby, he turned his elbow around and touched it to her hand. *That was awkward*, Katie thought, *but sweet.*

"And who is this little guy?" Katie asked.

"Little *girl*," the teen named Gibbs corrected her. "She doesn't have a name. We found her."

"You found her?" Katie asked.

"Yes. On the loading dock. Day before yesterday," Gibbs said matter-of-factly.

Katie was flummoxed. "But…whose baby is she?"

Gibbs shook his head. "We don't know. Sheriff Saks is checking around. Meanwhile, she's staying here with us."

"In the store?" Katie was incredulous. "With you?"

"Where else?" Gibbs shrugged. "*Who* else?"

Katie didn't know. *Surely there are government agencies,* she thought, but she didn't say it. Instead, she was struck by the tenderness with which this gangly teenager handled the child. She put her hand to her heart. It moved her. "And at night?"

"She stays with me and my ma," the kid said, without a hint of guile or shame. There was even a bit of pride in that voice.

How strange, she thought, *that Jerry brought me out here to talk about 'moon ornaments' when the real matter for discernment was so…huge, so obvious. Was that conscious? Probably not,* she reasoned. She was feeling a little unmoored by the strangeness of the situation, when a sweaty man in a Santa suit puffed into the room, throwing off his coat and untucking a Grateful Dead T-shirt from his red, fur-lined trousers.

"Sugar!" he announced. "I need sugar—now. No one is safe!" he made a beeline for the snack machine and fumbled in his pockets. "Dagnabbit!" he swore. "Anyone got any quarters? I'll be in your debt forever."

Katie fished in her handbag and emerged with five quarters and two dimes. "Will this help?" she asked.

"Oh, much obliged," the Santa-guy said to her, his eyes widening as he took in her collar, really noticing her only now. "I owe you."

"I make it a habit to forgive my debtors."

"Ha!" he burst out, turning back to the machine and inserting the quarters. "'Course you do. We say 'trespass' in my church."

"We do in ours, too, actually. I couldn't help myself, though."

"That's Nick," offered Myrtle, between pecks at her Melba toast. Then she whispered again. "He's a *Santa.*"

"Um…his secret is safe with me." She shot Nick a

confused look. He winked at her. "I was just meeting the little one here," she told him.

"She's a cutie," Nick said, snatching up a Snickers from the machine's chute and ripping the wrapper off of it with ferocity. He took a bite and with eyes closed, he backed up to the break table and sat down heavily on the bench, obviously savoring the sensations that had taken over his mouth.

"I wish I knew what to do," Katie said, realizing just how far outside her expertise this situation was. Then it occurred to her that it was the same for all of them. They all seemed to simply be doing the best they could with the knowledge they possessed—Jerry, this Gibbs kid, probably even the Sheriff.

She tried not to think of how rude he had been to her when he had slammed the door in her face the day before yesterday. After all, who knew what he was going through right now? It occurred to her that this was the first Christmas without his own child at home. She decided to give him the benefit of a doubt.

"Everyone has something they can do," Myrtle said. "I know!" She darted straight from the table to the break room door. Holding the door open with one hand, she stood poised on the threshold, one foot in the break room, one foot on the store's main floor. She cocked her head and appeared to be listening for something.

"What's she doing?" Katie asked Nick.

"Carolmancy," Nick said, rolling his eyes. "It never ends."

"What's 'carolmancy'?" Katie asked. She had never heard the word before.

"It's a form of divination," Nick explained. He opened his mouth to say more, but Myrtle burst back through.

"The song is 'Away in a Manger,'" she announced breathlessly, "to Murray's tune, not Kirkpatrick's, thank goodness. Anyway, it's the third stanza—the words are, 'Bless all the dear children in thy tender care, and fit us for heaven to live with thee there.'" Her face was shining as if she had just received a divine revelation.

Katie recognized the words, but she didn't see the significance. She looked at Gibbs, who seemed to be ignoring the whole episode, his attention riveted on the baby. She turned to Nick, her eyes pleading for an explanation. He stuffed the rest of the candy bar into his mouth and shook his head, which she took to mean, "I have no clue."

She turned back to Myrtle. *What an odd woman,* she thought, but she said, "I don't understand. Can you help me?"

"It's a Lutheran hymn, Pastor," Myrtle said, her hands on her hips. Katie couldn't tell if she were genuinely indignant or if she were teasing her. Then, as if explaining to a child, she spoke slowly. "Think, Pastor, how do you—in your job—'bless all the dear children' in order to 'fit them for heaven'?"

Katie looked at Nick, who held his hand up in a "don't look at me" gesture. Gibbs was still oblivious. She looked back at Myrtle. "Um…can you give me a clue?"

"You *baptize* them, you silly goose!" Myrtle said, seeming to be aghast. "Don't you have to go to school to be a minister?"

Suddenly, Katie understood. She looked at Myrtle as if seeing her for the first time. She still saw an eccentric, bird-like woman, but she also saw something more now, although she wasn't yet sure what that "more" actually was.

"You see?" Myrtle said, coming back into the break room, and taking Katie's arm in her own. "You *can* help her. That little girl has been through the ringer. Who knows what she went through before she showed up here? You can bless her, Pastor—you can give her God's grace." She turned and looked into Katie's eyes, pleadingly. "She needs all the help she can get."

"Can't hurt, Pastor," Nick said.

"What if her parents aren't Christian?" asked Gibbs, who, it seemed, had been listening after all.

"Silly, she don't look A-rab to me," Myrtle said, with a dismissive wave. "And the nearest synni-gog is in Flint. What else would her parents be?"

"Could be Unitarian," offered Nick.

"In which case they won't care about a little 'mumbo-jumbo,' will they?" Myrtle shot back.

Nick threw up his hands. "Can't hurt," he said again.

"No," Katie said. "It can't hurt." She smiled. "I'd be delighted to. Where? When?"

"No time like the present, with things like this," Myrtle said with confidence. "Nick and I can be god-parents. We've got water. What else do we need?"

Katie shook her head. "Nothing. That's all."

Myrtle gave a curt nod. "I'll go get Jerry, then. He'll want to see this. Nick, get us a bowl and water set up, please." And with that she rushed onto the floor.

"That's a woman I wouldn't want to cross," Katie said.

"Believe me, we don't," Nick said, glancing longingly at the snack machine again.

Katie leaned in and touched the baby on the cheek. The little eyes looked into her own, and she felt a rush of wonder. "You're wonderful with her," she said to Gibbs.

"She's a miracle," he said.

Katie touched his shoulder. "She certainly is."

She sat down next to Nick and tapped him on the shoulder. He turned from his longing, sugar-oriented gaze, and smiled at her. "You're name isn't really Nick, is it?" she asked him.

"No, it's Przemyslaw."

"Ah. I'll just call you Nick, then," she tried not to laugh, without much success.

"That's the spirit," he nodded.

"I'm guessing that's Polish?" He nodded. "Are you Roman Catholic?"

"No. My family was one of the founding members of the Polish National Catholic Church. Father Karol is our priest, over in Silas." With a grunt he rose and went to the sink. He opened a cupboard and rummaged around.

"Oh!" she said, a note of delight in her voice. "You're the Catholics that aren't Roman Catholics."

"The very ones," Nick agreed.

"You're a variety of Old Catholic, aren't you?"

"Used to be, until the European Old Catholics started ordaining women a few years ago. Then our bishops cut the apron strings." A look of pain crossed Nick's face. "Sorry, no offense intended. I'm sure you're an excellent pastor."

"None taken," Katie said, although it wasn't entirely true.

Nick pulled a large plastic bowl out and blew into it. Then he blinked rapidly as he had just blown the dust that had settled in the bottom of the bowl straight into his eyes. He stopped and wiped them with his hands before continuing the conversation.

"It's strange, because we're amazingly progressive on lots of other points," he said finally, sounding a little defensive. "We've been Universalists since the early twentieth century, for instance. There might be a Hell, but we don't think God actually sends anyone there. Of course, that doesn't mean that you can't walk there on your own two feet."

"Lots of people do," Katie said, thinking of a certain church secretary she knew.

"We also have eight sacraments," Nick said, his eyebrows rising hopefully. He turned on the faucet and began rinsing the bowl.

"Let me guess—the first seven are the same as Rome's?"

"Yes."

"And the eighth?"

"The preaching of the Word. Grace is communicated through the proclamation of the Gospel just as surely as through the bread and wine."

"Are you sure you're not just Protestants who like lace vestments?" Katie asked.

"Ah, no—now you're confusing us with Episcopalians," Nick said. "A common mistake."

Katie laughed. Nick held up the newly rinsed bowl. "Will this do?"

"Very nicely, I think."

He ran the hot water until he got the temperature just right and then filled the bowl halfway. He then placed the bowl on the table. Suddenly, Katie felt funny about what she was about to do. "I feel weird not doing this in the context of a church service—you know, a worshipping community."

Gibbs looked up at her, confused, but Nick sighed. "I know what you mean. She should be surrounded by the reality she's being brought into—or at least that part of it that's visible to us. But still, these are extreme circumstances. We don't know what's going to happen to her tomorrow. We may have to surrender her to Child Protective Services, and we'll have missed our one chance to give her this kind of help." He looked at Katie full in the face and squeezed her arm. "And we have to believe that it's a very real help. Otherwise, what is our faith about?"

She nodded. He was right, of course.

"Besides that, Pastor, she *is* surrounded by a worshipping community. Not everyone who works here is a Christian, but no one is hostile to the faith, or there's no way they could work here. And the rest of us, *most* of us, well, even though we're all of different denominations, we're still the one Body of Christ. We're all praying for her, loving her, upholding her. She has a worshipping community right here. In fact, I can't imagine a more appropriate place to baptize her. Besides," he chuckled, "in this store, we're surrounded by the singing of hymns all day, every day. Sometimes it's more like church than church. Sometimes it's enough to drive you nuts."

She laughed. Oh, she liked him. Yes, she liked him rather a lot. He reminded her of her own father, who, had he lived, would have been much the same age. They stood together in silence for a few moments, gazing at the child and Gibbs. It occurred to her that they looked for all the world like a post-modern Madonna and child. She sighed.

Then Jerry walked in from the floor, still clutching the first-aid kit. "Mr. Keller," Katie said, turning toward him, "is everyone going to live?" Myrtle was quick on his heels.

"Nothing serious," he said, looking very tired. "What's this about a baptism?"

Katie and Nick exchanged a look. Then, speaking at the same time, they both said, "It can't hurt."

Chapter Twenty-Three

Although he had feigned annoyance, Howard had been glad to hear Jerry's voice on the phone and thought his suggestion of lunch a fine one. He stomped his boots just inside the door at the Hungry Sow, and hung his hat and coat on the large rack in the foyer.

Jerry waved at him from across the room, and Howard scowled when he saw that he was not alone. A woman was with him. As he got closer, he saw that she was a young woman. As he approached the booth, he noticed that she looked familiar. Then he noticed her collar.

"Howard, I'd like you to meet our new Reverend, Katie Jorgenson," Jerry said cheerfully. He held his cup up where a waitress could see it and presumably see that it was empty.

The new Reverend held her hand out to him. "We've met," she said, giving him a wry smile. "But it's good to meet under better circumstances."

Howard wasn't sure what to say. How did he know her? He looked back and forth between Jerry and the Reverend.

"A few days ago," Katie prompted him. "I paid you a visit. It seemed like a not-very-convenient time."

Howard closed his eyes as the memory struck him. *This is the woman I sent away*, he thought. A wave of shame rolled through him. He mastered it and opened his eyes, looking directly into hers. "My deepest apologies, Reverend," he said with a little bow.

"We're Lutherans—please call me 'Pastor'—or just Katie." She smiled. "And please don't apologize. I've discovered that people talk in this town…and they say you and your wife have had a pretty tough time of it." Since he didn't offer his hand, she stood, reached out, and took it. "No apologies necessary. I hope you'll forgive the intrusion."

Howard thought of a million things to say: *T'wasn't no intrusion*, except that it was. *You meant no harm*, but that was obvious. *Nothing to forgive*, except that wasn't honest—he had been plenty annoyed by the visit. So instead of saying anything, he gave her a warm smile, a nod, and took a seat next to Jerry in the booth.

The Hungry Sow was a typical small-town diner—a little less polish than a Denny's, and a little more spit. Gingham tablecloths covered the tables, and they in turn were covered with clear plastic that was always a little sticky. A person could expect his eggs to be greasy and his oatmeal to be cold, but once you got used to that, anything else just seemed odd. One thing that Howard relied upon absolutely was that the coffee there at the Sow wasn't that froufrou swill they served over at Stöllen Goods. This stuff was strong and tart, straight from the Chock-Full-O-Nuts can, as American as football and flannel pajamas.

"I thought you and Pastor Katie here ought to get to know each other," Jerry said. "I invited her to the store to help me…decide?"

"Discern," Katie offered helpfully.

"That was it—to help me *discern* about the moon ornaments."

Howard looked confused. "Moon ornaments?"

Jerry waved it away. "Never mind that. She met the baby, of course, and she even baptized her!"

Howard looked at Pastor Katie, unsure what to think. She looked a little sheepish.

"When someone asks for a sacrament, it's a little hard to say no," she said—a little defensively, he thought.

"You act like you're not sure you did the right thing," Howard noted.

"That's because I'm not." Howard noticed the Pastor's cheeks flush red. "There's another matter for discernment."

"Well, I thought she did a fine job, and I'm not strictly speaking a believer," Jerry said in a chatty tone. "But it struck me that since we're...discerning...what to do about this baby, the Pastor here might be able to help us."

Howard nodded. That seemed reasonable. Even comforting. He smiled at the Pastor. "I didn't give you a very warm welcome before. But welcome to Munich. And apparently, welcome to our problems."

"One thing that I've learned about both towns and people, Sheriff, they're always mixed bags. Joy and Trouble only walk arm-in-arm."

"And sometimes Trouble gives Joy a pretty fierce pounding," Howard added. He looked at Jerry, who seemed to be frozen with his mouth open. "Sorry, did that come across a little harsh?"

Katie laughed and Jerry shut his mouth. Finally, a waitress approached them. Jerry set out his cup and made a little circular gesture with his hand. The waitress nodded, made a note on her pad, and then looked at Howard, who gave a thumbs up and nodded, turning his coffee cup right-side up. The waitress wrote on her pad again and turned her attention to Katie.

The Pastor looked confused. "Excuse me, are you two actually eating anything?"

The waitress looked at her pad and read aloud, "Two flapjacks, apple sausage and coffee; for the Sheriff one rare hamburger patty, topped with a fried egg and fruit cup. What can I get *you*, Pastor?"

Katie's eyes went wide. "Oh, my—I have got to find out where they sell the decoder rings." She scanned the menu. "I'll have a cup of coffee and a club sandwich, please. And could you bring some mayo on the side?"

The waitress looked at her like she was from Mars, but took her menu and stuffed it under her arm without complaint.

"Don't forget the 'on the side' thing, Deirdre," Howard told her. "She's not *from* here."

"You don't say?" Deirdre said curtly, and turned on the heel of her Keds.

"How are you settling in, Pastor?" Howard asked.

"Me? Oh…." Katie looked down at her empty coffee cup, and then back up at the Sheriff. "I'd rather talk about that little girl at the store."

Howard grunted, realizing there was more there than the Pastor wanted to say. He granted her privacy with grace. "Well, Jerry, I hate to say this, but I've had Czarnecki on the horn for two days now, running down missing persons, checking with Social Services, checking hospitals, and I'm sorry to say we've got a big fat zero."

Jerry folded his hands and rested his chin on them. "That's not *good* news exactly, is it?"

The waitress came by again, this time with a full pot of the strong black brew in her hand. She filled their cups and moved on without a word.

"You sound ambivalent, Jerry," Katie offered.

"Well…I am. I want to find the child's mother, sure. But…it's been awfully sweet having that little girl around, I've gotta say." He looked up at Howard. "And I know he's not your favorite person in the world, Howard, but she's done a world of good for Gibbs. That boy has been like a little lost sheep ever since… well, you know. And now he's back. There's fire in his eyes again. He's alive, and it does my heart good."

Howard grunted again and looked at his coffee. He took a swig. Katie did, too, and he couldn't help noticing the face she made as she swallowed. Then she coughed. "You all right?" he asked.

"Gah!" she said. "Someone should have warned me."

"Put hair on your chest," Howard said, toasting her with his cup.

"Oh, great…" she said, uncertain about taking another sip.

"Yeah, I've seen that," Howard said, finally responding to Jerry. "Gibbs is no Einstein, but I can't hold that against him. Heck, I can't hold much against him. I just wish…."

"Gibbs is the red-haired boy, right?" Katie asked.

Howard nodded. "Going steady with my Lucy just before she…before we lost her."

"Ah."

"This is going to be hard on the boy, I'm sure, but there's no way to avoid it. We've looked under every rock for a hundred miles around, and it's time to call in the county."

Jerry stared at the back of his hands. He looked up again. "I'm not sure I can do that."

"I don't think you have a choice," Howard said, grimacing after taking a sip. "She can't live in your break room any more. And it's not fair to foist her on Gibbs' mother, either. That woman works hard and makes peanuts."

Jerry nodded, but Howard could see his brain working.

"I'm going to make some calls this afternoon. Find

out where to take her. You're going to have to break it to Gibbs, Jerry. I can come by for the baby tomorrow, or I can give you the address and you can drop her off, either way."

Jerry shook his head, clearly not wanting to accept this, but Howard didn't hear any other ideas.

"It's gonna tear that kid up," Jerry said.

Katie touched Jerry on the elbow. "What if I picked Gibbs and the baby up tomorrow?" she suggested. "We could take her over together. He'll see that she'll be well taken care of, and we can talk on the way. If he's having feelings, I can probably help."

"*Having feelings,* Pastor? Did you go to seminary in California?" Howard teased.

She shot him a mock glare, but kept her attention on Jerry. He nodded. "I think that would be good. The only thing wrong with that is…" he trailed off.

"The only thing wrong with that is that you've got to tell Gibbs today," Howard finished. "C'mon, Jer, man up." He glanced at the pastor. "No offense, Pastor."

Jerry nodded. "You're right, Howard, of course you are."

Just then the waitress arrived with their food. She rattled off their orders as she put their plates in front of them. She finished up by pulling a bottle of ketchup out of her apron and setting it in front of Howard. Then she walked briskly away.

Katie was picking at her sandwich.

"Something wrong?" Howard asked.

"How can a club sandwich be *greasy*?" she grimaced. "Do they just arbitrarily *add* grease, like a condiment?"

"They butter the bread and fry it before making the sandwich," Howard informed her.

"That defeats the entire purpose of a club sandwich!" Katie complained. "This makes no sense."

"Eat up, Jerry," Howard said, turning his attention to his friend.

Jerry just stared at his food. "Suddenly I'm just not hungry," he said.

Chapter Twenty-Four

Karl Wysocki slammed the screen door. "Tulia!" he shouted. Usually, there was a foul black brew steaming in the Mr. Coffee at this time of the morning, but it was empty and cold. "Tulia!" he shouted again. *Where is that woman?* he thought. Through the doorway to the dining room he saw a note on the table. He strode to the table and picked it up. "Good morning honey-bear," it read. "It's my book club morning, so I'm at Stöllen Goods until lunchtime. You can fix your own coffee today. I promise it won't kill you."

Karl scowled at the note, remembering vaguely that this happened once a month, in spite of his efforts to deny that it did. It wasn't that he minded Tulia meeting with other women in the town—it was a good thing, he reckoned. He just didn't like the idea of her shirking her duties. After all, he never missed a day milking that cow of hers. "Least she could do is make me some dad-blasted coffee," he groused out loud.

Tulia's boxer puppy ran up to Karl and pounced on him. "Off me, you mangy animal!" he snapped at it. The puppy put its head on its paws and raised its tail high into the air, ready to play.

That's when Karl saw the living room. "Oh, lordy…." he said out loud. The puppy, apparently, had been having a field day with the Christmas wrapping. Shredded paper, bright and cheery, littered every corner of the room, and the remains of numerous gifts were scattered willy-nilly.

Karl ran his fingers through what remained of his hair and gave the puppy a black look. "I have two choices, the way I see it," he said to the dog, with surprising calm. "I can shoot you here and now, or I can pretend this never happened and let your mother 'discover' this when she gets home. Now which would you prefer? Should I just put you out of my misery?"

The puppy leaped up and licked his hand.

Just then the phone rang. "What?" he shouted into the receiver.

"Karl, this is May Knudsson, from over on Grizzly."

"What now, May? I just replaced that garbage disposal. Don't tell me it's the heater."

"No, the house is fine. Listen, I just thought you ought to know, I saw him."

"Saw who?" Karl's eyebrows bunched up with concern.

"The burglar. I saw him breaking into the old Gorski place."

Karl swore. "When?" he asked.

"Just now. He's still in there, I think. I mean…I'm not watching right now."

Cradling the phone against his ear, he stepped over a pile of shredded Christmas paper and crossed to the fireplace mantel where his shotgun hung. He lifted it down with one hand and cracked it open.

"Well, watch for him, please, May," Karl said, a steely anger in his voice. "I'll be there in a shake."

He noted with approval that there were two shells in it, one in each chamber. He snapped it closed again.

"Should I call the Sheriff?" May asked.

"Don't bother," Karl said. "I'm tired of his foot-dragging. It's my property, and I'm going to *finally* do something about this. See you in a minute, May."

He cradled the gun against the inside of his left arm and went to hang up, but then he stopped himself. "Oh, May? *May?* Listen, you keep your kids inside, you hear me? I don't want any young'uns getting hurt."

Chapter Twenty-Five

Gammy paused with her hands over her type-writer—should she write the bishop now? She certainly didn't want to waste any time beginning a search for a new pastor—*a proper pastor this time*, she thought, *not Miss Barbie-Doll "Let's Play Pastor." I'm not going to fall asleep on my watch again.*

But no. She removed her hands from the keys. There was a way things were supposed to be done, and this decision needs to come first from the Pastor. Gammy knew this was right, but she screwed up her mouth into a powerful pucker and looked out the window at the snowy street. She did not like the delay one bit. Patience was not her strong suit, but she didn't want the Lord Jesus to be displeased with her. She sighed and turned away from the typewriter.

Just then the door swung open and she squinted to see who it was. It was a man; she could see that. She stayed seated, watching with interest as whoever-it-was removed his hat and scarf. Finally, he had unpeeled enough for her to see that it was Kevin Schwartz, his glasses foggy from their sudden change in temperature.

"Afternoon, Gammy," he said, pulling a manila envelope out of his jacket. "Here's the estimate for the roof repair. Can you have those copied and ready to go for the next Council Meeting?"

Gammy stood and walked over to the foyer, taking the envelope from Kevin's mitten. Kevin was the President of the Church Council and had volunteered to get estimates on a repair that should have been done a year ago. *Like everyone else around here,* Gammy thought, *a day late and a dollar short.* "I'll handle it, Kevin. Eight copies?"

"Nine, now that the pastor's here."

"Well, about that," Gammy said, looking around as if she were concerned that they might be overheard. In fact, she knew that there was no one else in the building. She dropped her voice to a whisper. "You're not going to be needing that ninth copy—trust me."

"What do you mean?" Kevin cocked his head sideways.

Was that suspicion she saw on his face? *Nonsense,* she thought. *Kevin is a sensible sort.* "I have it on good authority that the pastor will be resigning soon after Christmas."

"Gammy, what are you talking about? She just got here!"

"She's been having some…personal adjustment troubles." Gammy gave him an "it's such a shame" kind of smile and shook her head slowly. "I knew it would be hard, being a Lady Pastor and all. I don't know why some people just line up for trouble, but they do. They surely do." She sighed. "Anyway, she's working on her resignation letter right now." She dropped her voice even lower, adding conspiratorially, "I saw it on her computer. I'm…helping with her spelling and such."

"Gammy, I don't believe a word of it." Kevin set his mittened hands on his hips.

"Well, you should! You saw how she just walked out of worship last Sunday! You can't reward unprofessional conduct like that, you just can't. The Lord Jesus—" she was about to say that the Lord Jesus would not be pleased, but she stopped herself. Her mother had warned her that the Lord Jesus didn't talk to other people the way he talked to Gammy. Other people just didn't know him and his divine love the way she did. She pitied them. And she knew that she had to hide her special relationship with Jesus from them, or they might be jealous, or frightened, or heaven knows what else. People were simply unpredictable, she found, and they got bent out of shape at the oddest things. "The Lord Jesus said we are to take up our cross, not hightail it out the back door when things get a little rough."

Kevin was watching her a little too closely for her

comfort, and he was scowling besides. "Gammy, are you harassing the new Pastor?"

She recoiled in horror. "Kevin Schwartz! I don't even know what you mean!"

His face softened, but his eyes did not. "Let me put it to you this way: if Pastor Katie announced today that she was leaving, would you be happy about it, or sad about it?"

"Well….I'd be…what I mean is…" She held her hand to her chest, mortally wounded by the unspoken accusation Kevin was making. "It's a very sad thing that she didn't work out."

"I agree with you there." He grabbed his scarf and began winding it again around his neck. "I hope you're wrong about this, Gammy, I really do. Last Sunday was a fluke—I talked to people from her last parish. It might have even been intentional—it certainly woke people up, and it was a great object lesson. People are calling it 'performance art,' and who am I to say it isn't? I know this, though: she's got people in this parish thinking and talking. And that's not a bad thing in my book." He put his hat on and opened the door. Then he shut it again, and turned back to her. "Gammy, a gentle reminder— you work for me, me and everyone on the church board. If our new pastor leaves and I get any wind that you had anything to do with it, you can kiss this job goodbye." And with that, he went out and shut the door behind him.

Gammy's mouth worked like she was grinding pencils in her teeth. *How dare he speak to me that way?* she raged inwardly. *How dare he?* It was she who kept this parish running—she alone. Without her, the whole thing would have collapsed years ago!

Blindly, she threw the envelope. It smacked against the far wall, knocking an icon of the Lord Jesus to the floor. Gammy's heart fell, and she sank to her knees, crawling over to the fallen icon. "I'm sorry, I'm sorry, I'm so sorry," she said, nearly weeping. She snatched up the icon and held it in her lap as she rocked back and forth on the floor.

She gazed at the blessed face of the Lord, and before her very eyes, it became animated. The Lord licked his lips, and blinked his eyes. She drew a huge breath and dabbed at a tear welling from her eye. She loved it when he "visited" her like this, and it had been too long.

The Lord sniffed, then he looked her straight in the eyes and said, "That pastor is a Little-Miss-Prissy-Pants. Send that letter." Then his eyes stopped moving, and it was just an icon again. She hugged it to her chest. "Yes, Lord Jesus," she said out loud, and gently laying the icon aside, she set her fingers once more to the type-writer keyboard.

Chapter Twenty-Six

She had been lucky. At first, she despaired at the prospect of finding more food in the abandoned hous-es, but once she put her mind to it, she was amazed at what she found. She had been through three of them today, and she clutched a cardboard box filled with treasure close to her chest as she entered the back door of a fourth.

In one house she had discovered a slightly rusted can of peaches, high up on a shelf in the garage. It was out of sight from the ground, but sitting right there when she climbed up for a closer look. She immediately started salivating when she saw it—so much so that she had to laugh at herself. She had wiped her mouth on her sleeve before reaching for the can.

In another house she had found two boxes of macaroni and cheese. There were some mouse nibbles on one box, but amazingly, they had not chewed all the way through. Her heart leaped when she saw it. "Comfort food!" her mother had called it, and she was comforted indeed to have found those boxes.

The third house seemed to be a bust at first. Then she got creative. She surmised that there must have been an alcoholic who lived in the house last, because she found a small flask-sized bottle of whiskey in the bottom of a toilet tank. She had never tasted whiskey, and wasn't sure she wanted to, but it was booty, so she put it in the box with the other stuff anyway.

She was just about to give up when she hit pay dirt. In the living room was a little sun alcove, complete with built-in benches that lifted up for storage underneath. Removing the cushions, she lifted up the bench, and flinched as it squeaked. Inside she found some wadded newspaper and a shoebox. She lifted out the shoebox, and breathlessly pulled the lid off of it. Inside was a cache of about twenty Hershey's bars.

"What was this, a house full of addicts?" she said out loud, but she wasn't complaining. It was a Christmas gift, she decided, that God had selected especially for her. The thought made her feel sad, because she was sure that God wouldn't be giving her any gifts. She was a whore, a runaway, a homeless person, a baby-aban-doner—what God could possibly love her? What God would want to give her anything but a one-way ticket to Hell?

She tasted the sourness of a spoiled moment, and without thinking further she put the candy bars in the cardboard box, shoebox and all.

One more house and she'd call it a day. She went first to the kitchen, but didn't have much hope, as she'd cleaned it out already. Still, she double-checked, and discovered a small can of sardines hiding on a top shelf. "Ewwww…" she said to the empty kitchen. "Thanks, I guess."

She tried the garage next. As she scoured the shelves, the cupboards, and the nooks, her mind drifted to the subject that she wanted most to avoid. It took a lot of effort not to think about the baby. Too much effort. Sometimes she could distract herself, but empty spaces—like this house—made that almost impossible. Thoughts of what she had left behind on that loading dock at Bremmer's flooded into the vacuum of the empty house. She batted the thoughts away, but they swept back in moments later.

Remorse and guilt flooded in with them. She worried, but comforted herself knowing that someone there would find her, would take care of her. She knew Gibbs would be there. No harm could possibly come to her.

She wiped the dust from her hands onto her jeans and tried the living room next. Heartened by the discovery of the stash in the living room of the last house, she searched eagerly for hidden doors or clever hiding places.

She sighed at the thought of Gibbs. At first, she had always thought he was goofy, when they were growing up. Other kids teased him because of his skinniness and his bright red hair. But in the last year or so, she had seen another quality in him she had never noticed before: he was kind. And it wasn't a kindness that was forced, in order to achieve some ulterior motive. It was real. And he was kind to everyone.

It was the strangest feeling, but the first time she noticed him being kind to her, she had simply melted. She smiled at the memory of it. It seemed like such a long time ago, but she knew it was only a year and a half or so. She stopped her search of the living room and clutched at her belly. It was so small. Kindness had made her grow large. The thought seemed to her profound.

It was too painful to hold onto. She had walked away from Gibbs, just as she had walked away from her baby, just as she had walked away from her parents. That stopped her. She was halfway up the stairs when she set her box down and sat, staring blankly at the afternoon light on the fireplace brickwork. She missed her parents the most. She fought against a welling of tears and wiped her nose on her sleeve. She simply couldn't face them. What they would think of her? What they would say to her? *What would* she *say to her?* she thought, recoiling at the thought of her mother's wrath.

"It's done now," she said out loud, with a note of

defiance. She stood and clomped noisily up the stairs. In the bathroom she found a half-used tube of tooth-paste. She put it in the box. She searched the bedrooms next, but they were empty of all but dust-bunnies and dead spiders. She was just about to call it a day when she heard a faint click as the deadbolt on the front door slid open. She stood stock-still and listened. The door banged open and a man's heavy boots sounded on the hardwood floor.

She swallowed hard and held her breath, backing up toward the far side of the back bedroom, as far from the door as she could get. As she moved, the floor beneath her squeaked. "Who's there?" A man's voice rang out, echoing slightly in the empty house. "Come down right now, or I swear to St. Peter I will blow your filthy head off!" She heard a clicking sound and she knew just what it was. She had watched her father cleaning his rifles on many a Saturday night.

Quickly, she looked over her shoulder. There was a window. She turned and looked out. There was a little ornamental lip midway around the roof—she could just see it poking out near the bottom of her view. She glanced up at the window's lock. Quickly she turned it. She expected it to stick, but it didn't, and she exhaled with relief as it slid without resistance. With both hands, she gripped the lower pane and pushed it up. It slid up with faint complaint from the counterweights in the walls.

Time seemed to slow down as she heard the man's tentative steps on the stairs. Once the window was fully open, she whisked up the cardboard box and threw it to the ground below. It seemed to take a long time to hit the ground, and when it did, the man on the stairs shouted, "What was that? What *was* that??" And then there was a thundering of steps as he rushed back downstairs to investigate.

She hadn't expected that reaction, but she was glad of it. It bought her a few precious seconds. She did not waste them. With an agility that surprised even her, she leaped through the window, twisting to hold fast to the sill. Her legs flailed at first, but quickly found their footing on the ornamental lip.

Crouching down on the lip, she noticed a drainpipe about four feet away. Hugging the outside wall of the house, she edged herself over to the drainpipe and tried to get a grip on it. She thought she could use it to scramble down, like a rope, but she couldn't get her fingers behind it, and didn't trust her grip on the front of it.

She panicked then, and a sensation of vertigo washed over her. Just then she heard a sound above her and to her left. Looking up, she saw the business end of a rifle sticking out of the window she had just jumped from. She waited to see if the man would stick his head out, but he didn't. She fought to control her breathing.

She had to do something. She became aware of her immediate surroundings again, and she realized she was down on one knee on the ornamental lip of the roof. She faced the wall and twisted until both knees were just barely holding her. Then, with a grunt, she placed her hands on either side of her knees, and with precision born of her years in gymnastics, and remembered only in her muscles, she pushed up, swung her legs out, and swung down, hanging on to the ornamental lip with her fingertips.

Swaying from the lip, she looked down and gauged the distance to be about four feet to the ground. She knew it looked higher than it was, and she squeezed her eyes closed and dropped. She was careful to roll when she hit the ground, but she still felt a jarring pain in her right ankle.

Without pausing to think, she snatched up the box and started running for the tree line for all she was worth. Behind her, she heard the man shouting, but couldn't make out his words above the puffing of her own breath.

Adrenaline pumped through her. Briefly, she recognized a feeling of euphoria, of aliveness, of something free and young and vital bursting through and beyond her and it felt good and wild and sad, all at once. And then she heard the explosion of a shotgun blast and felt a burst of buckshot and hot, sulfurous air blow past her left ear, entirely too close. She felt something on her cheek, and slowed just a little as she pulled her hand back and saw the blood.

But a new burst of energy came with the sight, and somehow she knew to jog evasively to the right. Another shot rang out, and although she felt the wind of it, she didn't feel anything strike her. She kept running and prayed the shotgun was a double-barrel and not an automatic and the man would have to reload.

The tree line joggled before her tantalizingly. She figured she was just ten yards from the first of the trees when another blast caught her in the shoulder. This time she felt it before she heard it. It felt like someone had slugged her on the shoulder with a frying pan, and it twisted her around. Ducking, she righted herself and dashed into the cover of the trees, praying to the God who hated her to protect her.

Chapter Twenty-Seven

Howard pushed open the door to the Sheriff's office and sighed deeply. He felt as if there were an enormous sandbag pressing down on his chest. He was having trouble breathing.

"Chief? Are you all right?" Diane called to him over her shoulder.

"You're not even looking at me! How do you know something's wrong?" he asked.

"A sigh like that could put out a candle in Silas," she answered, still not looking at him.

He forced a little smile for her benefit, which, he supposed, she could smell, or otherwise detect by non-visual means. "Mueller still out?"

"Down for the count."

"How bad?"

"Bad enough to go to the doctor. He went this morning."

"How do you know—never mind." He waved away the rest of the sentence.

"Hi, Chief," Czarnecki said, exiting the restroom.

"Maggie. What do you got for me?"

"I got an assortment of missing baby pictures—all of

them too old to be this one. Only one fits the time frame—and she's Korean," she said, pouring herself some coffee.

"So we still got nothin'." He sighed again.

"Chief, do you need a nap?" she asked, looking at him with concern. "Naps are the best medicine, Mother Herzog used to say."

Charlene Herzog had been Czarnecki's foster mother, Howard remembered. An amazing, brave, and giving woman. "Mother Herzog was onto something, there, but I've got too much to do, unfortunately."

"A power-nap only takes 20 minutes, and it'll do you a world of good," Czarnecki argued.

"I don't do 'power-' anythings. Besides, I lay down and I'm groggy for the rest of the day. I'll tough it out."

"Suit yourself," she tossed over her shoulder, and headed for her desk.

He sighed again.

"There goes another candle in Wade County."

"You can stop, Diane."

"Chief, can I see you in your office a minute?" To his great surprise, Diane was actually looking at him.

"Of course," he said. He watched as she rose and entered his office. He followed her and closed the door. "What's the matter?" he asked, and sank into his chair.

She stood. "Well, it's obvious you're not going to talk in front of your subordinates. So I thought some privacy might help. What's wrong with you?"

"Aren't you my subordinate?" He narrowed one eye at her.

She didn't flinch. "What's up with you, Chief?"

He sighed, noticed, and shot her a warning look. She

didn't say anything, but the tiniest curl of a smile touched her lip for a moment.

"Do you mean on top of the fact that we've got a baby we don't know how to help?"

"That's not so far out of the ordinary, and you know it. It's not what's eating at you. Is it Lara?"

He met her eyes. *How did she always nail it like that?* he wondered. He shifted uncomfortably. "I came home last night and she had packed up every trace of Lucy and then decorated the house for Christmas. She was... chipper. As if Lucy had never been."

"She needs to see a psychologist."

He scowled. "Do you think so?"

"I've thought that for a long time now. Chief, people see psychologists these days when they lose the lottery. It's not any kind of poor reflection on her—or on you."

"People are sad...." He stared off into space.

"No. People are often sensible. *Lara* is sad, and you need to get her help."

He didn't say anything. Instead, he looked at the poinsettia on his desk. A single leaf had withered and fallen to his blotter. "I need to water this plant."

"You overwatered that plant. You need to leave it alone. You need to help your wife, or you're going to lose her."

"Don't bully me, Diane."

"Stop being a stubborn mule, then. Face your fear, Chief. Your wife's life depends on it."

They stared at each other for a couple of long, uncomfortable minutes. "Anyone else talked to me like that, it'd be insubordination."

"Anyone else hasn't kept your office running like a

clock for twenty years," she said, not missing a beat. "And that includes moving parts like you."

"I had a thought on the way over here," he said, his eyes unfocusing.

She cocked her head and waited for it.

"I thought, you know, if that baby didn't have to go in to the county today, I…I don't know. I was thinking it might do Lara good…."

"It might do her good to go down to Bremmer's and help out with the baby?"

"Yeah," he looked down as his hands. *When had they gotten so wrinkled and rough?* he wondered.

"Well, it's a good thought. It would probably do her a world of good." She crossed her arms and smiled at him a little sadly. "I called the County, by the way." She indicated a slip on his desk with a flick of her chin. "There's the address. They're full up in Silas, so you'll have to go to Kent. They close at five, so you'll have to get a move on."

Howard glanced at the yellow slip of paper and picked up the telephone receiver. Then he hung it up again. "Thanks for this. Can you get me that new pastor on the phone?" She nodded, and paused at his door.

"Therapist."

"Pastor. Now."

She closed his office door and he watched her through the glass as she made her way back to her desk. In less than a minute, her voice crackled over the intercom. "Pastor Jorgenson on three."

He picked up the receiver and held it to his ear. "Howdy, Pastor."

Her voice was tinny but cheerful. "Sheriff, that was fast."

"You serious about driving Gibbs and that baby?"

"As a heart att—yes, I'm serious," she said.

His lip curled into a smile. "You're going to have to go to Kent. Here's the address...." He waited until she'd grabbed a pen and then rattled it off. "Can you go now? Good. You'll have to step on it—they close at five. You have just enough time. Can you call Bremmer's or do you want me to do it?"

"I'll phone them right now—I'm sure you have your hands full," she said cheerfully.

"I'm grateful for your help, Pastor."

"Glad to do it. I'll call you later with a report."

"You keep this kind of efficiency up and you'll be on the payroll."

She laughed. "The way my job is going, you shouldn't tempt me."

"I got a man down with flu—"

"Sheriff, stop. I'll call later."

He gave her his cell phone number and hung up. For a moment, he felt the stillness of the world. In his mind he knew that everything on earth was moving at millions of miles a second, but in the confines of this office, it seemed like time—and everything else—was standing still. Just then a shriveled petal from the poinsettia dropped onto his desk. He watched it fall, as if in slow motion. When it hit, his mind supplied a "boom." He sighed.

He looked up to see Diane waving at him with wide eyes. She had the telephone to her ear, and she looked grim. He bolted to the door and snatched it open.

"What's happening?"

She held up a finger, and then spoke into the receiver. "We'll have someone out immediately. Keep everyone indoors until we contact you." She hung up. "Grab your keys, Chief, we got gunfire up on Grizzly Flat."

Chapter Twenty-Eight

Katie pulled up to the loading dock and honked. Within moments, Gibbs was walking briskly to her car, baby bundled and safely cradled in his arms. She reached across and opened the car door and he stuck his head in. "Gotta put in the baby seat," he said curtly. She hit the button on her armrest and the rear passenger door clicked open. He gingerly laid the baby on the passenger seat, and in less than a minute, Gibbs had the seat installed, and had installed the baby in it.

Without a wasted moment, he shut the back door and slid in beside her. "Hi, Pastor," he said, and shut the car door.

"Hello, Mr. Gibbs," Katie said, wasting no time heading out of the parking lot. "I hear we've got to step on it. Do you know the way?"

He nodded. "Head for the highway."

She turned out onto Schillerstrasse heading West. Their drive to the highway was quiet. Katie respected the teen's silence, glancing at him now and then, twisted in his seat, cooing and touching the baby's little hand. She wondered at his kind attention. Soon they were approaching the onramp, and a minute later they were at the speed limit heading toward Kent.

"How long should this take us?" Katie asked.

Gibbs glanced at the digital clock on the dash. "About a half hour. We got time." Katie looked at the clock herself. It was 4:15. She raised her eyebrows and sighed. It was going to be close, all right. She edged forward on the accelerator and then kept it steady at 70.

Gibbs leaned over and eyed the speedometer. He gave her a surprised look.

"Who's going to stop us? The Sheriff? He'd give us a flashing-light escort if we asked him."

"I didn't say nothing," Gibbs said.

They rode in silence for a while longer. Then Gibbs looked over at her, as if he were studying her. "Pastor, how did you know you were going to be a pastor?"

She looked at him and saw that he was earnest. "At first I didn't—"

"You must have really liked going to church when you were a kid."

Katie laughed. "No! I hated it, in fact."

His red eyebrows scrunched together. "Then how—"

"Tell you the truth, I don't much like it now." She lowered her voice. "That's a secret just between you and me, of course."

"I don't get it."

She paused to think about how to answer him. "Before that baby came along, did you think, 'Hey, I'd like to take care of a baby?'"

"Heck no. I always thought they kinda stank."

Katie burst out with a laugh. "Well, yes, exactly. But now?"

He looked back at the little bundle in the rear seat. "Now, I can't imagine her not being here." He looked back to her and Katie held his eyes for a moment. "I don't want to do this."

"Me neither," she said, and patted his knee.

"So?" he said.

"Oh," she said, her train of thought suddenly back on track. "So it's like you and this baby. I was part of a great youth group when I was your age. I didn't much like church, but I liked the other things we did. One day, it was like a little voice said, 'Time to get serious about this.'"

"So what did you do?"

"I ignored it, of course." She smiled at him, then looked back at the road. "Are you crazy? It's way too scary to become a pastor. That's the last thing on earth I wanted to do."

"Except that it wasn't?" he asked.

She looked at him and noticed him looking at her intently. She nodded. "Once that voice started, it wouldn't shut up. It nagged at me. It was worse than my mother!"

"Word," Gibbs agreed.

"And once I started, I realized how much I loved it. I couldn't imagine doing anything else."

"I could never be a pastor."

"Why do you say that?"

"I'm not good enough."

Katie laughed. "Oh, you think I'm good, huh? I'll let you in on a secret. Pastors are just as screwed up as everyone else."

She glanced over and noticed that his eyes were big.

"They are?"

"Absolutely. It's just that…well, a lot of pastors try to pretend like they're not."

"Oh. My high school principle is like that. He cheated on his wife, and everyone knows it, but he just pretends that it didn't happen."

"I've known pastors like that, too."

"Wow," he chewed on this for a bit. "So if pastors aren't good, I mean, more good than other people, why are they pastors?"

"Well, I can only speak for myself. But I can tell you that I'm not particularly good, I'm not particularly smart, and a lot of the time I have no idea what I'm doing. In fact, I mess up all the time."

He looked at her then as if he were seeing her for the first time. "So why are you a pastor?"

"I think it's because I love."

She could see his shoulders relax as comprehension dawned in him.

"I don't know what I'm doing, either." He gestured to the back seat. "But I love her."

"It's just like that," Katie agreed.

For several minutes they were silent. Finally, Katie couldn't stand it any longer. "Tell me about your folks," she said, her voice bright and interested.

He looked out the side window, away from her. She wondered if she had said the wrong thing. Eventually, though, he spoke. "My mom's fun. She works too hard. She smokes too much. I think I ruined her life."

Katie's heart sank. "Why on earth would you say that?"

"She was about two years older than I am now when

she had me," he said. "My dad ran away when she told him about me."

"You've never met him?"

"No." He kept looking out the window, away from her. "I guess he was scared of us. I don't know why. My mom is fun and I work hard."

"Of course you do," she said, her voice soft and full of emotion.

"What do you think your mother would say if she heard you say you think you ruined her life?"

"She'd tell me not to be an idiot."

"I like your mom already," Katie said.

"That's the turnoff, coming up." Gibbs pointed. "Go left when we get to the bottom."

"Aye-aye," Katie said. She looked over at him again, concerned. "How do you feel about your dad now?"

"I hate him," he said, the pain in his voice evident. "I'm never going to be like him. Never."

Katie breathed out a deep breath. "I think you have every reason to be angry," she said. "But if you met him today, do you think you'd want to hear his side of the story?"

He looked at her strangely. "What do you mean?"

"I guess I mean, people don't just do things for no reason. Don't you think you'd want to hear what his reasons were?"

"I never thought about it," he said gravely.

"Everyone has their own version of a story to tell. And everyone's version is different, you know."

He looked like he wasn't sure about that.

"It's even in the Bible," she said, grinning.

"It is?" he asked.

"Yes, it is. Do you know how many gospels there are?"

He shook his head.

"Gibbs, are you telling me you've never been to Sunday school?"

He shook his head again. "Mom never took me to church."

She pursed her lips. "Well, there are four gospels in the New Testament of the Bible. They all tell the story of Jesus' life, from beginning to end."

"They tell the same story four times?" he asked, looking at her uncertainly.

She took the off-ramp and prepared to turn left. "Yessir, they sure do. And do you know why?" Out of the corner of her eye he saw him shake his head. She turned left. "Because every one of them tells the story from the perspective of a different person. And the stories are all different. The writers all have different ideas about who Jesus is and what he's here for. And sometimes they contradict each other."

"So how do you know which one is true?"

"Well, you never know what really happened. You only ever know what someone's experience is. It's like this: I'm talking to you now, and I'm hearing your side of the story. Tomorrow, what if I bumped into your dad? I would hear his side of the story. How would I know which story was true?"

She looked over at him, and saw his eyes darting back and forth, deep in thought. "I don't know."

"Right. I would have to be humble and truthful and say I didn't know. I'd have to be open to the possibility of either of you being right or either of you being wrong. But maybe both of you are telling the truth as you see it, too."

He said nothing, obviously chewing this over. He pointed, indicating she should turn right at the stop sign. He pulled a scrap of paper out of his coat pocket and consulted it. "Almost there," he said.

She turned right and waited for the next instruction. A few minutes later, they pulled into the driveway of a squat, cinderblock building. Mounds of plowed snow, made black from exhaust fumes, adorned both sides of the drive. She stopped the car and glanced over at Gibbs. "Here we are," she said, and slid out.

A little too slowly, he opened his door and deliberately disengaged the child from the car seat. He held her to his breast.

Katie started to walk toward the door, but he did not budge from the side of the car. "C'mon, Gibbs, they're almost closed." That's when she noticed the tears spilling from his eyes.

He clutched the baby closer to him. "I can't do it," he said, his voice thick and gravelly. "I can't be... I can't be like him."

Katie melted inside. She walked back to him and passed her hand over his red hair. "Oh, Gibbs, you're not like him at all."

"I don't know that. I don't know his side of the story."

"No, you don't," she agreed. "But this isn't your baby, either. Your father abandoned you knowing who you were. This child doesn't belong to you. You have had the joy of caring for her for a couple of days, but now it's time to let her find a home with people who can love her and care for her for the long haul." She smiled at him. "You can't keep her if she isn't yours, Gibbs. You just can't. That's the law."

He buried his face in the blankets that swaddled the baby. She waited for the wave of sobs to pass. Then she put her arm around his waist and nudged him toward the door. "Let's go, honey," she said gently.

With short little steps his feet began to move. As they approached the glass double doors, Katie noted that the Christmas lights spread along the top of the door-way seemed perfunctory and cheerless—as if their sole function was to mock all who passed through these doors.

There are no tidings of comfort or joy here, she thought. She opened the door and held it for Gibbs. Reluctantly, he stepped over the threshold.

Chapter Twenty-Nine

Siren wailing and strobe light flashing, Howard drove as fast as safety allowed toward Grizzly Flat. Since no one else was around, he cursed aloud, rehears-ing what he'd *like* to say to Wysocki, but never would. Karl was impulsive, reckless, a hothead. And he was determined to get someone killed.

But he had always been that way, Howard remem-bered. He flashed back to a time when, as teenagers, they had gone deer hunting and Karl had narrowly escaped blowing the head off of another hunter, who—

he had to admit—*was* stupid enough to be out in the woods without a hunter's-orange vest.

Still, Karl could not be trusted with a gun—never could, couldn't now. The problem was, he couldn't think of a single legal way to part him from it. *Sometimes the Second Amendment is more trouble that it's worth,* he mused.

He pulled up when he saw Wysocki's car, and no sooner had he stepped down from his Range Rover than Karl was walking over to him, shotgun cradled in his arm like a baby. "Karl," Howard said by way of greeting. His mind flashed on all the things he had rehearsed on the way over, but he let them go like cobwebs trailing away from his memory.

"I got 'im, Sheriff!" Wysocki crowed, a mean, satisfied smile stretched over his face. "Winged 'im good, too. I only regret I didn't kill the crook!"

Howard sighed. "You *hit* him, Karl? With a shotgun?"

"Sure did, right in the shoulder. Knocked 'im down for a moment, but he was up on his feet again before I could reload. Made for the tree line back of the house."

Howard looked up and squinted to see the trees in the fading light. Dark had just about descended, and except for the Christmas lights of the neighbors about a half mile away, nothing was very clear. "Well, I'm sorry to hear that, Karl. I really am. I hope you didn't do anything you'll regret, or I'll have to do something *I'll* regret."

"Vague threats don't mean nothing to me, Howie. You want to scare me, be clear about it. Otherwise you can either help me or get out of the way."

Howard ignored him and headed for the house. "It open?" he called over his shoulder.

"Yeah, I opened it."

"Lights?"

"Nope, but I've got a flashlight."

Howard took his own flashlight from his belt and leveled it at the door. No sign of forced entry. He pushed it open and stepped into the foyer. He made his way to the back door, shining the flashlight back and forth. *No sign of damage,* he thought. He paused by the back door—a broken pane near the inside handle told the story.

"Did you touch this, Karl?" he asked without looking at Wysocki.

"Nope."

"Good. I'll get Czarnecki out here tomorrow to dust for prints. If it's a known felon, we'll at least have an idea of who we're dealing with and how dangerous he is."

Wysocki nodded.

"Where were you when the shooting happened?"

"Upstairs, back bedroom window."

"Take me. And be careful not to touch anything." Howard followed Wysocki up the stairs, all the while shining his flashlight on every surface he passed, looking for some sign of damage or something out of the ordinary—but he saw nothing.

At the top of the landing, Howard pushed in front of Wysocki and examined the doorframe. The doorknob was unmolested, as he expected, but it might have been touched. He shone his flashlight around and saw a small box on the floor near the window. He pulled out a handkerchief and used it to pick up the box. The label read "sardines."

"Well, we either got a thief with no culinary sensibilities, or he's really, really hungry," Howard said, almost to himself.

"Don't like sardines, Sheriff?"

"Does anyone?"

"I do."

Howard cocked an eyebrow. "No need to prove my point, Karl." He set the box down again where he had found it. He'd have Czarnecki dust it as well. *The window too*, he thought, and rose to examine it. Again, there was no damage. He grunted and turned back toward the stairs.

"What'cha going to do, Sheriff?"

"I'm going to go home and have supper, Karl."

Wysocki positioned himself between Howard and the stairs. Howard stopped and Wysocki stabbed a pudgy finger at his chest. "You been dragging your feet too long on this, Howard. You do something about this tonight or I will. It's your choice. You either find and arrest this guy, or you can collect his body in the morning. 'Cause I got no problem going from house to house until I find him, and when I do, I'm not going to hesitate to separate his head from his shoulders."

"You do, Karl, and I'll charge you with murder. This is a police matter, and you need to leave it to me."

"Leave it to you to do a lot of nothing! Meanwhile we've got a thief terrorizing the flats, breaking and entering, looting and vandalizing. If you won't protect folks up here, it falls to us to do it." He gripped the barrel of his shotgun in both hands and he trained a steely eye on Howard's. "It falls to me. And I won't fail."

Howard fought the temptation to wrest the shotgun from his hands, to confiscate it, to call in a 5150, anything to keep Wysocki from behaving impulsively. They stood there for what seemed like hours, their eyes locked on one another, neither man willing to budge. But eventually, Howard blinked first. "All right, Karl. I'll make a deal with you. You give me the keys to your properties up here, and then you go home. I'll go round to each of the houses—I'll make sure they're empty and secure. If I see anything out of the ordinary, I'll flag it for Czarnecki tomorrow."

Wysocki backed up a pace and felt at the scruff of his beard, considering. Howard continued. "And you're *in* for the night—no excuses, no objections. Tomorrow I'll keep you in the loop when we run the prints. This is my number one case, and I'll check in with you every day. Deal?"

"Number one case?"

"Top of my list."

"You're not just yankin' my chain?"

"Swear on my mother's grave."

Wysocki looked down at the flashlight beams on his shoes. Curtly, he looked up and gave a nod. "That's good enough for me, Howard. For now."

"Now is all we got, Karl."

Karl started down the stairs. "I hate it when you get philosophical. That degree did you no good."

Karl was talking about his first degree at the University of Michigan, in Philosophy. It hadn't taken Howard long to realize that he could not feed a family with a Philosophy degree, and he went back for his master's in criminal science—a much more marketable field.

By the time Howard finished reminiscing, they were outside, standing on the porch of the house, and Wysocki was locking up. He presented the keys to Howard. "They're all on the Flat," he said, "and the addresses are on the tags." He pointed to the little white paper circles attached to the keys with a thin circle of metal. Addresses were written in ink in a neat hand. *Not Wysocki's hand,* Howard thought, *obviously.* "I know where they are, Karl."

"All right then," Wysocki said, the barrel of his shotgun waving around wildly as he turned. Howard closed his eyes and counted to five in order not to blow up at him for his recklessness. Wysocki looked as if he didn't know what to say. *He is certainly not going to say 'thank you,'* Howard thought to himself. "Go home, Karl. I'll call you if I find anything."

Wysocki nodded curtly. "You do that."

"I will."

"See that you do."

"Good night, Karl."

"Sheriff." Howard watched as Wysocki reluctantly got in his car and pulled out of the drive toward home.

Chapter Thirty

Myrtle dodged a falling Christmas tree and shrieked as the bulbs shattered on the linoleum in front of her. Revealed to her sight once the tree had fallen was a red-faced little girl who held her hands up to her mouth, her eyes wide, mittens dangling from their ties at her wrists. "I didn't do it!" she squeaked, although it was obvious to Myrtle that she had.

"Young lady!" Myrtle glared at her with her hands on her hips. The little girl gave a shriek and fled behind another tree, nearly knocking it over, too. Myrtle sighed. Then she leaned over and righted the fallen tree. "More sweeping," she said to herself, looking at the shattered glass on the floor. She looked toward heaven. "Don't even need to listen for guidance this time—I know what to do."

She turned toward the back rooms and marveled at the spectacle the store had become. Between her and her goal was an obstacle course of winter-bundled people, darting children, and careening baskets, some of them stacked precariously with fragile items.

By the time she reached the break room, she had narrowly avoided two collisions and taken note of three kiosks that needed restocking. Breathlessly she stumbled into the break room.

"Jerry, thank goodness you're here," she said, seeing Jerry seated at the break table, staring off into space. "We've had a tree upset, and I've got to clear some broken bulbs," she panted, making her way past him to the stockroom where the brooms were kept. She called over her shoulder as she walked, "But we've got urgent restocking on the meat products ornament kiosk, the Bulgarian kiosk, and the helping professions wall—we are plumb out of physical therapist ornaments."

A moment later she re-emerged, and her mouth dropped open when she saw that Jerry had not budged. She cocked her bird-like head, which was oscillating quickly from side to side. She stepped toward him and placed a hand on his shoulder.

"Oh, huh?" he asked.

"Jerry, are you all right?" Myrtle asked.

"It's so quiet," he said, that distant look coming back into his eyes.

"Have you been out on the floor lately?" she asked incredulously.

He didn't seem to hear her. With a puff of impatience, she sat next to him and turned his chin to face her. Comprehension resolved in his eyes. "Hi, Myrtle," he said.

"Jerry Keller, you listen to me. It's like the finale of *Les Misérables* out there. I want to know what's wrong with you right now, or I'm calling Carol."

"Without the baby…." he said, as if completing a sentence. "It's so quiet."

"Ooooo, you're going to hate me for this," Myrtle said. She stood and stomped on his foot with every bit of strength that was in her.

"Ahhhhhhh!" Jerry said, doubling over and clutching at his boot.

"Meat products! Keller! Now!" Myrtle shouted at the back of his bobbing head, and then zoomed from the room, brandishing her dustpan and broom.

Chapter Thirty-One

Pastor Katie ushered Gibbs and the baby before her as they approached the information desk. When it was their turn, Gibbs stared at the angular woman at the window and said nothing. Katie pushed herself in beside him. "We have an abandoned baby to admit," she said, not at all sure of the proper terminology in this situation.

Tight-lipped, the angular woman looked up at the clock, narrowed her eyes at them, and pointed to a corridor, at the end of which was a single door. "Thank you," Katie said, and tugged at the shoulder of Gibb's coat.

Within moments they were in the waiting room and lined up at yet another window. Gibbs gently rocked the baby, held close to his chest, while Katie looked around. The room was absolutely packed. Katie flinched at the din, as children of all ages wailed, screamed, and shrieked. The adults who attended them did little to control or comfort them. Most were reading magazines. A couple of them were screaming back at the children, or simply scolding.

Katie counted the number ahead of her in line. Five. She looked at the clock. Five minutes until five o'clock. She wondered what would happen in five minutes. Would they send everyone home? Would they lock the front doors and finish with those who were there? She didn't know. She felt a spirit of desolation sweep through her as she watched the chaos around her. The garland hanging above the window seemed to mock her.

She watched the minutes crawl by on the clock as, inch by inch, they progressed in the line. At five o'clock sharp they finally reached the window. The bored woman facing them looked like she needed a week's worth of sleep. "Hi," Katie said to her, "I'm wondering—"

"Sit over there," the woman interrupted her, and thrust a clipboard at her. "Fill these out. Bring them up when you're done. Next."

Gibbs shot her a look that said, *I'm not too sure about this.* Katie didn't budge, but addressed the woman in the window again. "Um…I'm sorry, is it always this busy?"

The woman scowled at her. "Welcome to the economic downturn. *Next!*"

Katie's face bunched up with anger. She had grown used to being treated with respect, ever since she had begun wearing her clerical collar. But this woman either didn't see it or didn't care. *Or maybe she just has it in for female clergy,* she thought, and then her shoulders sank as she remembered just how prevalent an attitude that was in this place. Gibbs freed one hand and tugged at her sleeve, "C'mon, Pastor, let's sit down."

There really wasn't any place to sit down. They circumambulated the room, like a clot moving through an artery, looking for a place, any place, to rest. Not knowing exactly why, Katie made a decision. "Gibbs, I'm going to find a bathroom. Wait here." He nodded and she headed toward the door. Just then another door she hadn't noticed before opened, and a drably dressed woman with mousy brown hair stepped through.

"Turner!" she called, looking at her clipboard. One

harried woman with two children in tow got up. Gibbs made a beeline to the woman's vacated seat, and Katie beat her to the door. "I need a restroom," she said to the mousy woman. The woman pointed at the hall through which Katie and Gibbs had come mere minutes ago. Katie gave her a pained smile. "It's broken. Is there one back there I could use?"

The woman looked beyond Katie at the doorway leading to the hallway, as if her x-ray vision could confirm that the toilet was broken, but then she looked back at Katie's earnest features. Her eyes dropped to the clerical collar, then back up to Katie's pleading eyes. "Come through," she said, pointing down a hallway to her right. "Take a right when you get to the end."

"Thank you so much," Katie said, ducking slightly out of deference and walking quickly down the hallway. Along the way, however, she scanned the rooms she passed. The window set into one door revealed a scene evocative of an out-of-control kindergarten class. One child was clearly being bullied, and another was sitting on the floor crying so loudly that Katie could hear through the shut door. No adults attended them.

The next window showed into a room packed with cribs. Katie looked around, and saw that she was alone in the hallway. She went over for a closer look at the small window, noting the chicken wire embedded into the glass. Again, there were no adults present. Each crib held two or even three infants. She tried the door, but it was locked. The crying was very loud, however, and the smell of unchanged diapers clearly detectable from where she was.

Katie gulped. *This is what we are leaving her to,* she

thought. She quickly calculated a rough ratio of children to caretakers in the office—twenty to one? Probably more. Her lips pressed together with increasing firmness as she progressed down the hall. By the time she reached the restroom, she could barely contain her rage or her tears. She stared at herself in the mirror and noticed how haggard she looked. *It's probably the fluorescents,* she thought. *God, let it be the fluorescents.*

That unrelated thought was enough to break the compulsive grip of anger that squeezed her only moments ago. Her thinking momentarily cleared, she knew what she had to do: there was no way they could leave that baby here.

Is there any way out of here without being seen? she wondered. It hardly mattered if Gibbs hadn't yet filled out the paperwork. But then she remembered her clerical collar and she cursed herself for not removing it, since it made her conspicuous and memorable to the average person on the street. There wouldn't be many women ministers around, not in a place like this. She wouldn't be hard to trace.

Her senses buzzing, her nerves painfully alert, she stepped back into the hallway. For all the children behind every door, the halls were eerily vacant. On her way back to the waiting room, she saw a red box, a little over waist high midway down the hall. She glanced up—no cameras. She glanced back—no cameras there, either. In an effortless, fluid motion, she removed her coat, used it as a barrier to catch the spray of telltale stain, and through its fabric felt for the catch on the fire alarm. She pulled it, felt the glass rod burst, heard the shriek of the alarm, and headed for the door.

In moments she was in a herd of panicked people, all jostling for the outer door. She didn't bother looking for Gibbs, but just let the river of people carry her through the outer corridor and into the parking lot. Holding her coat in front of her, she rocked back and forth in the cold, watching her breath emerging in great, gushing clouds of smoke, and waited for her heart to stop pounding. In a few minutes she saw Gibbs and the baby standing off by themselves, his face surprised and slightly bemused. She also noted, with a great sigh of relief, that he was still holding the clipboard with his unfinished paperwork under one arm.

Briskly she walked toward him and saw him smile when he saw her. "Where's the fire?" he asked. "Did you see a fire?"

"Let's go," she said, grabbing the clipboard and turning toward the car.

"Go?" he asked. "But we—"

"Gibbs! Now!" she thundered. His eyebrows shot up, but his feet started moving toward the car without further protest.

"There's no fire, is there?" he asked, catching up to her. Without intending to, Katie started giggling. She held her hand to her mouth and glanced over at Gibbs, then burst out laughing again.

"Wait a minute, *you* did that?" he asked, his eyes widening. "*You* pulled that alarm?"

Her face was red now, and she looked around to make sure no one was watching. She turned back to Gibbs and gave him a conspiratorial look. "Well, you know, Martin Luther said, 'If you're going to sin, sin boldly,'" she said. They were able to contain themselves only until they slammed closed the car doors. Then they collapsed into hopeless gales of laughter.

Chapter Thirty-Two

She stumbled through the back door of the house and instantly tripped. She couldn't see what she had tripped over, so she crawled the rest of the way to the kitchen. Her arm seemed to be working fine, although her shoulder had gone numb. She felt around on the floor for the box of matches, and with shaking hands she struck one and lit the wick of a stubby candle.

Her breath was visible as she cast around for something to burn. There were still some pieces left from the upper part of the stairwell, so she shoved those into the stove, bunched some brown paper bags underneath, and held the candle flame to the paper until it caught.

As soon as the wood was burning well, she put a pot of water on to boil. The steam warmed the room with a wet, sticky heat. *It feels wonderful,* she thought, standing above the pot, steam rising into her face.

Slowly the chill faded from her bones, and she was warm enough to take off her coat. It was trickier than she had anticipated. At first she tried extricating her left arm, but the movement caused a stab of pain in her upper arm, despite the continued numbness in her shoulder.

Gritting her teeth, she relaxed her arm, and turned her attention to her other arm. Raising her elbow, she lifted it easily from her sleeve. Once free, the coat simply fell free of her, dropping off her wounded limb. She repeated the strategy with her blouse, noting the hand-sized bloodstain at the shoulder as it fell to the floor. A wave of nausea rolled through her and she waited for it to pass.

She felt dizzy and realized she was hyperventilating. She held onto the table with her good hand and closed her eyes, forcing her breathing to slow. In a moment she felt better, and she allowed herself to sink onto a large plastic bucket she had been using for a stool ever since she had used the kitchen chairs for firewood.

Not really wanting to see, but knowing she must, she glanced over at her shoulder. *It looks like hamburger,* she thought, and she had to fight not to panic. She knew she needed to do something, but what? She should go to the hospital, but she knew that was impossible. They would find her. They would force her back…home.

She felt her throat thicken and her lip trembled. *No, I've got to handle this myself,* she thought. *There's no other choice. I can't face him. And I really, really can't face her.*

Rags, she thought. And a mirror. With every other thought forced from her mind, she rose and found some rags. One she had found here, in the basement. Another was the remnant of one of her T-shirts that had ripped months ago. She rinsed them in the sink and then dropped them in the pot of boiling water. Then she went upstairs to the master bedroom. She had seen a handheld mirror there, she was sure of that.

Indeed, it was lying just where she'd pictured it. She was about to hurry downstairs when the vanity drawer caught her eye. *You never know,* she thought, and yanked it open. The old makeup was useless to her, but as she rummaged, she also came across some ribbon, fingernail scissors, and tweezers. She stuffed these into the back pocket of her jeans and kept looking. A box of Band-Aids was almost empty, but two medium sized bandages remained. She snatched at them, and, standing on tiptoe to see better, she felt around at the top shelf of the medicine cabinet. A roll of gauze bandage fell to the floor. She almost cheered, but just then her fingers lit on a plastic bottle. She pulled it down.

"Witch hazel," the label said. Her eyebrows bunched up in confusion. She twisted off the knob and sniffed at it, instantly recoiling at the acrid, alcohol-like stink of it. "If that's not rubbing alcohol it might as well be," she said out loud. She reached down for the gauze and quickly headed downstairs.

She removed the pot from the burner and waited for the water to cool somewhat. When the water was bearable, she wrung out one of the rags, and held it ready in her left hand. With her right, she gingerly lifted the strap of her bra and pulled it down until it hung against her arm. Then taking the steaming rag in her right hand, she gingerly touched it to her shoulder.

She expected a stabbing flash of pain, but the numbness prevailed. She did feel a dull, aching heat as she dabbed at the wound. In a few minutes, she had succeeded in wiping away most of the blood.

She was amazed at how calm she was. In her mind, she saw herself running in panicked circles around the kitchen making loud "whoop-whoop" noises in an irrational frenzy. But no, she wasn't even feeling faint as she wrung the bloody rag out in the pot. With slow, deliberate actions, she finished cleaning the wound, and using some of the gauze bandage wadded into a pad, she dabbed at her shoulder with witch hazel.

That's when the pain hit. She screamed. Then she screamed again. She swore. Her vision went snowy, and she panted until the burning subsided. When her vision cleared, she wiped at the tweezers with the witch hazel, and looked back at her shoulder.

To her great relief, it looked much more like a normal shoulder now. She took up the hand mirror and circled her shoulder with it. By the candle's light, she could clearly see four breaks in the skin where, she imagined, the buckshot had entered. Awkwardly holding the mirror in her left hand, her arm pinned tightly to her side as she attempted to get it into a useful angle, she held the tweezers in her right hand, and brought them up to her shoulder.

It took a few minutes to coordinate her movements with the mirror, since all of her actions went in the opposite direction she intended. Eventually, however, she got the halting hang of it and drew her lips back around her gritted teeth as she watched the tweezer's tip disappear into her skin. The pain was excruciating, but she bore it, sweating and shaking slightly. She fought to keep her fingers steady, and stabbed into the wound, pinching the tweezers and drawing them up. As soon as she got them free she felt the tweezers give and a BB dropped to the floor with a much louder "clack" than she would have thought possible.

She breathed quickly and shallowly, wiping at her sweat with the wrist of her right hand. *One down,* she said to herself, *three to go.*

The second BB came out just as easily, but the third one evaded her. She simply couldn't find it, and the pain became overwhelming as she stabbed deeper and deeper into her muscle. Finally, on the edge of passing out, she began talking to herself aloud. "Slow down. Stop breathing so fast. Slow down. That BB already fell out. That's why you can't find it. It's already gone. Just let it go…" She chattered away at herself for awhile until she was ready to tend to the last entry wound. Once again she took up her tweezers. Once again, she held the mirror close to her shoulder. Once again she willed her hand to stop shaking.

But the angle was all wrong. She had to reach too far around. The wound wasn't on her shoulder proper, but her shoulder blade, where she couldn't really see it. Fighting down her panic, she dabbed her fingers with the witch hazel and felt for the hole. Her front teeth biting into her lower lip, she felt for the wound with the tip of the tweezers. She stabbed inwards, squeezed, and a BB shot to the floor as soon as the tweezers cleared the confines of her skin.

She convulsed with relief, and allowed herself a few moments of rest. Then, rolling up a fresh wad of gauze, she wetted it with the witch hazel and applied it to her shoulder. Fire raged through her brain as she made sure that every wound was soaked in the foul-smelling liquid. Finally, she took the rest of the gauze and wrapped it around her shoulder.

It was a sloppy job; she could see that. But she didn't care. Briefly, she wondered what her mother would have said. But she dashed that thought from her head as soon as it entered, knowing how pointless and useless that would be.

She didn't have any clean clothes, but she found a cleanish T-shirt and pulled it on, her bra strap hanging out of the end of the sleeve. She hoped that the pain would subside once the dabbing and the poking were over. But she was wrong. If anything, it was only growing worse. I've got to do something for this pain, she thought. She fought to remember what she had seen in the medicine cabinet, but she couldn't. Wearily, she climbed the stairs and rooted around.

She found a bottle of Ibuprofen with about twenty capsules in it, but that was all. She nodded. It would help. Then, inspiration flashed. Whiskey, she thought. I have whiskey. She'd never drunk whiskey. She didn't know how much to drink. She didn't even know if it would help. Walking deliberately downstairs, aspirin bottle in her pocket, feeling at the wall for support, she decided it certainly couldn't hurt.

Back at the table, she popped three of the tan Ibuprofen tablets and swallowed, not bothering with water. She rooted around for the cardboard box of booty, and quickly found the flask of whiskey. Grabbing a coffee cup, she decided that prudence was the best strategy, and filled the cup only halfway. She gulped at the whiskey, and instantly spit most of it out in a revolting spray.

"What in the world???" she exclaimed out loud. "Why in the world would *anybody* drink anything so awful??" She turned her nose up at the mere smell of it, but steeled herself. The second attempt went down easier, because she was ready for it. She drained the rest of it, her face screwing up into a nasty mask of revulsion. "Gah!" she spat.

And yet, within what seemed like mere minutes, she felt warm, she started to relax, and the edge of the pain began to subside and back away from her brain. Relief flooded her, and suddenly all seemed right. It felt like things were going to be okay. She gazed at the candle and rocked back and forth, a slight smile alighting on her face. A tune played in her mind, and without thinking she started singing, "Silent night, holy night...."

It seemed so fitting. She didn't know the second verse, so she sang the first verse again. And again, each time with more gusto. When she finished her third time through the song, she laughed out loud. Then she glanced at the whiskey bottle. "You are dangerous," she said to it.

Just then she heard a car door slam. She froze and listened intently. The sound of boots on the porch reverberated through the floor. Without thinking she sprang into action, snuffing the candle, pouring water onto the fire, grabbing her coat, and fleeing out into the silent, starry night.

Chapter Thirty-Three

By the time Howard pulled up at the third of Karl's five properties, weariness had overtaken him. Feeling like he had lead weights strapped to his boots, he lowered his feet from the Range Rover and trudged toward the porch. His flashlight revealed nothing. The property was dark and silent. He saw no lights in the windows, heard no sound. He fumbled for the key ring when his cell phone range.

Flipping it open, he leaned his tired back against the front door. "Saks, here," he said.

"Sheriff, hi," said a reedy female voice. It took him a moment to place it. The Pastor.

"Reverend. How did it go?"

"Uh…huh. Well, it didn't." Her voice was halting, as if she were confessing to cutting a High School class.

Suddenly, Howard was not aware of the pain in his lower back. "What do you mean? What happened?"

"Oh, Sheriff, you have no idea!" She paused, clearly trying to figure out how to say what she needed to say.

"Just spit it out, Pastor. We can clean it up later."

"We couldn't leave her there," Katie said. "The conditions were horrendous. We just couldn't do it."

"I see…." *How bad could it be?* he wondered. He was sure she'd tell him all about it eventually, but now was not the time. "Okay, Pastor, I get it. I'll want a full report tomorrow."

"Aye aye, sir," the Pastor said, relief in her voice. "Anyone ever tell you you'd make a good bishop?"

"I don't do dresses. Or purple."

"Point taken," she said, and chuckled.

"Where is the child now?"

"I dropped her off with Gibbs at his house."

"Did you leave…any traces?"

She paused for a long moment. "No," she said.

He relaxed a bit. "Well, let's hope this don't come back to bite us."

"I'll do better than that. I'll pray for it. And for her. I'll pray for you while I'm at it." Howard could hear the warm smile in her voice.

"I could use it, Pastor," he said. "I am bone weary, and I don't mind saying so."

"That makes two of us," she agreed.

"Thanks for calling, Pastor. I'll talk with you tomorrow."

"Yes, sir," she said, and he heard the line go dead.

He folded the phone and put it back in his pocket. As he thought about searching yet another house, he felt the pain return to his back. He realized he had no heart for this tonight. "First thing tomorrow," he said to the porch. It was a promise.

Chapter Thirty-Four

She ran. She was careful not to bump into anything, not to make any noise. Once behind a shed in the back yard she took a moment and listened. Faintly, she heard voices—or a voice, she couldn't tell. Looking up, she saw a grove of trees that bordered the property, and she ran for them, careful to keep the shed between herself and the house.

Once in the trees, she looked back, but she couldn't see anything. She imagined that whoever it was had by now discovered her nest. It was lost. She set her teeth and forced back a frustrated sob. Her eyes darted back and forth, wondering what to do, where to go. Without knowing why, she chose a direction and set off, her boots crunching in the snow underfoot.

She was cold, and she wrapped her arms around her chest as she walked. The walking started to help. Before long, she even unzipped her coat a bit, and she felt sweat running down her back.

It felt good to be moving. The alcohol had left her with a vague, dull headache, though, and she felt a little sick. She wondered what would happen if she just lay down and went to sleep. *I would freeze,* she thought. *But would that be so bad? It's painless, isn't it?*

It *was* a tempting notion. She fantasized about how her mother would react when she got the news. In her mind's eye she watched her mother sink to her knees and wail, pulling at her hair in her grief. The fantasy felt good. It was the ultimate revenge, and she could taste its bitter sweetness.

But knowing her mother, it wouldn't be like that at all. She might just sniff, and say something mean like "serves the little tramp right." She trudged on through the snow and shook her head. That wasn't a satisfying fantasy at all. She couldn't risk an outcome like that.

Soon, she saw a golden light floating in space before her. As she walked it would be obscured by trees, but then suddenly it would appear again. It drew her as if she were a moth. It seemed like hours later that she finally passed through the trees and could see the light clearly. And then it winked out. She found herself staring at a large, dark house, its inhabitants no doubt turning in for the night. She sank back into the cover of the trees to think.

But she didn't think. Not really. She sat on a log and

watched her breath as it drifted from her mouth and obscured the light of a distant streetlamp. Her shoulder ached and she flashed on the blood. She wondered how badly she was bleeding now. It reminded her of when the baby had come, and she had cleaned up that blood with the same stoic efficiency.

The baby. She tried to push the thought away, but none of her usual tricks worked. The image of her filled her brain and she could not banish it. So small, so helpless, so *hers*. And now, not hers. A gush of grief pushed up through her throat and she nearly choked on it. *I'm evil*, she thought. *I'm a bad person who hurts the people I love.* She thought of her dad, and for the first time allowed herself to imagine how he must have felt when she left. She felt no similar remorse about her mom, but she felt almost sick when she thought of Gibbs.

She buried her head in her hands and her face screwed up in grief. Tears came. *I didn't mean to get pregnant*, she thought. *I just wanted to show him…that I loved him.* And she did. She loved him. And she missed him. She ached for him. For the first time in months, she allowed herself to feel everything that she had been beating back by sheer force of will. Her will that had been deflated by buckshot.

She didn't know how long she cried. She only noticed when she got cold. *I can't walk in the woods all night*, she thought. *Can I?* She didn't know. Surely, sometime, she'd fall asleep. *Then I'll be dead*, she thought. Suddenly the idea seemed less appealing now that she'd let herself feel something about the people she really cared about.

She looked at the dark, sleeping house and realized

there was no way she could get into it, not without being caught. Her eyes naturally drifted toward the streetlamp, and beneath it she caught the amber reflection of the streetlamp on chrome. There was a car there.

Without thinking about it she rose and started walking toward the car. Within a few minutes she could see it clearly. It was parked on the street, outside of another dark house. As she got closer, she saw it was a big sedan, an old-style Cadillac. Looking in the window, she froze. The peg of the door lock was *up*. She looked around to make sure no one was looking out of any of the windows. Everything was as still as death. Tiny snowflakes floated down from the sky. Everything was silent.

She reached out and grabbed the handle, grimacing at the metallic cold. It took both hands and two thumbs to depress the button. When it opened, it sounded like the echoing boom of an ancient tomb uncovered after centuries of repose. She panicked at the sound of it and looked around. Again, nothing stirred. She forced herself to breathe slowly and regularly. Then she crawled onto the long bench seat and shut the door behind her, flinching as it clicked shut.

She held her breath. Everything was cold. Everything was quiet. And for the first time since she had bandaged up her shoulder tonight, she felt safe. She felt her muscles relax, and the tension run out of them onto the vinyl of the seat cushions.

Looking down, she could see a bunch of what looked like trash on the floor. It smelled a little, like day-old burgers. It was a very, very welcome smell, but it made her stomach lurch. She reached down with her good hand, and started to sort through what was there. She found half a bag of peanuts, and marveled at the treasure. She stuffed them into her mouth faster than she could chew.

Reaching down again, her fingers lit upon something cold, hard, and compact. She pulled it up into the light of the streetlamp and squinted at it. "A cell phone," she whispered aloud. She sat bolt upright, then. "A cell phone!" Her mind raced. *Don't call anyone,* she thought at first, but the loneliness and guilt that had swept through her less than an hour ago had other ideas. She desperately wanted to connect with someone. She ached for someone she cared about to know she was alive, that she was okay, especially since she almost wasn't, after being shot.

"Gibbs…" she breathed. She had to be careful, though. Who knew what forces her father could marshal to find her? She flipped open the phone and sighed in relief. It had Internet browsing capabilities. Her thumbs flashed over the keyboard and within minutes she had located a site, and from within it, typed a quick Instant Message: "Gibbs, it's me. I got shot, but I'm okay. I miss you. Lucy."

Chapter Thirty-Five

Gibbs shut the door behind him, cradling the baby close to him. Hopping slightly, he got both boots off without recourse to hands.

"What's that racket?" His mother's voice sang over the sound of the radio, coming from the kitchen. He ducked his head sheepishly as he walked toward the sound.

The baby started crying. "O, my…." his mother said as he entered the kitchen. "You didn't pick up another baby, did you? If you did, we have to have a talk."

"Same baby," Gibbs said, sitting at the table. "I think she's hungry."

His mother nodded and started a pot of water to boil. "So what happened? I thought you had to drop her off at the county today."

"We did. But Pastor Katie—"

"That's that new Lutheran minister, right?"

"Yeah. She—"

"Word is that she's kind of weird."

Gibbs' mouth was open, but nothing came out of it. "She's not weird," he finally said. Then he looked down. "Well, she is *kinda* weird. For a minister she's *way* weird, but for a normal lady she's…I don't know….normal."

His mother looked at him uncertainly. "Huh." She placed a formula packet in the water to warm. Suddenly her face screwed up. "Ew…you better change her."

"I'm on it," he said, and with an exaggerated grunt, heaved himself and the child to his feet, ambling toward his room. He spread out a towel on his bed, then laid the baby on it and, pulling a new diaper from a bag on the floor, changed her quickly and efficiently.

That's when he noticed the alert on his computer screen. A text message was waiting. Gibbs looked over at the baby, who was now gurgling contentedly. *You might be hungry,* he thought at her, *but we've taken care of your main complaint now.* He knew he should go feed her immediately, but curiosity got the better of him. He sat down and squinted at the screen. The message was from a user he didn't recognize. He clicked on it and suddenly felt all the strength drain from his bones.

"Lucy…" he said aloud. He read the message again. And again. He read it for clues about where she might be. He read it hoping to discover how she was. But there seemed very little there. *She got shot??* His mind raced. He fought to control it. *But she's okay, she's okay. She misses me….*

He typed back furiously, but there was no response. He went to her Facebook page, untouched for six months, and still dormant except for grieving well-wishers who had been posting to her wall. He e-mailed her, but there was nothing.

He pounded on his keyboard. Despite his effort, his control broke. His eyes watered and his mouth worked as an irrational rage surged in his brain. Months of frustration, of worry, of helplessness, of guilt melted into one seething clot of fury burning in his gut. Gibbs roared and hammered his fist into the wall of the trailer.

Chapter Thirty-Six

Carol passed a hand in front of her husband's face. Jerry didn't seem to see it, and she sighed. She hated when he checked out like this. In any other town, in any other job, he wouldn't be indulged like this, she knew. She was grateful for Munich and for Bremmer's, but his inclination to dissociate at the slightest occasion of stress worried her. "Oh, honey…" she said, her voice tinged with both love and pity. She cocked her head and her lips turned up in a mischievous smile. "Merry Christmas, love."

That did it. "Huh?" Jerry looked up at her. "Oh. Yes. Merry Christmas, honey." She shook her head, watching as Jerry picked up the paper and apparently picked up where he had left off ten minutes ago before checking out.

Carol sat down. "Jerry, we need to talk about something."

He lowered the paper and looked at her with concern. "We do?"

"Yes. I'm worried about you."

"Don't be silly," he said, looking back at his paper. "I'm fine."

She waited a couple of seconds, then grabbed the paper from him and threw it to the floor. "Sorry," she apologized. "But I can't see your eyes through the newsprint."

His eyes, which were now plainly visible to her, were wide and slightly alarmed.

"I don't think you heard me," she said with measured calm.

"You're worried."

"Yes."

"About me."

"Right."

He stared at her. Then he looked from side to side. "Um…why?"

"Jerry, you're the manager of a multi-million-dollar-a-year business. You can't just check out when you're upset about something."

"Do I do that?" He smiled at her.

Her eyes narrowed. "Don't make me hit you."

"You've never hit me in your life," he countered.

"Don't make me start now. I don't believe in domestic abuse, and it'll shatter my self-image."

"We wouldn't want that," he agreed. "Why do you think I check out?"

"Why do I…. Jerry, whenever something stressful happens at work, you sit down on the floor in front of everyone and take a Hawaiian vacation."

"I don't think it's Hawaii," he said, looking doubtful. "I don't think they speak English."

"Don't mess with me," she warned.

"Rumor has it I'm dissociative, but I'm not stupid."

"I want you to see someone," she said, getting to the point.

"Anyone in particular?" he asked.

"A psychologist," she said. "I'll ask around and find someone good."

"You're serious, aren't you?" The playfulness had gone out of Jerry's voice.

"Yes, honey, I'm serious. I—"

A loud pounding on the door interrupted them. Jerry

looked at her with alarm. They both jumped to their feet and made for the door. Carol opened it, and Gibbs spilled into it, grimacing with pain, and holding his right hand like the broken wing of a sparrow.

Behind him, his mother stood, a baby in her arms.

"Gibbs!" Carol shouted, pulling him to the couch.

"The baby!" Jerry sang, and rushed to embrace Gibbs' mother. After a moment, he released her and retreated a step, his eyes only on the child. He spoke to the woman, though. "Do I know you?"

"I'm Leonard's mother," she said, a little flustered by his surprise display of affection.

"Who's Leonard?" asked Jerry.

"Gibbs, what happened?" Carol said, pushing the young man's left hand away, and examining his injury.

"He punched a wall," his mother explained. "He's a very loving boy, but sometimes not too bright," she added, a note of chagrin in her voice. "We live in a double-wide out on McCormack, and the walls are *not* made of sheet rock."

"Oh, Gibbs, what were you thinking?" Carol asked rhetorically, noting the swelling already begun. "You can't take care of a baby with one hand."

"She wrote me," he said, between grimaces.

"Who wrote you?" Jerry asked, still looking at the baby.

"Lucy."

Jerry's head snapped toward the boy. Carol stopped and met her husband's eyes.

"Lucy?" Jerry asked. "Howard's Lucy?"

"My Lucy," Gibbs nodded.

"She's alive?" Carol asked.

"She said she was shot," Gibbs kept nodding. "But she says she's okay. She says she…misses me. Do you think she still loves me?"

Carol softened and touched the boy's cheek with her hand. "She wrote to you, didn't she? As far as we know, she didn't write to anyone else. She certainly didn't contact me or Jerry."

The boy looked confused. "Why would she?"

Carol laughed. "She wouldn't. I'm just saying…. Oh look, Gibbs, look at how that hand is bruising already. Let's get you to the emergency room. Jerry, get the car."

"Getting the car," he said, grabbing his hat and scarf.

Chapter Thirty-Seven

Howard pushed the button to close the garage door and bent down to remove his boots. It was late. *Is she still up?* he wondered. His wife was never a night owl, but in her recent state of mania, or whatever it was, he could never be sure. He took a deep breath and opened the door.

A remnant of a fire was burning itself out in the fireplace. The air smelled of mulling spices, sweet enough to indicate that they had been used in apple cider rather than red wine. He grunted his approval at this. In Lara's current state, lapsing into drinking would only have compounded their problems.

He flipped on the light in the kitchen. Everything was immaculate and in its place. On the table was a mug, the correct amount of cocoa powder already measured out within it. The electric teapot was filled and ready for him to push the button. Cocoa in three minutes. On the saucer beside the mug was a piece of chocolate, wrapped in bright foil. He smiled.

Lara had always been thoughtful. Theirs had been a happy marriage until the contest of wills between her and Lucy had erupted soon after Lucy had crossed that inevitable line of puberty—invisible to him, but monumental in consequence. His previously harmonious home life seemed to disappear overnight. Within mere weeks, the claws on both mother and daughter were out and slashing. Howard had withdrawn and waited for the storm to pass. It never had.

Lara, it seemed, had won when Lucy disappeared. Truly, however, they had all lost. Terribly. Howard did not push the button on the electric teapot. He turned out the light and with tired, loping steps, headed for the bedroom.

When he opened the door, Lara looked up at him, smiled and closed her paperback. She removed her reading glasses. "How was your day?" she asked.

It was simply too exhausting to recount. "Nothing much," he said.

"That's not what I heard," she said, looking dubious.

"You caught me," he said, sitting on the bed and stripping off his socks. "You?"

"Just baking," she said.

Howard scowled. She had been baking for the past two days. The Feast of Christmas might be twelve days long, but there was no way that the two of them were going to consume the quantity of cookies, fudge, and cake she was producing—not without emergency medical treatment.

"What are you going to do with all that you're baking?" he asked.

She looked confused. "They're for you, silly."

"Death by diabetic coma could still be looked upon as murder in this state," he said, a little too grumpily.

"Why are you being so nasty?" she asked, her face clouding over.

"It was a joke, darlin'," he said, and gave her a weary smile. "I tell you what, it's almost Christmas, let's take some of them to church. And let's take a plate or two of the blondies to Bremmer's for Jerry and the crew."

She paused to consider this. "I don't think we have quite enough—"

"We have enough four times over," he interrupted her.

She looked hurt. He sighed. *I have to be careful,* he reminded himself. *She's fragile.* "Listen, honey, I've got a favor to ask you."

She brightened up. "What is it?" She seemed eager to please. He took it for a good sign. "I don't know if you've heard, but a baby was abandoned at Bremmer's a few days back. They've been caring for him at the store, but it's been rough on them because of the Christmas rush."

"A baby?"

"Yup, a newborn, too. They've been doing a bang-up job over there, but they could use some help."

"What can I do?" She sounded suspicious.

"Well, you could take a plate of goodies over in the morning and see if maybe you can help. It's been a long

time since you've cared for a baby, and I was thinking....
I don't know, it might be good for them and good for
you, too. Just a few hours, there in the break room.
What do you think?"

"You aren't suggesting we bring him home?"

"No.... *She* stays there. You could just help."

She gazed off into space for a moment, and it
appeared to him that years of experiences passed over
her face as he watched. "What happens to the baby at
night?"

"She goes home with the Gibbs boy."

Her eyes flashed anger at him, and her lips were thin
and tight. "I don't want to see him."

He softened and reached for her hand. "I under-
stand why you're angry with him. I am too. I was..."
He trailed off and considered his words for a moment.
"I *was* angry with him. Now I think he's a pretty good
kid who made some pretty normal adolescent choices."
He brushed her hair back from her cheek. "Truth is,
honey, I think his only real crime was that he loved our
Lucy."

She looked away. He realized that her current state
of mental equilibrium seemed built on some kind of
fantasy that Lucy never existed. *I'm not going to play that
game,* he thought, steeling his resolve. "Promise me
you'll go over there in the morning."

She didn't. In fact, she didn't do anything. She didn't
say anything. *She's pouting,* he said to himself, his brows
edging toward each other in disapproval. He sighed.
"Please think about it, honey. This baby needs you. The
Bremmers' folks need you. You can do some good
there."

Silence. He stood up and untucked his shirt, heading for the bath. Just then his cell phone rang. He scowled at it and looked at the number, but he didn't recognize it. Wearily, he flipped it open. "Saks."

"Howard, it's Carol," a woman's voice said.

"Carol? Carol Keller?"

"Yes. I'm sorry to call you so late."

"Well, so long as you don't make a habit of it. What's up?"

"I'm at the hospital, I've got Leonard Gibbs, here."

Howard's body surged with electricity. "Gibbs? Is the baby ok—"

"Relax, Howard, the baby is fine. She's here with Mrs. Gibbs."

His shoulders dropped again and his breath returned. "And Gibbs?"

"He hurt his hand. Nothing broken, just a bad sprain. A word to the wise—never attempt to punch through prefabricated walls."

Howard looked back and forth, trying to make sense of this. "Um…can you back up, please?"

"Gibbs tried to punch through the wall of their double-wide."

"Whyever for?"

"He was angry."

"I'm waiting."

"Howard, are you sitting down?"

"No. Should I be?" He locked eyes with his wife, who was clearly curious by now.

"I think so. Gibbs got an instant message. He thinks it's from Lucy."

Howard grabbed at the door frame of the bathroom

door to steady himself. *Yes*, he thought, *I should have been sitting down.* "What did she say?"

"She says she was shot."

Chapter Thirty-Eight

It was half past eleven when Howard's boots mounted the darkened porch once more. He cursed himself for abandoning his search of Wysocki's properties earlier. "I might have found her," he muttered out loud. "I might have found her before..." *What? Before she bled to death?* He pushed the thought aside and fumbled with the key ring.

He wasn't finished with cursing. He cursed Wysocki and his trigger-happy recklessness. He cursed his own reticence to rein in a loose cannon like that sooner. He cursed his own humanity, his fallibility, his shocking, staggering ineptitude at the simple task of making peace in his own family.

The lock clicked and the door yielded as he pushed inside and was met with utter darkness. He listened, but heard nothing. Cautiously, he shone the flashlight around, and saw nothing out of the ordinary. Then the beam swung around to the staircase.

"What in the world?" he said aloud, his voice echoing in the empty foyer. He trained the beam up the stairs, staring incredulously at the sheer destruction of it. Every one of the staircase balusters had been ripped away, and enormous, jagged shards of wood stood up at crazy angles from each step, all the way from the first floor to the next. It looked as if a tornado had torn through it.

He swung the flashlight around at the walls, then around to the living room again. All was perfect. Only the staircase looked like it had hosted a chainsaw duel. Howard whistled. He trained the beam down the hall, and, placing his ear on the swinging door that he surmised must lead to the kitchen, listened. Nothing but a slow drip-drip-drip of water.

He opened the door slowly. The room was empty. He stepped inside and flashed the light around. "Looks like a rat's nest," he said. He noted the blackened König stove and the pile of kindling beneath it. He saw the pot with a film of water in the bottom of it. There was a rag in it, too. He went to reach for it, but stopped himself. Remembering his professionalism, he snagged a set of latex gloves from his coat pocket and put them on. Then he lifted the rag. In the too-bright beam of the flashlight, he saw it was stained red. Blood. He dropped it back into the pot.

He felt faint. He struggled to master himself. He trained the beam of his flashlight on the floor and saw the bloody trail of what was clearly a buckshot BB. Panic surged through him, and he steadied himself with one hand on the floor. He intentionally breathed more slowly until his light-headedness passed. Then he started looking around again.

He found a cardboard box with a rusted can of peaches in it. Beside it was a half-full flask of whiskey. He scowled at this. Sadness welled within him. His throat felt thick. He began a systematic search of the cupboards, finding little. Then he opened the door to the broom closet, and a sour, rancid smell spilled out into the frigid air.

Nostrils twitching, he knelt and shone the beam inside. The closet did indeed contain brooms—two of them, and a mop. But the smell was clearly coming from a pile of rags. He picked one of them up, and saw that it was covered with blood. On closer inspection, he saw not just blood but some kind of effluvia—some kind of tissue, which had turned and was beginning to decay.

This isn't blood from today, he thought, his brows knitting together. *It isn't blood from a gunshot wound, either. It looks like someone cleaned up after having a baby*—and at that thought, he froze, an icy chill momentarily paralyzing him. *A baby. The baby. The baby at Bremmer's.*

In a state of horrified wonder, he reached for another of the blood-soaked rags, and held it up. After a second, its crustiness gave way and it unfurled, flag-like, revealing its emblem to him. It was a concert T-shirt from a rock band, and the logo looked strangely familiar. Suddenly he remembered where he had seen it. It was the Grief Patrol logo. *The same one that Lucy….*

In one instant, everything in his brain clicked into place. Howard's legs turned to water, and he sank to the floor, an animal-like sob escaping from his throat. "Lucy…Oh, Jesus, please, Lucy…." He clutched the soiled T-shirt to his chest and curled up around it, in the fetal position on the floor of the kitchen, the rat's nest, the home of his daughter.

Chapter Thirty-Nine

Sleep was not an option. Howard spent the rest of the night searching the last of Wysocki's houses. Finding nothing there, he went back to all five again, giving them the fine-tooth-comb treatment, now that he had some idea of what he was looking for. Finally, he came back to the "Rat's Nest," as he had started calling it in his own mind.

Searching every inch of the kitchen, he found other clues that could only have been left by Lucy: an earring that he remembered buying her at the mall in Silas, a scrap of paper with her writing on it. It seemed to be a love poem, but whether it was by Lucy or just something she had copied from somewhere, he couldn't tell.

There was no weariness in him as he climbed into the cab of his Rover. The sun was just peeking up over the horizon, sending a pink spray of light shooting through the threatening cloud cover. Driving back to town, his features were stoic, but beneath them, wildly conflicting emotions battled for advantage. He needed to tell someone. *Should I call Lara?* He asked himself. He decided against it. Not until he knew more. Not until he knew what to tell her. *Who then? Gibbs?*

The thought struck him as preposterous. Again, he decided to wait until he knew more. He pulled up to his office and found Diane's car already parked in its space. *Was she always there this early?* he wondered. *If so, I have got to give that woman a raise.*

But he didn't stop. He didn't consciously know where he was going, but his body seemed to be doing just fine. It was with some surprise that he pulled up to the curb in front of St. Gabriel's. He noted a light on in the office, and, trudging through the snow up the drive, he knocked on the door.

A harsh, wizened face appeared in the crack of the doorway. "Oh, Sheriff, what a pleasure." She didn't open the door any wider.

"Ms. Gammerbrau," Howard said, removing his hat. His head was cold, so he put it back on. "I'd like to speak to the Pastor, please."

"Ewww…that's too bad." Her features scrunched up in a feigned look of pain. "I'm afraid the Pastor isn't going to be here much longer." She shook her head, as if it were simply too, too sad. Then she brightened up. "But I've written to the bishop, and thank the Lord Jesus, we should have a new interim in a week or so. I'm sure whatever moral crisis or family tragedy you're experiencing will still be with you then. Have a blessed day!" And with that she shut the door in his face.

Howard stood blinking in the morning cold, staring at the door. "She does work for me, doesn't she?" he asked the door. "I mean, I am a parishioner, right?" The door did not answer. He took his hat off. It was cold. He put it back on. He looked at his truck. He looked the other way. He saw the parsonage. "Goin' to the source," he said, and set off across a knee-high snowdrift toward the Pastor's house.

It only took her a moment to answer. Katie's hair was a tangled mass held behind her head by a rubber band, strands of which fell in front of her face. She wore no makeup, and Howard noted how pale she looked. A quilted housecoat and bunny slippers completed her early-morning look. "Sheriff?" she asked, concerned.

"Um…I just spoke to Ms. Gammerbrau. She said you weren't going to be with us very much longer."

"Did she now?" A defiant grin passed over the Pastor's face, as she looked past him at the office. Then she looked at him, and softened when she saw his eyes. "Oh, dear," she said, noting the miasma of emotion churning behind them. "Coffee, now." She held the door open for him and he stepped inside.

"I don't really need coff—"

"Well, I certainly do. Come in."

He did. She led him to the kitchen and installed him at the table. Within moments she placed two steaming mugs of Stöllen Goods' best grind in front of them. The cream and sugar were already there. Katie sat and crossed her legs. Howard noted the razor stubble peeking out from her housecoat. For some reason, that relaxed him. The Pastor was just a regular woman after all.

"It's Lucy…" he started, and with that, the floodgates were open. He told her all about Lucy and Gibbs' romance, how he had opposed it, how Lucy and Lara had fought. He told her about the night Lucy ran away, and how she had seemed to simply disappear off the face of the earth. He talked about Lara's decline into an Ozzie and Harriet fantasy, and his feelings of failure, both as a father and a husband.

Through it all, Pastor Katie smiled her compassion and concern. She nodded when he told her about the shooting. Her jaw dropped when he told her about finding the Rat's Nest.

"You mean…the baby…" she started, her eyes wide with sudden comprehension.

"It's Lucy's. I'm sure of it," Howard said, nodding grimly. His fingers played over the brim of his hat.

"And that means the baby is Gibbs', too." He nodded again.

"Oh, my…" Katie's hand went to her neck, but there was no collar there to pick at. She dropped her hand and it found her coffee cup again. "Well, in a way, that's good news. I'm not sure it's possible to part him from her, not now."

He gave a curt nod.

Katie reached out tentatively and touched his forearm. "That means that the baby is your granddaughter, Howard."

Howard's eyes were watery as he looked from side to side, considering. "I'm not ready for this."

"And you were ready to be a parent?"

"Well, now that you mention it, no."

"I don't think any of us is ever ready for real life. It happens to us and we cope as best we can. And usually we muck it up pretty badly before we finally figure it out."

"I've only known I was a grandfather for four hours and already I feel like a failure at it."

"Relax, you have plenty of time to feel even worse about yourself," she smiled a pained smile.

"I don't know why that's comforting," Howard said, chuckling and wiping at his eyes. "But it is."

"Yeah, it is. Jesus became human because human was not a bad thing to be. It's just messy. And inconvenient. And hard." She placed both her hands on top of his and squeezed. "And terribly, terribly right."

He sat back, both arms dropping to his sides. He

could almost feel the grief pouring from his fingertips to the floor. "How do I get her home?" he asked.

"You can't," Katie said. "Not unless she wants to come home."

"I've got to let her know I'm not angry with her. I need her to know that she'll be welcome, no questions asked."

"That sounds like a good start, but even if she knew that, I'm not sure it would be enough."

Howard looked at her with tired desperation in his eyes. His lip quivered. "Why is that?"

"Because the problem with human beings isn't really guilt, it's shame."

Howard's brow furrowed at this. "I don't follow you, preacher."

Pastor Katie leaned back and sighed. "Do you know the story of the prodigal son?"

"Sure, of course," Howard said. "A boy demands his inheritance early and goes off and squanders it."

"Right. And even after the money is gone, he stays in that far country, surviving on the refuse that the people feed to their pigs." Katie sipped at her coffee. "Why do you think he stays there so long?"

"I always assumed it was because he was afraid his father would be angry at him," Howard said, cocking his head.

"But you know that when he does finally return, his father isn't mad at all, but overjoyed. He knows his father's temperament. He's grown up with this man his whole life. He's not afraid of his father's anger. So why does he stay away?"

Howard's shoulders sank and his features relaxed.

"Because he's ashamed?"

"Yes. Human beings aren't alienated from God because of our guilt. God isn't holding us at arm's length saying, 'You icky people shouldn't come near me because you're sinful.' The God that Jesus revealed to us is the same as the father in the story. God is always waiting for us to return to him. He always has his arms open to embrace us. He isn't pushing us away because of our sin—never has and never will. We *run* away because we're ashamed. *We* hold *God* at arm's length because of that shame. The block to communion between people and God isn't in God—it's in us."

Howard nodded, a faraway look in his eyes. "You're saying that Lucy didn't run away because she was afraid of what I would do when I found out…."

Katie shook her head.

"…you're saying she ran away because she was ashamed of what…what happened."

"Of what she had done," Katie corrected him. "*She* did it. *She* had sex with Gibbs. *She* got herself pregnant. And she couldn't bear the shame of it, so she ran away."

Howard's hands had nearly folded his hat in two, but his eyes met Katie's. "She knows me. She knows I wouldn't hurt her…."

"Right," Katie said, touching his elbow.

"But my wife…" Howard looked down.

"Do you think she would have hurt her?"

"Not physically, no. But she can be…emotionally…."

"Abusive?"

"That's a California word."

"What word would you use?"

He didn't answer her, but he sat up straighter in his chair. He hadn't touched the coffee, but he looked at it.

"How can we...how do we...we need to get her home," Howard said. "Before some crazy nut like Wysocki hits her with another round of buckshot."

"Or before her own hunger and desperation drive her to become a real criminal," Katie added.

Alarm played on Howard's face. "I hadn't really thought of it that way. But you're right, of course. So what do we do?"

Katie shook her head. "I don't know. But I think we should pray about it, and think about it, and talk about it, and just be open to ideas." She smiled at him. "And I think we should go see your granddaughter."

Chapter Forty

"Christmas Eve," Jerry said with a satisfied sigh, taking in the sight of excited customers rushing onto the shopping floor. Above him, Andy Williams was crooning about "The Most Wonderful Time of the Year." "The most busiest *day* of the year, you mean," Jerry said to the 6-foot plastic snowman to his right. He felt a surge of energy, a high percentage of which, he realized, was most likely caffeine. But he was also aware that the rest of it was old-fashioned Christmas joy. "It never gets old," he told the snowman.

The snowman was grinning, as usual, corncob pipe in place and his top hat set at a jaunty angle. Jerry resisted an urge to throw an arm around his plastic companion. Instead, he brushed a bit of lint from its rounded shoulder.

Just then Nick hurried by, his T-shirt untucked, wiggling into his suspender straps. "Unprofessional, Santa!" Jerry called, and shook his head. Nick waved an apology but didn't slow down for a second on his way to his North Pole Photo Center.

Jerry set off to patrol the store's perimeter, walking clockwise against the mad dash of enthusiastic shoppers. There was Gibbs at the Orno-matic, his right arm in a sling. Nevertheless, he was organizing his materials, and Jerry noted with satisfaction that Gibbs' customers were just arriving and starting to form a line. Jerry was too far away to hear what was said, but he saw Gibbs look up with a broad smile on his face, mouthing cheerfully, "How can I help you?"

Jerry allowed himself a feeling of bliss. There was no place on earth he'd rather be. No time he loved more than this season, this day. He was surrounded by people he trusted and loved. There was a baby in the break room. Everything was perfect.

Jerry turned his head as Myrtle zoomed past, her arms filled with packages of blue tinsel. She saw him and skidded to a halt. "I see a cloud of trouble hanging over your head, Jerry Keller," she said to him, an ominous, bird-like Sybil.

"What are you even talking about, Myrtle? Everything's fine. I feel great. It's Christmas Eve!"

"It isn't 'fine,' and somewhere inside you, you know it isn't." She cocked her head and listened to the Christmas carol playing. "You hear that? *Deck the Halls.*

That's the answer. Whatever it is that's troubling you, Jerry, that's the answer. Mark my word!" And with that she zoomed off again.

As he watched her go, he asked himself exactly why it was that he kept such an odd woman on the payroll. "Because she's family," he said out loud to a giant stuffed Mouse King, his sword drawn, ready to battle any nutcracker comers.

Just then "Deck the Halls" was interrupted by a snarling crackle. "Jerry Keller to Nativity. Jerry Keller to Nativity, urgent!" With a pop, the music was back.

"Oh, heavens." Jerry glanced at his watch. They had been open less than five minutes. *What could have happened in five minutes that requires urgency?* he wondered as he set off toward the Nativity scene section.

He traversed the distance in two minutes and was met by the anxious fluttering of Mia Federer, a seasonal cashier who commuted from Kent. "Oh, Mr. Keller, I don't know what to do!" she said, her arms almost flapping in alarm.

"Well, how bad can it be?" Jerry said, trying to calm her. "Tell me what's happening." She grabbed his sleeve and pulled him over to one of the side aisles. There he saw an elderly woman kneeling in front of a young boy of about five years. The woman wore a scarf over her curlers, and Jerry noted the straps attached to hosiery too sheer to hide her exaggerated varicose veins.

"What's she doing?" Jerry asked Mia, although it looked for all the world as if the old woman were digging in his nose.

"It's stuck," Mia explained.

"What's stuck?" Jerry asked. By then he was standing

next to the kneeling woman. She looked up and saw him, eyed his red vest, and then looked back to his face. "You must be the manager," she said.

"Yes. I'm Jerry Keller. How can I—"

"I'm going to sue every butt you have," she said.

"I'm pretty sure I only have the one," Jerry said, "although I will concede that the good Lord allotted me more than one portion." He gave her a conciliatory smile. "What seems to be the trouble?"

"That!" she said, standing up shakily. Jerry caught her by the elbow and steadied her. He then turned his attention to the boy. Yes, there seemed to be something emerging from his nose. Jerry leaned over and elevated his head in order to make use of his bifocals.

"Feet," he said aloud. "Son, there appear to be feet coming out of your nose."

Boots, in fact, Jerry noted. "Hand-painted," he added. "Probably Italian. Porcelain, by the look of them." Jerry looked around at the Nativity sets near the boy. Yes, over the child's left ear was an Italian porcelain miniature set. Jerry turned to inspect it. "Just as I thought," he said, although to no one in particular. "A shepherd seems conspicuously absent."

He opened the cupboard above and fished about for the right box. Pulling it down, he studied the picture printed on the front, stopping every now and then to squint at the feet hanging from the boy's nose. Calmly, Jerry replaced the box and, turning to the boy, he delicately took the boots between his thumb and forefinger and gave a gentle tug.

"Ow!" the boy said, drawing back. Jerry wondered if the copper shepherd's crook might have gotten snagged in the child's nasal cavity. The child was portly, Jerry noticed, with a soiled parka, a poor haircut, and a pouty demeanor. He resisted the temptation to yank on the little shepherd's feet again.

Jerry straightened up and placed his hands on his hips. "Young man. We have been open five whole minutes. Are you telling me you raced through the door, came straight here, and shoved a shepherd up your nose?"

The boy looked at his grandmother uncertainly. Then he looked back at Jerry and nodded.

"Whatever possessed you to do such a thing?" Jerry asked, but he didn't expect an answer. This was not, he could see, an articulate child.

"It's your fault," the old woman said to Jerry, and she swung her purse at his head. It connected with a sound like the rattling of chains.

"Ow!" Jerry said, one hand raised in defense, the other holding his head where he'd just been struck. "Now, listen, Mrs…. What is your name, please?"

"Brown. Clara Brown."

"Mrs. Brown, I'm going to do everything I can to help your grandson," he assumed the child was her grandson, and when she did not protest, he felt a momentary feeling of relief. At least he had got that much right.

"How dare you keep dangerous toys out where young children can get ahold of them and hurt themselves?"

"Well, Mrs. Brown," Jerry said, gesturing with his defensive hand, "there are a number of things wrong with that sentence. First, the nativity set is not a toy, it is a rather pricey set of handmade figurines. That shepherd hanging from your grandson's nose runs about $200 wholesale. Second, your grandson is not a young child, but old enough to know the limits of…"—he wasn't sure how to put it—"nasal play."

The woman's face was bright purple, and it occurred to Jerry that a spelunking shepherd may be the least of their worries if this woman had a stroke. "I've got an idea," Jerry said, "Why don't we have Mia here drive you and your grandson to the emergency room? I'll call ahead, so they'll be expecting you, and they'll free that Italian intruder in no time. What do you think?"

"No waiting?" the woman sneered.

"Hardly any at all, I'm sure of it." He winked at her. "I've got an inside track over there."

"Who's going to pay for this?" the woman snapped.

"Bremmer's will be glad to pay for the…extraction and return of our shepherd."

The woman nodded, shooting him a suspicious "don't try anything" look. "Mia, does that sound all right to you?" Mia nodded, looking relieved. "Good. We'll reimburse you for mileage." Jerry patted her shoulder.

Jerry turned away and felt for his cell phone. Pushing his speed dial, he got Carol's voice mail and left a message, hoping she would retrieve it before the old woman and her grandson arrived. *Well, I can't control everything*, he said to himself.

As he walked back toward his office, he wondered about Myrtle's "prophesy." "The *halls* are not what needs decking in this situation," he said out loud to himself, and let out a brief guffaw. But he wasn't really *that* annoyed with the boy, not really. In fact, he felt a small surge of pride. *That wasn't a major event,* he thought, *but I didn't check out. I just dealt with it. I'm getting better.* He didn't quite believe it, but he wanted to.

Just outside the break room, he stopped, not sure of what he was seeing. It looked like Lara Saks, holding a canvas tote bag and pacing back and forth in front of the door leading to the back rooms. "Lara?" he asked, placing a tentative hand on her elbow as he came closer.

She must have been deep in thought, because she jumped a bit at his touch, and seemed to take a moment to even recognize him. "Oh, Jerry. I'm sorry, I was…I guess I'm not sure why I'm here."

Jerry smiled. "You must have heard about our baby."

A thin smile formed on her tight mouth. "Yes. I heard. Howard thought…he thought I might be able to help."

Jerry's head moved in a slight sideways motion. He had known Lara Saks for most of his life and had never known her to volunteer her efforts for anything. "Oh!" she said, as if just remembering something, "I brought these." She handed the tote bag to Jerry. "Well, let's just see what we've got here," he said brightly, and motioned for her to follow him into the back rooms.

The break room was nearly deserted. Only Margaret Dunny, the cashier from Silas, was there, holding the baby, cooing at her, and bouncing her slightly on her knee. She looked up and smiled at them. "Hello," she said. "This has got to be the happiest baby I have ever seen."

"Well," answered Jerry, "she certainly has a lot of people around to love her."

Jerry looked at Lara. From the moment she had stepped in, she had not looked away from the child. Her face looked like it was glowing. Her lips relaxed and fell back into the first genuine smile Jerry had seen on her in a very long time.

"May I…?" She didn't finish the sentence, but held her arms out. Margaret looked at Jerry. He shrugged and nodded affirmatively. Margaret stood and placed the babe in Lara's arms. The tension drained from the air, Jerry could feel it, just as Lara's shoulders relaxed and her face softened. "I haven't held a baby since… since…." She didn't say, "since Lucy," but Jerry understood. He gave her a compassionate smile.

"I'd better get back out on the floor," said Margaret. Jerry nodded at her. "Thank you, Margaret." When she'd left, Jerry sat down next to Lara. "You've got great timing, Lara. I'm really glad you're here," he said. "It's our craziest day, and I need everyone out on the floor. I don't know how long you can stay, but…I'm grateful for your help." He motioned to the baby, who was all eyes and dribbles. "I know she is, too."

He wasn't sure if Lara had even heard him. Her world seemed to have become a suddenly compact place for two. Jerry, strangely, felt like an interloper in his own break room. "Well, I'm just going to…I have some office stuff…bottles and formula are on the counter, over there. Please let me know if you need…" he trailed off, as Lara gave no indication of having heard him.

Chapter Forty-One

Gibbs took advantage of the momentary gap in customers to put up his "Back in 15 minutes" sign and head for the back rooms for a much-needed break. His uninjured hand was sore from pulling double-duty, and he craved sugar. *I'm turning into Nick,* he chuckled to himself.

The store was a madhouse in full swing. Twice he narrowly avoided collisions with careening baskets, and more than once he was nearly knocked off of his feet by people who simply body-checked him in their rush to get to another section of the store.

Other than his temporarily-wounded hand, though, he was lithe and agile and was able to weave and dodge with more success than any other employee would have, and made it to the break room door with a minimum of trouble, given the circumstances. Still, he was panting as he walked inside.

He stopped as if an invisible brick wall was barricading the threshold. The last person on earth he ever expected to see in the store—in *his* store—was there, holding *his* baby. Gibbs stepped back and shook his head. *Is this real?* he wondered. He stepped in again. *Yes, that's Lucy's mom.*

Instantly, a variety of conflicting emotions surged through him. Shame first, because he blamed himself for the conflict in Lucy's home. *If we hadn't been going out, Lucy and her mom wouldn't have fought nearly so much,* he told himself, although he didn't know if that was actually true. Following hard on shame's heels was anger. This was the woman whose sheer meanness had driven Lucy away. *Her prissy superperfectionism made it impossible for Lucy to live up to her standards,* Gibbs told himself. *I would have run away, too, if my mom were like that.*

Gibbs had to pause for a moment, as it occurred to him that most people looked down on his mom. And yet he'd take one of her for a hundred of Lara Saks any day.

Lara looked up and saw him. Gibbs felt trapped. He couldn't just back out into the store again—she *had* seen him, after all. And he simply couldn't make his legs work to step forward into the room. *Sugar,* he reminded himself. *A Snickers bar. I've just come in for a Snickers bar.* He commanded his legs to work. They did.

He shot Mrs. Saks a pained, forced smile. She did not return it. But she did speak.

"Hello, Leonard," she said.

"Mrs. Saks," Gibbs said, nodding in her direction. He made a wide berth around her to the candy machine and inserted some quarters. The candy bar dropped into the tray below and he bent over to scoop it up. Then he remembered his manners. "Split a Snickers?" he asked her, holding the candy bar up enticingly.

"No, thank you," Lara said curtly.

"I'll bet that little one needs a snack, though," Gibbs said. He walked over and smoothed the baby's bright red hair over her head. This put him uncomfortably close to Mrs. Saks, but he ignored that, focusing only on the baby.

"That's beyond you, I suppose," Lara Saks sighed, disapprovingly.

Gibbs stepped back as if he had been slapped. He

surveyed her for a moment, a hurt look masking his normally genial face. "That was a really mean thing to say," he told her. Then, without another word, he went to the counter and began preparing the formula.

Neither of them spoke as he worked. Gibbs could feel Mrs. Saks' eyes on him, burning a hole through the back of his head. There was so much he wanted to say to her, but since he would probably end up screaming it, he kept it to himself.

In a moment he was finished, and without hesitation, he walked over to where Lara and the baby were sitting. He set the bottle on the table and scooped up the baby from her arms without asking permission, or indeed any words at all. Once seated with her in a comfortable position, her head propped up by his wounded hand, he reached for the bottle with his right and began to feed her.

The whole time, he spoke to the infant softly, kindly, encouragingly. For several long minutes, he forgot that Mrs. Saks was there at all. When he finally remembered that she was, he let down his guard enough to look up at her.

Tears were streaming down her face. Incomprehension and compassion flooded Gibbs, in spite of his feelings for her. "Mrs. Saks, what's wrong?" he asked.

She reached in her purse for a Kleenex, but she didn't answer him. He respected her privacy and returned his attention to the baby. When the bottle was finished, Gibbs threw a towel over his left shoulder and held the baby up to burp her.

"She needs a name," Gibbs said to Mrs. Saks. "I'm

getting tired of calling her 'the baby.' Besides, I need something to say to her when I'm talking to her. It feels weird to say, 'Hey there, anonymous baby, I really love you,' you know?"

Lara seemed to have collected herself. "Do you have any ideas? For a name?"

"I like Jughead, but I think she'll outgrow that one pretty fast," Gibbs said with a smile, a genuine one this time. "My grandma's name was Sarah. I kind of like that."

"My mother's name was Sarah," Mrs. Saks said. "I always liked it." She gazed at the baby's face, and Gibbs could see the emotions playing just under the surface. "I think it fits her," she added.

"Well, then, until someone else comes along with a right to change it, how about you and me name her right now?"

"It feels kind of conspiratorial," Mrs. Saks said, the small beginnings of a smile touching her lips.

"I like that," Gibbs said, meeting her small smile with a larger one of his own.

"Leonard, I'm surprised…" she stopped herself. "You're really good with her."

He brushed away his impulse to take offense. She had changed tack, after all. "Thank you," he said nobly, acknowledging with both voice and posture that he knew it was true. "She means the whole world to me. And I can't explain why."

Mrs. Saks rose and faced away from him, fumbling at the straps of her purse. "I'm sorry for what I said to you. It *was* mean. I'm just so…angry."

Gibbs didn't say anything. Instead, he waited for several minutes. Without turning around, she continued. "But I'm not angry with you, not really. So you liked my daughter, that's normal, I suppose. That's what teenagers do." She turned around and faced him, although she looked down at her purse and did not meet his eyes. "I wished she had waited another year or two before she wanted to date, but that's not your fault. I'm mostly mad at *her*."

Gibbs noted that Mrs. Saks couldn't bring herself to say her name. So Gibbs said it for her. "At Lucy."

"Yes."

"Why?"

She looked up at him now, a flash of irritation in her eyes. "You couldn't possibly understand."

"When my cousin Teddy was fourteen he shot my Uncle Fred in the back with a .22 because Uncle Fred wouldn't let him play the violin."

Lara's eyes widened, and her mouth opened in protest, but nothing came out.

"So I figure it's like that. Besides," Gibbs looked her straight in the eye, "I want to hear your side of the story."

Mrs. Saks closed her mouth, but before she could say anything, Howard stepped through the door, the Pastor close behind him. Howard stopped short as he took in the fact that both his wife and Gibbs were in the same room. He looked back and forth from one face to another, trying, it seemed to Gibbs, to assess the mood in the room. Gibbs spoke up quickly, "We're good, Sheriff. We named the baby. Meet Sarah."

Gibbs saw Howard swallow hard. "Hello, Sarah," he

said, with a thickness in his voice that Gibbs did not understand.

"Getting a cold, Sheriff?" he asked.

"I'm definitely coming down with something, but I don't think it's a cold. Listen, Gibbs, the Pastor and I need to speak to you. Lara, do you mind watching the baby?"

Lara's eyes narrowed a bit at her husband's words, but when she reached for the baby, she did so eagerly.

Chapter Forty-Two

Howard checked his watch. He knew it was important to meet with Gibbs, with Lara, but he sure wished he could delegate it to someone else. He itched to get back out on Grizzly Flat, to just drive and drive until... he wasn't sure. *Until I find her,* he thought.

Gibbs closed the door to Jerry's office behind him and looked around, probably for a place to sit, Howard surmised. It *was* a bit crowded with all four of them in there. Jerry motioned Howard to take his chair behind the desk, as if in deference to the Sheriff's station. He waved Katie and Gibbs over to the couch, and then leaned against the door, his unbuttoned red vest hanging beside his paunch like two sails in full wind.

Gibbs looked at Howard nervously, then to Katie with eyes that were slightly pleading. She saw, and patted his knee. "Everything's fine, Gibbs. We just have some news. Big news. *Good* news." She leaned over, grasped his cheeks in both her hands and kissed him directly on top of his head. Instantly, Gibbs blushed, his skin and hair nearly matching now.

"Uh…okay, what?" He looked at Howard.

Howard pulled in a deep breath. *Where to start?* he wondered. "Well, Gibbs, after you got that Instant Message from Lucy, I went out looking for her. I found where she's been living."

Gibbs sat bolt upright. "You did? Where is she?"

Howard held up a hand. "Down, boy. I said I found where she's been living. I didn't find *her*." He crossed his hands over his stomach and made a steeple with his forefingers. "But I will. You can bet on that."

Gibbs nodded. He waited. Finally he said, "Is that it?"

Howard glanced at Katie. This time she drew in a deep breath and replaced her hand on Gibb's knee. "Not quite," she said. She met Howard's eyes, then glanced at Jerry.

Howard looked over at Jerry, who was all grins and seemed barely able to contain himself. "So, spill it!" Jerry enthused.

"Well, it's tricky," Katie started. She looked back at Gibbs. "Gibbs, that place where Lucy was living— Howard found something there. He found…well, evidence, I suppose. Evidence that Lucy had…that she had a baby." She paused to let that sink in.

Howard studied Gibbs face closely. He saw the boy's jaw drop, then he saw all the color drain from his face. "Uh…Gibbs," Howard said, "that would be *your* baby."

Gibbs turned his head toward Howard, his mouth still wide open. *He looks like an idiot,* Howard thought to

himself. *There he is, my probable future son-in-law, the idiot.*
"Son, do you have anything to say?"

Gibbs let loose with a whoop that nearly deafened
Howard in that small room. He picked at his ear for
some remaining hearing. "Like we said, it's good news,
kind of." Howard gave the boy a pained smile.

Gibbs had stood during his whooping, his uninjured
hand raised to the ceiling. He nearly touched it,
Howard noted. But the boy was suddenly serious again.
"Um…Sheriff?"

"Yes, son?"

"Why haven't you slugged me yet?"

Howard looked over at Katie, who nodded at him.
"First, because I'm tired of being angry with everyone
that matters to me. Second, I have it on good authority
that there's just not enough forgiveness in this world.
And third: because, son, I think you've suffered
enough."

Gibbs dropped his hand and looked at his shoes for
a moment. "So…is Lucy okay? Isn't it dangerous having a baby if you're not at a hospital?"

"People have been doing it for millions of years, all
the way up until County General opened. Seems like
everything worked exactly how God intended, for
which I'm grateful. So, yes, except for being shot by a
man with a brain the size of a hairball, I think she's
fine. She's just…spooked, I think."

"You know who shot her?" Gibbs asked, his face suddenly red with anger.

Howard held up his hand. "You let me worry about
that. The important thing now is figuring out how to

convince Lucy to come home. Have you had any luck getting a message to her?"

"No. I think she registered a one-time anonymous account so I couldn't trace her."

Howard looked over at Jerry, who was grinning like the Cheshire Cat. "Do you know, Jerry, I wouldn't know how to do a thing like that to save my life."

Jerry laughed and shook his head. "Howard, I know you just said something, but I wasn't paying any attention to it."

Howard squinted at him. "Thank you for your honesty. I think."

He turned back to Gibbs. "Do you have any ideas how we can get her home?"

Gibbs sat back down. "Well, I think she won't come home as long as she thinks you're mad at her. Or that her mom hates her."

"Her mom doesn't hate her," Howard said bitterly. "And I'm not mad at her."

Katie spoke up. "But Lucy doesn't know that." She laid a hand on Gibbs' bandaged hand. "And how about you, Gibbs? Are you angry at her?"

Gibbs looked away, ashamed. Howard studied the boy—he had tried to punch through a wall, after all. *Is he likely to try to punch my daughter?* he wondered.

Gibbs looked at his shoes when he spoke. "No. I love her. I was just frustrated that I couldn't reach her." He looked up at Katie. "So how do we find her?"

Out of the corner of his eye, Howard saw Jerry raise his hand. His eyes followed the movement, and he saw Jerry, glassy eyed, reaching for some invisible object. "Oh, great," Howard said out loud. "There he goes."

Katie looked at him, her mouth forming a questioning "O."

"Fugue state," Howard explained. "Happens when he's stressed."

"No," Jerry said, still clutching at something only he could see. "No, I'm here, I'm just...*Deck the Halls.*"

"Huh?" Howard grunted, not following.

Jerry's eyes refocused, and he looked over at Howard, a wicked grin playing on his lips. "Deck the Halls!" he said with vigor. "That's it! Myrtle, I could kiss you!"

He leaned over, planting both hands on the top of the desk, looking straight into Howard's eyes. "I have an idea! I know how to get Lucy to come home. C'mon, Gibbs, I need you!" He grabbed the boy's good arm and, flinging open the door, dragged him into the stockroom.

Howard met Katie's eyes and they both shrugged. Then they roused themselves quickly and followed Gibbs out of the room, jogging to catch up. Entering the break room, he saw everyone stop cold. "Where's Sarah?" Gibbs asked. "Where is Mrs. Saks?"

That's when it hit Howard. His wife was gone. And she had taken the baby.

Chapter Forty-Three

The steering wheel almost leaped out of Howard's hand when he hit a pothole, but he quickly gained control and did not slow down as he sped toward downtown. He pushed the button on his radio. "Unit 101."

In a moment, Diane's voice crackled back at him. "Unit 101, proceed."

"Diane, where's Czarnecki?"

"11-82 out on Morganson."

A minor fender-bender, Howard translated the code automatically. *No one hurt.*

Howard grimaced. That would tie her up for a while. His shoulders drooped. *What was I thinking? Czarnecki and I would single-handedly close and monitor all the roads out of Munich?* "Diane, will you go to the window and tell me if my wife's car is in the drive?"

"10-4, 101. One moment."

It was only about twenty seconds before Diane's voice crackled again in his ears, but it seemed like an eternity. "Affirmative, Chief. Car is present. What's up?"

"Suspected 207A. 10-26, though, thank God."

"10-9, Chief?" Howard translated, *Come again?*

"You heard me right, Diane. Suspected kidnapping. If she's there, though, it's all right."

"Do you need backup?"

"Nah. I'll handle it. Consider me 10-10A." Diane would understand this, he knew. He was home and off duty.

"10-4, Unit 101. Good night, Chief."

"'Night, Diane."

"You call me and I'll trot right over."

"Good to know. 101 out."

Three minutes later he was pulling into his driveway. His wife's car was there, just as Diane had said. He swung his feet to the snow, and with a great sigh, heaved himself out of the seat.

He didn't know what he was going to say when he confronted her. He also didn't know what he was feeling. *Too many things to sort out,* he thought.

The house seemed empty, but when he stopped to listen, he heard someone singing softly. It was Lara's voice, and he followed it to their bedroom. "Hello, love," he said, as he filled up the doorway.

Lara was sitting on the bed, trying to comfort the fussing child. He sat next to her, and laid his hand on her thigh. She ignored him.

"Lara, why did you bring the baby here?"

For the first time she looked at him, but then she returned her gaze to the child. "That store is no place for a baby."

"Well, I agree it's not ideal. But she's loved there, and that's the most important thing."

"She needs a mother," Lara countered.

"She has a mother," Howard said.

"Well, of course she has a mother," Lara said as if he were an idiot. "We just don't know who it is."

"Well, actually, honey, we do."

Her eyes leapt to his face and searched it. "You do?"

"Yes. The problem is, we can't find her," Howard said carefully. "Turns out she…ran away about six months ago."

Howard watched the blood drain from his wife's face. "You mean…."

"Yes. Sarah is your granddaughter." Howard watched as a procession of emotions played out on her face: shock, wonder, pity, anger, sadness, each in its turn. He knew them all intimately.

"Well, then, she should be here…until…until…."

"Actually, honey, I think it's fine that she's visiting us. But next time, you'll need to ask her father for permission."

"Her father? Who's her fath—" Then she stopped, her face screwing up in a mixture of confusion and outrage. "You can't mean Leonard?" Howard watched as she took in the color of the infant's hair. She felt its fine, silky strands between her fingers. She nodded. "Of course," she said. "He is…he's good with her."

"He is, and I know for a fact that he's worried sick about her, and with good reason. Officially, you're guilty of child kidnapping, darlin'." He rubbed her leg and then put his hand on her shoulder, pulling her into him. "Let's get her back before anyone does anything we'll regret, like filing a report or something."

"But, Howard, we can care for her so much better here. It's not fair to the baby—"

"Sarah belongs with her father, honey. That's the law, and that's the truth." He smoothed her hair. "And when we find Lucy, she'll belong with her."

"Do you think you will…find Lucy?" There. She had said her name.

Howard smiled. "We have a plan. It's a little far-fetched, but it might just work." He stood. "In the meantime, this little one needs her father."

Howard could see the indecision on her face. Minute expressions indicated defiance, fear, and finally resignation. She extended her arms toward him, and he scooped up the child, who had stopped fussing and was reaching for something he couldn't see. *Kind of like Jerry,* he thought.

He paused at the door. "I'll be back in about a half hour. Why don't you put on something nice? We'll drive into Silas and have a nice dinner, and then we'll come back for the Christmas Eve service."

He could see she was on the verge of tears. He knew she was about as fragile as she had ever been. He worried about her. He loved her. *Do I forgive her?* he wondered. He didn't know. There was a lot that needed healing. *Well, we can start tonight,* he decided. He walked back to the bed, leaned down, and kissed the top of Lara's head.

Chapter Forty-Four

From behind the line of trees Lucy peered at the house that she had called home for so many months. It looked abandoned. She couldn't see any cars. *But that doesn't mean there aren't any out front,* she thought. She weighed the risks. *Too great,* she decided, and slunk back into the concealing blanket of brush.

It was Christmas, she knew, but she didn't know how she knew it. As she trudged through the snow, she smelled more wood smoke on the breeze than usual—a lot more. And somehow, the snow shone in the sunlight with more sparkle than it had yesterday. Within herself she felt both elated and depressed at the same time.

Elated because it was Christmas, and depressed because she was spending it alone.

She forced herself to think of what she was going to do. For two nights now, the backseat of that old sedan had given her shelter. If she didn't find something else, she'd have to take a chance that it would be there again tonight. And if it wasn't? She stopped in her tracks, a moment of panic seizing her. She inhaled deeply, and let her breath out slowly. *Calm,* she told herself. *Keep calm and think clearly.* Her life depended on it, she knew.

Dusk was coming. The daylight had brought the temperature up, but she knew it would plummet very quickly. She ached to be out of the cold. She tormented herself, thinking of a fire in a fireplace, cookies, hot cocoa…. She reached for a tree to steady herself. *Stop it,* her interior voice almost screamed at her. *Stop it now.*

Ahead she could see the trees beginning to thin. Beyond she saw a two-story colonial. There were no cars in front of it, but neither was it abandoned. The house was dark, but a new cord of wood was stacked by its side, and there were fresh tire tracks in yesterday's snow. She headed off to her left to stay within the tree cover while she wove her way around to the back of the house. *No sign of life,* she thought. *So far so good.*

Once again, she wrestled with herself about breaking into a house. She had long ago justified squatting—no one was living there, so what did it hurt? She intentionally ignored the objection raised by her conscience regarding the demolition of one staircase.

She weighed the relative harm, breaking in and stealing some food and warmth, or freezing to death?

Her tummy rumbled. The choice became less trouble-some as the twilight faded and the temperature fell.

What if they come home? she thought. *It's the dead of winter, the sun is down at five o'clock, which means that it's about 4:30 now, maybe 4:45. If they went to a relative's house for Christmas dinner, that's usually about 3pm for most people, but they never actually sit down to eat until 4 o'clock,* she calculated. *They'll just now be finishing up, which means they'll be visiting for at least another hour, and then will have to drive home, which could be anywhere from a half hour to two hours.*

So at the very least, she concluded, *I've got an hour and a half, and at the most, I've got three and a half hours.* And who knows? She might find a place to hide out once she got warm. She nodded as the back of the house came into view.

Again, all was dark, except for the winking of tiny Christmas lights that she could see through the sliding glass door leading out onto a redwood deck. She smiled when she saw a storage shed to the far side of the house, out of the line of sight of any of the windows.

Taking one last look around, she dashed across the yard, straight to the shed. It was locked. She fought down a surge of panic, and realized that the key must be hanging somewhere in the house, probably by the door or in the kitchen. She would just have to find it. *Well then,* she thought, *that is the first order of business.*

She trudged across a snowdrift and made her way to the back door. The light was fading fast. She tried the door. It was locked. She looked over to the sliding glass door and quickly mounted the stairs to the deck. She heaved the door, and to her great amazement, it slid along its track without protest.

A great wave of warm air buffeted her. She gasped and basked in it. Then she remembered herself and stepped inside, sliding the door closed behind her. Not thinking about the snow on her boots, she turned and looked at the wall by the sliding door—there was no hook holding a key. *That would be too easy*, she thought.

Briskly, she strode to the kitchen and looked at the wall there. Nothing. She undid the deadbolt, however, so that she could make a quick exit by this door if she needed to. Then she turned her attention to the cupboards.

That's when she noticed the smells. They were almost intoxicating: chocolate, cinnamon, butterscotch, and apple. She stopped and closed her eyes, filling her nostrils with the luxuriant aromas. Saliva sprang to her tongue with such a great quantity that she literally drooled. She giggled and wiped the spit from her mouth with a grimy mitten.

Focus, she said to herself, and opened one cabinet door after another. "Yes!" she screamed aloud. There was a key rack, screwed into the back of the cabinet drawer holding the spices. There were several keys there, one marked with a hasty hand on the tag hanging from it, "Shed." She put it in her pocket and ran upstairs looking for blankets and a pillow.

She found what she was looking for in the linen closet and rushed back downstairs, clutching them to her chest. She put them in a pile near the back door—her exit plans shaping up very nicely.

She allowed herself a moment to relax. She dare not take her boots off, but she did remove her coat, since she was beginning to sweat. It was a good feeling. Then her stomach growled again.

Time to explore this kitchen, she thought, and opened the refrigerator. "Chocolate milk?" she said out loud. "That can't be real." But it was. She pulled it out, opened it, and downed the whole carton where she stood.

She set the empty carton in the sink, and turned back to the fridge. Half a ham stared at her, daring her to eat it. She did not hesitate, but pulled it from its shelf, and grabbed a knife. Then, on the table she saw a whole plate of baked treats, under a glass lid: cookies, brownies, and things that looked like tiny little pies.

Balancing the plate holding the ham in one hand, she removed the glass lid and picked up the whole plate of goodies and carried both into the living room where she could eat by the light of the winking Christmas tree. She didn't want to turn on any lights, after all. And the tree was cheery. "It really feels like Christmas," she said out loud as she planted herself on the couch. She put the plates on the coffee table and she paused a moment to look at the tree before digging in.

She smiled and said a blessing of sorts. "God, thank you for Christmas." She sighed, and was just about to tuck in to the ham, when she caught something out of the corner of her eye. "What is that?" she said out loud, and turned toward it. She thought she had seen a picture of someone who looked a lot like she did. *Or like I used to,* she thought. She squinted and realized she was looking at a Christmas tree bulb, hanging from a bough on the left side of the tree.

Without thinking she rose and went over to it. Bending over, she looked at it more closely in the blinking colored light of the tree. A picture of herself smiled up at her, the winking of the lights giving it an illusion of motion. A feeling of horror rolled through her. She pulled at the ornament, and the bough snapped back lazily as she pulled it free.

Too stricken for caution, she walked to the kitchen and switched on the overhead light. She held the ornament in her hand, and, her heart feeling like it was going to pound straight through her chest, she turned it over and over.

On one side was her picture. She remembered when it was taken—on vacation by Lake Superior the summer before last. She hardly recognized the breezy, carefree girl that smiled up at her. Who was she? It certainly wasn't *her*. Except that it was.

On the other side, in rolling cursive script, was written, *Lucy, come home. I love you. Dad.*

A sob choked her and she dropped the ornament. It shattered on the linoleum, shards scattering in a hundred sparkling directions. She held her hands to her face and sank to the floor as months of loneliness and guilt erupted up through her throat and flooded from her eyes.

She wailed and did not hold back, her voice an animal cry of pain and loss, inarticulate and primal. She moaned and rocked herself for a long, timeless stretch. When the obscuring mask of pain lifted from her, she found herself in the fetal position on the floor, her head hanging over the molding into the carpeted living room. Her hands were clutching at her empty gut, void of either food or baby. She wailed again, but it was a short, vestigial cry, the last dregs shaken out.

Then she heard a click. Instantly, her mind was empty of everything but the impulse to flight. She grabbed a handful of cookies and stuffed them into her coat pocket. With her other hand, she clasped the blankets to her chest, turned the knob of the back door, and silently pulled it to behind her. She descended the steps of the deck in two large, rapid steps and ducked beneath it. She noted her breath issuing from her mouth like a steam locomotive, and she forced herself to control her breathing, to exhale through her nose. It helped.

She heard shouting from within. Her thefts, minor as they were, had been discovered. Probably the glass from the broken ornament, too. As she knew it would, the sliding glass door opened. She heard the frantic clomping of boots on the deck above her. She thought her heart was going to pound through her chest. She willed it to be quiet. The clomper above her circumambulated the deck a couple of times and finally went back inside. She exhaled in a relieved puff and began to breathe normally again.

But then, to her surprise, she heard the door slide open again. Someone else came out. She heard a lighter step above her. A woman's voice called out, clearly audible above the wind in the trees. "Lucy! We know it's you! Please, come home! No one is mad at you. Your family loves you. Please come home!"

Lucy's head swam. First the ornament, and now this. Who was this woman? How did she know who she was? How did she know it was her? How did she know what was happening in her family? There were too many questions, and Lucy felt paralyzed in the face of them. In a moment, the woman went back inside.

Lucy waited a few minutes, and when there were no more excursions onto the deck, she picked her way through the scrub growing beneath the redwood slats over to its far end. There she could clearly see the shed. She slid out from under the deck and edged her way along the wall toward the small metal structure. She couldn't see any windows, which meant they couldn't see her, either. She continued to control her breath, as she knew that the steam might float within sight of a window and give her away.

Then she was beside the shed. She fished the key out of her pocket and inserted it into the padlock. It fit. She turned it. The door swung outward toward her. And then she almost screamed with frustration. The shed was filled from floor to ceiling with…"stuff," Lucy said out loud. *Why do people store up years of garbage?* she asked herself. Her heart sank. Then, despite the cold something melted within her.

"I'm just like them," she breathed. "I'm storing up garbage." A couple of the strands by which she bound her resentment to herself frayed, snapped. And then the danger of her situation reasserted itself.

There was no way she could remove enough of that stuff to crawl inside, not without making so much noise that she'd be discovered. She looked back at the dark side of the house. She looked at the impenetrable pile in the shed. She looked at the night sky through the trees. She looked at the road beyond the shed.

She wasn't thinking then, just acting. She left the door of the shed hanging open and made for the road.

Soon, she passed another house. The family was home. Smoke wafted from the chimney, filling the air with a sweet, warm smell. It smelled like comfort. She could see the lights of the Christmas tree through the window. Like a moth to a flame she walked toward it. She wasn't going to break in, so she wasn't worried about being seen, not really. She walked right up to the glass, peered in at the tree, and found herself staring at herself.

It was another Christmas ornament, sporting another photo of herself—one that Gibbs had snapped on his cell phone outside her high school. "This is very very weird," she said out loud. In a daze, she turned from the window and continued to follow the streetlights down the road.

The thought of Gibbs made her ache. She had always thought he was both sweet and goofy. She hadn't really realized how much she loved him until she tried to stay away from him, from everyone. Loneliness pressed on her shoulders, on her chest, becoming almost more than she could carry.

She passed a fir tree on the side of the road and stopped. There, hanging from one branch, square in the middle of the tree, was a single ornament. She was irresistibly drawn to it. She plucked it like a ripe fruit and held it up to the glow of the streetlamp. It was a picture of a baby. A very, very young baby. Her spine tingled as she realized it was *her* baby. She was smiling, holding her little fist aloft. Turning the ornament, Lucy saw the glittering script. "Mommie, I need you. Please come home."

She brushed at her eyes with her mittens and looked

at the photo of the baby—her baby—again. Gingerly, she put it in her pocket and kept walking.

She didn't know where she was headed, but gradually, she realized she was getting closer to town. She kept finding ornaments—peeking out of people's garlanded windows, hanging on wreaths fixed to their doors, fixed to random telephone poles, tree limbs, fence pickets, the driver's side mirrors of cars.

The closer she got to town, the more of them she found. Their frequency increased as the houses became denser. She gathered them until her pockets couldn't possibly hold another one without breaking it, and then she just let them be. But she touched every one, read them, cried over them. One had a picture of her Dad, and she had kissed it.

Soon, she found herself on the main street. There were ornaments everywhere. Like a trail of breadcrumbs she followed them to the main Christmas tree in the middle of the town square. In wonder she raised her face to its peak. Lowering her gaze, she saw herself reflected in its branches all the way down.

The tree was ablaze with light, and for every light there was an ornament bearing her likeness or the face of someone she loved. Every one entreated her to come home. Every one told her she was loved. She reached out and took one down. Her father's face smiled up at her, and his eyes looked pleading and wet. The script said, "I love you, darlin'. Lucy, please come back to us."

She didn't wail then, or sob, or faint. She just clutched the ornament to her breast and cried.

She had no idea how long she stood there. But after a while she realized she was not alone. A young woman in a long coat and bunny slippers was standing beside her, looking at the tree. "It's beautiful, isn't it?" she said.

Lucy nodded, still clutching at the ornament.

"I brought you a blanket," the young woman said, and she gingerly laid it over Lucy's shoulders. Lucy gathered it around herself, and with a thick, hoarse voice said simply, "Thank you."

"You must be Lucy," the young woman said.

Lucy nodded, not looking away from the tree.

"I've so been hoping to meet you. I'm Katie. How about some hot cocoa?"

It sounded *so* good. Lucy nodded. The young woman put her arm around her shoulders, and steered her toward an open door, which beckoned them with cheer and warmth and light.

Chapter Forty-Five

Once inside, Katie led Lucy to the kitchen, and within minutes, they were both seated at the table with a steaming mug of hot chocolate in front of them. Lucy looked around at the homey decorations as if she were in a dream. "Are we at the church?" she asked.

"We're *by* the church. This is the parsonage," Katie answered, testing the cocoa. It was still a bit too hot to drink. She blew on it, keeping her eyes on Lucy. Was it her imagination, or was the girl a little dissociated? *Well, who can blame her?* she thought. *It's probably just the shock of all the ornaments. Real love, when it meets us, can be disorienting.*

"Why are we at the parsonage?" Lucy asked.

"Because I'm the Pastor," Katie smiled at her.

"You are not," Lucy said, her eyes narrowing. "The Pastor is an old guy."

"Not anymore he isn't," Katie met her gaze with equal ferocity, then she tried to clamp down on a smile. She did not succeed.

Lucy saw, and smiled, too. "All those ornaments ….why?"

Katie cocked her head at her. "Can't you guess?"

Lucy shook her head. She looked like she was about to cry. "You have a lot of people who love you, Lucy. A lot of people. And they love you very much."

Lucy looked away. "That's all over."

"Why is that?" Katie asked. She rose and got a plate of sandwiches out of the fridge. She set them on the table. Lucy looked up at her for permission. Katie nodded and smiled. Lucy grabbed one and instantly stuffed it in her mouth.

When she could speak again, Katie repeated her question. "Why is it all over?"

"Because I…I don't know how to say it," Lucy looked down at the crumbs on her plate. "I'm not good enough for it."

"Do you mean to tell me," Katie said, hunkering down to look her in the eyes. "That you aren't good enough to be loved?"

Lucy nodded.

"Who told you that goodness had anything to do with being loved?"

"I don't deserve it," Lucy said to the crumbs.

"Can I let you in on a secret?" Katie asked.

Lucy looked up at her and nodded, her mouth pouty and her eyes sorrowful.

"Neither do I."

Lucy looked at her without comprehension. "What do you mean?"

"I mean that I am a royal screw-up. I do things I hate to do. I hurt people's feelings, like, *all the time*. I let people down—people that really matter to me." Katie pushed out her lower lip earnestly. "Sound familiar?"

"But you're a *pastor*," Lucy protested.

"Yes, I am," Katie agreed. "And I'm a *sinner*."

Lucy looked up at her strangely.

"You think I should be ashamed when I say that?" Katie asked. "I'm not. Being a sinner doesn't make me a bad person, it just makes me human." Katie smiled. "Look, I have black hair. I wet the bed until I was six. I swear like a longshoreman when there's no one around but God to hear me. I'm left-handed. And, I'm a sinner." She grabbed one of the sandwiches off the plate, but she didn't take a bite yet. She just looked at it. "I'm not proud of it. I'm just not ashamed of it. It's a fact of life. Kind of like being dyslexic or having the flu."

Lucy sipped at the hot cocoa. Her eyes went wide at the taste.

"Oh, is that cool enough to drink now?" Katie asked, and took a sip herself. "It's my mom's recipe. Never tasted anything like it, have you?"

Lucy shook her head and took another sip.

"Black pepper is the secret. Promise you won't tell."

"Okay," Lucy said, trying not to gulp the stuff now. She wiped her mouth on her wrist and looked back up at Katie. "What do you mean, it's 'like having the flu'?"

"Sin is like a disease. You aren't born with it, really. You catch it pretty early, though. It's a chronic condition. You suffer with it all your life. It's fatal, ultimately, but with proper treatment, you can live a long and reasonably healthy life," Katie smiled at her. "The thing is, sin is catching. And everyone has it. And everyone suffers from it. So, no, I'm not ashamed of it. It's part of being human."

She reached over and brushed Lucy's cheek with her hand. "So do you deserve to be loved? Oh, yes, honey. It's not your fault you're sick."

Lucy looked back and forth, obviously trying to take this in.

Katie leaned back and took another sip of her cocoa. "If I had to be good enough to be loved, I wouldn't have anyone in my life who loved me. Not the way I screw things up."

"And you're not ashamed, really?" Lucy looked down at her plate again.

"Well, sometimes I am. But I don't let that stop me. Shame is a terrible temptation, and it only serves to separate us from the people we love. Boyfriends, parents, friends...even God. Sin is a fact of life. Shame is the real enemy. Don't give in to it, Lucy. Whatever you do, *don't let it win*."

"You don't talk *anything* like the old Pastor."

"Thank God," laughed Katie. "I'm sorry—" She gave Lucy a suddenly contrite look. "—I've heard he was a very nice man."

Lucy couldn't stop herself. She giggled. She grabbed another sandwich, and then she got serious again. "So, if we can't do anything about...sin..." Katie noted that it was hard for Lucy to even say the word. "Why even try to be good?"

"Well, you can't *be* good, exactly," Katie said, "so really, you should just give that up."

Lucy looked at her as if she had been slapped. "Are you *really* a pastor?"

Katie held up two fingers. "Brownies honor." She shared a smile with Lucy at that. But then she too got serious. "What I mean is, if you go through life just saying, 'Don't do this, it's evil. Don't do that, it's bad,' you'll end up being a very sour person, and people won't want to be around you. But if you ask yourself, 'What kind of person do I want to be?' and strive for that, you'll have a lot of love in your life. You'll have to keep in mind that you won't do it perfectly, and you have to be okay with that."

"What kind of person do you want to be, Pastor?"

"I want to be the kind of person that loves deeply and well."

"Even when you screw up?"

"Especially then."

Lucy was silent for a while. Katie could almost see the wheels turning in her head. "More cocoa?" Katie asked. Lucy nodded.

Katie went to the stove and poured the rest of the hot chocolate. She replaced the mug on the table. She knew it was time to bring things back around to Lucy's situation, but wasn't sure how to do it.

"Honey," she said, reaching for Lucy's hand, "I know you probably won't want to hear this, but we need to call your father."

A primal look of fear filled the girl's eyes. "Why?"

"Because he loves you and he's worried sick about you," she gently stroked Lucy's arm. "We made those ornaments together."

"You can't make me," Lucy said.

"Nope, I can't. And I won't try." She saw Lucy relax just a little. But it was just a feint. As soon as Katie looked away, Lucy bolted for the door.

"Oh, Lord," Katie swore, and sprang after her. The Pastor's legs were longer, her strides wider, and before Lucy was halfway to the door, Katie had tackled her. They both went flying, landing in a heap on a frayed oriental carpet. Katie wrestled with her, got behind her, and wrapped both her arms and legs around the girl, pinning her tight.

"Let me *go*!" Lucy shouted.

"Okay, I will," Katie panted, "but first you have to promise me you'll talk to your father for a half hour. That's all. Then, after a half hour, if you want to leave, I won't stop you."

"You just told me you wouldn't stop me!"

"I lied!"

"How can you be a pastor?!" Lucy tried to wriggle free.

"I told you I wasn't *good*." She squeezed until Lucy stopped struggling. "I just try to love well…and that's— ugh—what I'm *trying* to do—ow!—right now. Not *per-fectly*…just—"

Suddenly there was a knock on the door.

"Come in!" Katie shouted without loosening her hold.

"Ouch!" Lucy complained. "Did you have to yell right in my ear?!"

"Sorry, honey," Katie said, still struggling. The door squeaked on its hinges as it swung inward. Katie looked up from the pile of arms and legs and saw Howard's face, upside down.

"Lucy, darlin'…" he said, his upside down features softening.

"Daddy…" Lucy said, her voice tentative. She stopped struggling.

"Pastor, what's…is everything all right down there?"

"Everything's just ducky, Howard."

But Katie could see he wasn't listening. He only had eyes for his daughter. "Lucy, it's so good to see you, honey," he squatted beside them and he stroked the girl's hair. Lucy's eyes went wide with fear, and her lower lip started trembling.

"You don't…hate me?" she said, barely understandable through the emotion welling up in her throat.

"Oh, honey, I could never hate you. I feel like I failed you. You tried to tell me how you were feeling, and I didn't listen." He sat down cross-legged next to their heads and put his hat on the floor. "I was so intent on keeping peace with your mother that I couldn't see…I couldn't *let* myself see how much you were suffering. I let you down. I'm sorry, baby. I'm really, really sorry." He touched her cheek. "Can you forgive me?"

"Forgive *you*…?" Katie couldn't see Lucy's face now, but she felt her chest contract with the beginnings of sobs. "Oh, Daddy, I'm so sorry…."

And there goes the dam, Katie thought as the sobs began in earnest. In moments, Howard was lying on the floor with them, his arm around them both, his forehead touching his daughter's. "How about I forgive you and you forgive me, and we start fresh right now?"

"Oh, Daddy…" Lucy wailed, and her arms wrapped around him. Katie let her go, then, and sat up, watching their embrace through tears of her own. *More cocoa,* she thought, and rose, heading for the kitchen. Once out of sight, she flipped open her cell phone and sent a quick text message.

Chapter Forty-Six

The milk was just starting to bubble, when father and daughter sat down at the table together. Lucy looked more freaked out than ever, but also relieved and happy—an unlikely mélange of emotions.

"Three mugs, coming up," Katie said. No one said anything until Katie had served them all and taken a seat.

"I'm not coming home," Lucy said to her father. "I can't live with her anymore."

Katie assumed she was talking about her mother. She glanced at Howard. His lower lip protruded slightly as he thought this over. "Okay," he said. "But where will you live? You can't squat out on the Flats anymore, or Wysocki is likely to shoot you again."

Lucy nodded a quick agreement with that, but she didn't offer any ideas. Just then the tension in Katie's chest released as an idea occurred to her. "Can I make a suggestion?" Father and daughter both turned toward her. She licked her lips and weighed her words. "This parsonage is too big for one person. It was built for a largish family, and by myself here I get lonely and kind of depressed."

Lucy was nodding. Obviously she knew those feelings well.

"The house needs a baby," Katie continued. "It was made for children. It would be a happier house with a child and a young mother in it. I wonder if we could make a trade—some housework, which I am terrible at, in exchange for rent. What do you think, Lucy?"

The girl looked dubious. *She doesn't know me, after all,* Katie thought. *But we're even, there, I don't know her, either. This whole Munich experiment is either going to work or it's going to blow up in my face, with nothing in between. If I were Catholic, I'd call this a Hail Mary pass.*

Lucy's eyes flicked back and forth as she thought about it. Finally, she spoke. "You can't boss me around."

Katie shook her head. "If we're going to be roommates, we're going to be roommates. Both adults. I help you and you help me. You set your boundaries and I'll set mine. If I have a problem with something you are doing or not doing, I'll talk to you about it with kindness and respect, woman-to-woman. What do you say?"

Lucy looked amazed, but she nodded in agreement. Katie turned to Howard. "Sheriff?"

Howard shifted uncomfortably. "I need to talk to Lara about it, but…I guess I just have to let go of…well, of the idea it will ever be what it used to be."

Katie put her hand on his arm and squeezed.

"Howard, it will never be like that again. But with God's help, it will be better than that."

He returned her squeeze and sniffed. "Anybody ever tell you that you was a crackerjack minister?"

"Not in so many words, no," Katie smiled. "But thank you. I pretty much just try to show up and get out of God's way."

"Well, I'd say that strategy works pretty well." Howard let go of Katie's hand and looked back at his daughter. "I want to heal everything between us, honey. I want you and your mom to heal, too, but I know that's going to take some time. And I know you need some distance for that to happen. So…I think this is a good solution. But I expect you to really *work* for your rent, and to negotiate like a grown-up with Pastor Katie."

Lucy nodded solemnly. Her dad did the same. "And we'll settle up later for board, Pastor."

"That sounds fine, Howard."

For a moment no one said anything. The room held the kind of calm that comes to one after a long, hard crying jag—a quiet touched by weariness.

It was broken a few minutes later by a brisk knock. Lucy jumped and her cocoa flew to the floor, the mug shattering and the brown liquid splashing all over.

"I'm so sorry," Lucy said.

"I think you've got your first cleanup job," Howard said to her with a wry smile, patting her shoulder to instill some calm.

"Don't worry about that," Katie said. "I'm sure the door is for you. I know you'll want to open it." She went to the sink for a sponge, and Howard gestured to the door. "Go on, honey, open it."

Hesistant, Lucy finally pushed back her kitchen chair and lithely stepped to the door. She turned the knob and peered out. Katie strained to hear what was being said, but she couldn't make anything out.

In a moment, however, Lucy pushed the door open the rest of the way, and Gibbs walked in, followed by his mother. As soon as he crossed the threshold, Lucy embraced him. He was a little stiff, and didn't have a free hand, since he was holding the baby. While normally he would have hugged her, he leaned into her instead.

"Sheriff," Gibb's mother said in greeting. "Pastor."

"Becky," Howard shook her hand.

Lucy's attention was on the baby. "There you are. There you *are*. I've been wondering how you…what…" But she couldn't say any more. Finally she just said, "I'm so glad you're here."

She went to take the baby in her arms, and Gibbs acquiesced. Katie could see Lucy's lip trembling. "You are so beautiful," Lucy said through her tears.

"Just like her mom," Gibbs said.

Lucy looked up at him. "Oh, Gibbs—what happened to your arm?" Her eyes widened as she took in his sling.

"Long story. Involves an Instant Message you might know something about. I can explain later."

She reached up and touched his face. "Gibbs, I'm so sorry…."

"I *am* kind of mad at you," he said to her, although there was no heat behind it. It was a matter-of-fact comment, Katie realized, like "I prefer chocolate to vanilla."

"I know," she said. "I'd be mad, too." She renewed her lean into his side. This time he had a free hand with which to hold her to him. "Will you let me try to… make it okay again?"

"You'd better," he said, a look of mock hurt on his face. She gave a sad smile and touched his cheek. He kissed her.

"I am *not* ready for that!" Howard said, and turned his back on the couple. Gibbs' mother laughed and Katie winked at him.

Katie stepped up and touched Gibbs' arm. "Gibbs, Lucy and I are going to be roomies."

Both Gibbs and his mother looked surprised. "Here?" he asked.

Katie nodded. "So Sarah can have her own room."

"Sarah?" Lucy asked. "The baby's name is Sarah?"

Gibbs nodded. "Your mo—I figured it was a good name, being in both of our families. Do you like it?"

Lucy looked at her father. He smiled.

"Yes, it's perfect," she said.

"About Sarah," Gibbs turned serious. "I…if you don't want to care for her, you don't have to. I will."

Lucy closed her eyes and shook her head, resolute. "No. Every minute I've been away from her has been… it's hurt." She looked over at Katie. "It was wrong."

Katie nodded encouragingly. Lucy continued. "I just want to do the right thing, now."

"The two of you will need to work together to make sure Sarah's care is covered while you work, Gibbs, and Lucy finishes school," Katie said. "I know your folks will want to help. Even your mom, Lucy."

Lucy didn't look certain, but she agreed. "We'll do fine," she said, putting an arm around Gibbs.

"With God's help, I think you will," Katie agreed.

Chapter Forty-Seven

The first Sunday after Christmas dawned brisk and bright, and Pastor Katie sipped her morning tea in satisfaction, listening to all the noise in the house. A baby wailed. A timer buzzed. A Grief Patrol CD was pounding out melancholic fury in another room. It sounded like heaven.

She stuck her head into the room that they had dubbed "the nursery." She saw Lucy changing a diaper, and the early morning sun made the image shine like an icon. "Hey there, St. Lucy," Katie said, "I'm off to work. You two need anything?"

"Nope, we're good," Lucy said, pulling Sarah's footy pajamas back in place. "Gibbs and his mom are going to come, so we'll see you over there."

"You know that you're not obligated to come to church, just because you're living here—not ever," Katie said, her face turning serious.

"I know. It's okay," Lucy reassured her. "We *want* to be there…at least today we do."

"Good enough for me!" Katie called back as she bounded down the hall toward the door.

There was always so much to do, getting ready for a service. *The people in the pews have no idea*, Katie thought.

But maybe that was good—if they did, she wouldn't be doing her job well. Once in her office, she ran through her mental checklist and set about getting all her "little tasks" done.

She made sure the bulletins were folded properly (they were) and carried them to the front door. She restocked the "tract rack" and made sure there were enough "visitor's packets" in place for the ushers. She placed a copy of her sermon on the pulpit and made sure the Altar Guild ladies had set out everything properly.

Everything was pristine, except that they had neglected to put out a glass of water for her. *That's an easy oversight,* she thought, remembering several times she had forgotten that herself when she was on altar duty. She filled a little glass with water and set it out on the credence table in easy reach of her presider's chair.

At ten 'til, the organ began its majestic strains, and the first of the parishioners began to wander in. Katie took in the beauty of the sanctuary, the hanging boughs of evergreen, the red ribbon, the Lucy ornaments hung by the windows for the Christmas Eve service, when they had handed them out to all the parishioners.

She had been relieved when they eagerly took them—she wasn't sure how that would be received. *But my people came through,* she thought. Then she realized she had just called them "her people." Yes, that felt right.

The ornaments she had sent over to Father Gene at the Roman Catholic church and to Reverend McElroy at the Baptist church were also enthusiastically taken up, she had heard. *What a relief that was,* she thought, and turned into the vestry to put on her vestments.

Properly adorned for worship in a glittering white chasuble, Katie sat for several minutes in meditation to prepare her soul for worship. Then, basking in the calm of those few minutes in God's presence, she exited the back door and walked around the building to the front door for the entry procession. Two teenage girls were serving as acolytes for the service, giggling with each other in their red cassocks, holding the rods of their processional candlesticks—almost taller than they were, like the walking staffs of pilgrims.

"Ahem!" Katie cleared her throat, and the acolytes blushed, suppressed their giggles and got in line in front of the currently inchoate mass of people in choir robes. In mere seconds, however, the choir sorted itself out into formation, and when the first organ blast of the entrance hymn sounded, every person was in place, attentive and ready to march.

And march they did. Katie's breath was taken away as she saw the packed sanctuary. It was literally standing room only. As she processed, she sang boldly and although no emotions other than the warm glow of praise showed on her face, her mind was abuzz with doubt. Everyone had heard of her last sermon, she knew. Were all these people here to see her fall on her face again? Were they here because of the community spirit roused by the Lucy ornament campaign? Or were they simply here to celebrate Christmas?

She didn't know, and that she didn't know unsettled her. Nevertheless, she put a courageous face on it, and forced such thoughts out of her mind. There was enough to think about in a worship service without nagging doubts plaguing her, none of which she could do anything about.

As they sang the final verse, she looked around. She saw Jerry and his wife—*Carol, was that her name?*—near the back, where they could safely escape if things got too churchy, she supposed. Gibbs and Lucy were there to her left, Sarah cradled in Lucy's arms. She was surprised to see them on the second row. Halfway through the last verse she saw Howard and Lara duck in, looking apologetic. They stood against the wall at the back, flying cherubs hanging over their heads, threatening to bomb them with golden styrofoam balls.

When the organ resolved its final chord, Katie paused to let the reverberations tremble through the building. Then she stepped forward and welcomed the people. *Her* people.

"Merry Christmas!" she shouted.

There was a confused murmuring in the crowd, with a few straggling, "Merry Christmases" returned to her. "As you know, Christmas is not a day, it is a season. Christmas is the second greatest feast in the Christian year, and it lasts twelve days. I believe today is 'Three French Hens,' so you can guess what we're having for supper in the parsonage tonight."

It wasn't much of a joke, Katie knew, but it got some chuckles from the congregation. "Today we continue our celebration of that marvelous event, the most important in human history, when the Lord of heaven laid his glory by and became one of us, uniting himself, marrying himself to creation forever. Never more can divinity and humanity be separate, never more can they be estranged. For two thousand years ago, in a lowly stable, our need and God's grace met and kissed and made a life together—the life of the one we call Jesus. Blessed be the name of the Lord!"

They responded with enthusiasm now. *Or what passed for enthusiasm among Lutherans,* she corrected herself. Still, they were grinning, they were receptive, they were *with* her. She relaxed as she read the opening prayer.

One by one the readers came forward to proclaim the scriptures. Katie tried to pay attention, but she couldn't. *That's okay,* she told herself. *You've spent plenty of time meditating on them this week.* After three of the lessons had been read by the lectors, Katie rose to proclaim the Gospel. The text from St. Luke told of the holy family coming back from exile in Egypt, where they had fled for safety. It had reminded her of Lucy, who had fled to an Egypt of her own for similar reasons.

Closing the Book of the Gospels, she handed it to an acolyte and then turned to mount the steps into the pulpit. As she stepped up to it, she experienced a moment of panic. Her sermon was not there. She closed her eyes to still her anger. Yet, she was surprised that what she felt was more pity than anger. *Oh, Gammy,* she thought to herself. *Why do you hate me so much?*

She opened her eyes and looked directly at Ms. Gammerbrau, whose eyebrow was arched, a wicked grin twisting her face. A restless wave went through the crowd at the unexpected pause in the flow of the service.

This had only happened to Katie once before. Katie's mind flashed back to the scene of her internship, where she and a rival seminarian named Ed Schmidt had been—childishly—competing for the approval of their senior pastor. When she had gotten up to preach, she discovered that Ed had swiped her sermon. The next eight minutes had been the longest of her life as she hemmed and hawed her way through what little bit of her sermon outline she could remember.

Never again, she had told herself, *especially in a hostile work situation.* Looking Gammy straight in the eye, Katie put her hand in through the slit in her alb, found her back pocket and pulled out the backup copy of her sermon she had placed there this morning. Katie's smile broadened as Gammy's faltered.

I must decrease so he can increase, Katie thought to herself, and had to stifle a giggle. She launched into her sermon with confidence, with a story about Martin Luther's own exile at Wartberg Castle when he was on the run for his life, how God had used his time there well, translating the Bible and effectively inventing the German language out of the scraps of competing dialects, and how he had returned because his people needed him.

"Exile is always painful," Katie affirmed, "but it can also be a time of healing and productivity. God, after all, is the master of taking painful situations and creating beauty out of them. Exile can be physical, as in the case of Israel's captivity in Babylon. But it can also be emotional. We can leave relationships without physically leaving them. We can shut ourselves off from the people who love us most. And the worst part of it is, we do it to ourselves."

She needed to let that sink in for a moment, so she descended from the pulpit and, with slow, deliberate steps, walked over to the credence table. She took a long drink from the glass of water, and then unhurriedly walked back to the pulpit. *They already think I'm weird*, she thought. *Might as well confirm it for them.* When she resumed her sermon, she did it with gusto.

"Did you ever think that maybe God felt like an exile from us? Did you ever wonder if perhaps that is why he was born as one of us? After all, we couldn't close the gap between God and us ourselves. Only he could do that. Could it be that God longed for us so much, wanted to be family with us so much, that he gave up everything, and made himself as vulnerable as it is possible to be, just to be with us?

"Who would have believed that the simple birth of a child could have closed such a large gap? Who would have believed that a tiny babe could hold so much importance? Who would have believed that, for love of a helpless infant, angels would fill the skies with song, shepherds would abandon their flocks, or that kings would leave their thrones and travel a thousand miles?

"Who would believe that a child from a young family could bring so much healing? Who would believe that a babe born out of wedlock could melt the hearts of so many, could make strangers into friends? Who would have believed that a baby everyone thought such a tragedy would turn into such a blessing?

"*I believe,*" Katie said forcefully, her voice ringing out like thunder.

After the offertory, she walked out into the middle of the aisle. A ripple of whispers wafted through the congregation. This was not part of the liturgy. "My friends, a few days after Jesus was born, his parents brought him to the temple to dedicate him to God, and to name him before the high priest. In our tradition, we usually do this at a child's baptism, but in this case—let us say circumstances interfered," she smiled at Lucy and Gibbs, who stared back in wide-eyed terror. A twinge of doubt struck Katie—should she have prepped them for this? Probably. *Well, too late now*, she thought.

"Lucy and Gibbs, will you bring your baby forward?" With every eye upon them, they didn't dare to disobey. Looking like they both wished they could find convenient rocks to crawl under, they climbed over the others in their row and stumbled out into the aisle.

Katie led them to stand in front of the altar, facing the congregation. "Lucy and Leonard," Katie said solemnly. "Last week, without the benefit of name, I baptized your daughter by water and the Holy Spirit into the Body of Christ. This morning, we acknowledge her as our sister in the faith and a part of our family."

Katie smiled warmly at them both. They seemed less nervous now, but they still looked as out of place as humans could be without actually crawling out of their skins. "What name have you given this child?" she asked them.

"S-Sarah," Lucy and Gibbs seemed to stutter in unison. Sarah burbled.

"In accepting Sarah as a gift from God, do you also accept the responsibility that God has placed upon you to care for her, and love her, to teach her right from wrong, and to instruct her in the way of the Spirit, as you discern which tradition your family will practice together?"

"I do," Lucy said, while Gibbs mumbled, "Sure, I guess so."

Katie turned to the congregation. "Members of Christ's family, I present to you Lucy and Leonard, together with Sarah, whose coming into their home they celebrate with gratitude and hope." She placed her hand upon Sarah's head, and prayed, "Sarah, may the eternal God bless you and watch over you. May you grow up to assume your part in Jesus' mission of healing and reconciliation. May the Holy Spirit sanctify you and bring you to life everlasting. Amen."

Hearty "Amens" were erupting from the congregation. *Obviously not Lutherans*, Katie thought to herself. "Let us bless the Lord!" she intoned.

"Thanks be to God!" the people called back.

There now, those are the Lutherans, Katie thought.

She waved Lucy and Gibbs toward their pew again, and gave each of them a kiss as they passed her. She then went to her place behind the altar, raised her hands and said, "The Lord be with you!"

"And also with you!" they almost shouted back.

"Lift up your hearts!" she said, with equal joy, and her heart leapt indeed as she led them in the prayers over the bread and wine.

As the great, dissonant chords of the final hymn thundered through the building, Katie felt a surge of exhilaration. *This* was what church was supposed to feel like. She shook hands until her wrist was sore, but she never tired of seeing the smiles on the people's faces. And she had to admit that she didn't mind the "wonderful sermon, Pastor" comments one little bit.

When Lucy and Gibbs appeared, Sarah seemed to

be sleeping. Katie looked contrite. "I hope you guys are still speaking to me," she said. "I didn't really plan that—it just seemed like the thing to do."

Gibbs poked her chasuble with his finger. "Okay, but don't do that again!" he said, but he couldn't stop himself from smiling as he said it.

"I'll make you pay at home," Lucy said, mock-darkly.

"Yikes," Katie said, but she was smiling, too. She noted with relief that as the young couple moved on, they were walking toward Lucy's parents. "Let the healing continue, Lord," she breathed quietly, but quickly turned her attention back to the next parishioner in line.

Just as the queue was beginning to thin out, Kevin Schwartz, the President of the Church Council leaned in toward her and whispered, "May I speak to you in your office, please?"

A twinge of fear pricked at Katie. *Maybe they* are *going to fire me*, she thought. "Oh, of course, Kevin. Let me get out of these vestments and I'll be right in."

She usually hung her vestments up neatly, but this time she simply draped them over a chair in the vestry. If the Altar Guild didn't see to them, she'd hang them up properly later. Willing herself to be calm, she walked through Gammy's untended office and pushed open the door to her own.

There she saw Kevin, sitting in one chair across from her desk. Gammy was in the other. *Oh dear*, Katie thought, *they're double-teaming me here*. She tried not to panic, tried to manage her anxiety and frustration without letting any of it show.

She sat down in the chair behind her desk, realizing

that it gave her the illusion of power in the room. She wished she felt it. She glanced at Kevin, who was sorting through some papers, a look of grim necessity on his face. She looked next to Gammy, who looked uncertain.

"Pastor, that was a fabulous service today," Kevin said, without looking up from his papers.

"Thank you, Kevin," Katie allowed herself to relax, but only a bit.

"Wasn't that a fine, sermon, Ms. Gammerbrau?" Kevin pointed his question.

"Well…it was…the best one the Pastor has given here yet," Gammy offered.

Ouch, thought Katie. Since she had walked out on her first sermon, it was a pretty backhanded compliment.

"Pastor, I've asked Ms. Gammerbrau to join us to discuss her…continued employment with the parish."

Katie saw Gammy's eyebrows jump nearly off of her head.

"What are you talking about, Kevin?" Gammy snapped.

"I got a fax from the Bishop's home office last night," he said, handing a copy to Katie and another to Gammy. He had a third copy that he looked at himself. "I thought maybe we could read through it together and discuss it. Gammy, perhaps you would do the honors?"

Katie looked down at the letter, its blurred, distorted letters still clearly readable. It appeared to be a letter from Gammy to the Bishop. Before Katie could get into the meat of the text, Gammy distracted her by noisily

wadding up the paper into a ball. "This is a private correspondence."

"It's not private if the Bishop decided to share it with
me, Gammy," Kevin countered. "Never mind, I'll read
it. It says, 'Dear Bishop Merckle, The Lord Jesus has
instructed me to write to you concerning our new
Pastor, the Reverend Katheryn Jorgenson. I'm sure that
her ordaining congregation saw something in her, but
I'm stumped as to what that could possibly have been.
Since her arrival, she has visited no parishioners,
attended no church meetings, and even walked out
right in the middle of her first sermon. She made a fool
of our parish at the lighting of the town Christmas tree,
and I have it on good authority that she is a man-hater
(and you know what that means). The Lord Jesus would
like you to remove her from her post at St. Gabriel's
effective immediately before she brings further shame
and ruin upon the good name of this parish. I know
you are a good man and you always do what the Lord
Jesus tells you. You should do it now. Your humble ser-
vant in the Lord Jesus, Evelyn Gammerbrau.'"

Katie was speechless. "I hardly know where to
begin…" she breathed.

Kevin held his hand up to stop her. "I don't think any
explanations are necessary from you, Pastor. I think it's
Ms. Gammerbrau we need to hear from."

"She hasn't visited any parishioners!" Gammy
protested.

"You made sure of that," Katie agreed.

"And she hasn't attended one church meeting!"
Gammy's voice was becoming hysterical.

"I've got the parish calendar for December in front

of me here, Evelyn," Kevin said calmly. "It's Christmas. There *are* no church meetings. No committees, no parish Council meetings. There hasn't been a meeting scheduled since the Pastor arrived."

"She walked out on her first sermon!" Gammy screeched.

"And she had every right to. People were being as rude as jackals, from what I hear—you especially." He turned to Katie and said. "That took a lot of guts, Pastor. It woke a lot of people up, got them talking— and I mean in a good way."

Gammy's protests had disintegrated into inarticulate squeaks. Finally, she gathered her forces for one last jab. "She is a man-hater!"

Kevin turned to Katie. "Pastor, are you a man-hater?"

"I like you a lot, Kevin."

"Well, there you have it." He turned back to Gammy. "Evelyn, the church Council held an emergency meeting by conference call last night regarding this little matter," he held up his copy of the letter. "And the consensus of the council is that, while we hope you will continue to be a faithful parishioner here at St. Gabriel's, your services as secretary are no longer required."

Gammy's face had grown beet red, and her mouth worked like a cow chewing her cud. Somehow, her hair had responded to her distress by sticking straight out from her head. It looked to Katie like she was about to blow a gasket.

Kevin raised his voice. "Sheriff!" Katie's office door opened, and Howard was there, badge stuck to his blue suit pocket. His right hand held back the coat of his suit jacket casually, so that his weapon was clearly visible. "Sheriff, will you please escort Ms. Gammerbrau to her desk and watch as she empties it of her personal effects?"

"I'll be glad to," Howard held the door open for Gammy, who did not budge at first. Finally, though, her shoulders deflated. She shot a hateful look at Katie and a wounded one at Kevin. Then she stood, brushed the wrinkles from her skirt, held her head high, and pushed past Howard.

As the door to her office clicked shut again, Katie let out an involuntary sigh.

Kevin laughed at the sound of it. "It's been a full morning, Pastor."

"It has," she agreed.

"I hope you're planning to stay," he said.

"If you had asked me last week, I would have said no, but now…" she looked him in the eye. "I have friends here."

"It's a good place to raise a family," Kevin added. "And St. Gabriel's is a fine parish. I think you're going to do just fine."

Katie nodded her agreement. She certainly hoped that was true. "Kevin…thank you. I've seen church situations where something like this could get…well…."

"Messy?" he offered.

"Exactly," she said, relieved.

"Pastor, you may not have noticed, but people have been watching you pretty closely this past week. We've heard about how you helped Howard and Lara, the time you've spent down at Bremmer's, your taking in

Lucy and her baby. It's easy to pay lip service to the Gospel. Living it is hard." He reached out and shook her hand in both of his. "We see that you live it. You are exactly the kind of pastor most of us have been hoping for. We know there are going to be some who…well, who don't want anything to change. But I want you to know that the rest of us, we've got your back."

Katie breathed a deep sigh. "Thank you, Kevin. That means a lot to me."

"See you at the Council meeting on Thursday?"

"My first meeting! I can't wait," she smiled, and turned toward the parsonage.

Standing by the doorway, Jerry and Carol were speaking to Gibbs. Jerry said something, and the three of them laughed. Katie approached and took Gibbs' arm in hers.

"Fine service, Pastor," Jerry said. "You might just make religious people of us yet."

Katie rolled her eyes. "God help us all. That's the last thing I want."

Gibbs turned toward her. "Thanks, Pastor. For… everything."

Katie squeezed his arm and patted it with her other hand. "I'm just happy everything seemed to work out so well. The only thing I'm sad about is that Christmas is almost over."

"Oh, no, Pastor," said Jerry, squeezing his wife's shoulder. "Not in this town it isn't. Not ever."

CPSIA information can be obtained at www.ICGtesting.com
Printed in the USA
BVOW03s1545231114

376327BV00003B/33/P